THE
SECOND
MURDERER

A
Philip Marlowe
MYSTERY

THE
SECOND
MURDERER

DENISE MINA

MULHOLLAND BOOKS

LITTLE, BROWN AND COMPANY

NEW YORK BOSTON LONDON

Copyright © 2023 by Denise Mina and Raymond Chandler Ltd.

Mulholland Books / Little, Brown and Company
Hachette Book Group
1290 Avenue of the Americas, New York, NY 10104
littlebrown.com

First North American Edition: August 2023
Originally published in the United Kingdom by Harvill Secker: July 2023

Mulholland Books is an imprint of Little, Brown and Company, a division of Hachette Book Group, Inc. The Mulholland name and logo are trademarks of Hachette Book Group, Inc.

Philip Marlowe and Marlowe are trademarks of Raymond Chandler Ltd.

The publisher is not responsible for websites (or their content) that are not owned by the publisher.

The Hachette Speakers Bureau provides a wide range of authors for speaking events. To find out more, go to hachettespeakersbureau.com or email hachettespeakers@hbgusa.com.

Little, Brown and Company books may be purchased in bulk for business, educational, or promotional use. For information, please contact your local bookseller or the Hachette Book Group Special Markets Department at special.markets@hbgusa.com.

ISBN 9780316265645
LCCN 2023933883

Printing 1, 2023

LSC-C

Printed in the United States of America

For Oni

THE
SECOND
MURDERER

1.

I was in my office, feet up, making use of a bottle of mood-straightener I kept in the desk. A mid-September heatwave had descended on the city. Brittle heat rolled down from parched hills, lifting thin dust from roads and sidewalks, suspending it in the rising air and turning the sky yellow. Sounds became crisp and metallic. Everywhere people were gliding along through a gritty yellow fog, mean and squinting, spitting on sidewalks, waiting for the heat to break.

I don't usually drink in the office at ten thirty in the morning but I had a bad taste to wash away. The Pasco Pete case was solved, the murderer was arrested and everyone else had moved on but me. I couldn't. There was something wrong, something bad in it, like a mouthful of soup with a stray hair that brushes your lip on the way in and then disappears. The facts rolled around in my head, tumbling over each other, in a smaller circle every time. Something was wrong.

I'd narrowed it down to the sighting of Pasco Pete the day after he had been murdered. Pete was being driven by a busty blonde with a badly mended cleft lip in a jalopy, careening down Alameda, and they were both laughing so hard at a joke that they almost crashed. In a good lie the victim would be spotted with a man in a hat, a brunette or a tall man, they'd be seen with a generic person. Black Jack's mistake was in making it too specific.

But the case was solved and closed, neat and tidy. No one was giving it a second thought but me, rolling it over and over in my head.

It had started with the heatwave. I arrived at the office one morning and found Baby Maude waiting patiently, sitting on a wooden fold-down, upright in her whale-bone stays with her purse perched on her knee.

Maude was a sixty-year-old child star. She wore a good quality purple day suit that was faded and mended and carefully pressed. Her hatless hair was an unmoving permanent wave dyed blackest black but she hadn't had time for the beauty parlour recently. Her roots were so white and bright they shone like stars in a black sky. Heavy face powder nestled in the wrinkles and folds of her face except for the tracks of hastily dabbed away tears on each cheek.

Maude had been weeping while she waited and she didn't seem the type for it.

In my office, trembling and trying to hide it, she explained that her man had disappeared. Either Pasco Pete had taken off with a new sweetie or else he must have died because that ol' rascal had no place else to go. The way she fussed with her handkerchief told me how dearly she hoped he'd run out on her. When she admitted that he might be dead her hands stilled and lay on her knees like dead birds. I don't think she really wanted to know where he was but she had to find out for the insurance company. Maude owed all sorts of money. Her house was falling down and she needed the cash to move on. If it hadn't been for that she'd have taken it on the chin like a big girl and allowed herself the luxury of hoping that he'd come back one day. But she needed to know. If he was alive she'd get nothing. If he wasn't she'd get a pay-out. She said it was all the same to her but her bloodshot eyes gave away that she hoped Pasco was alive, laughing at her in a bar somewhere with his new floozy. I don't think she'd slept for a week.

I warned Maude fair and square: I can only find the truth. She said okay to that. That was what she agreed to. I made it clear what I did.

She gave me a cheque she could ill afford and told me what she knew.

Pasco Pete was an extra in western movies.

He'd last been seen leaving a film set out in Idle Valley but he didn't make it home and she hadn't seen him since. The next day he was spotted heading north on Alameda, in a banged-up Model T, being driven by a big blonde half his age, a busty girl with a badly mended cleft lip, and they were both as drunk as monkeys at a rum convention. According to Black Jack Beau, the fellow cowpoke-turned-actor who saw them, they were cracking up, the girl laughing so hard she swerved the car halfway across the midline and nearly hit a truck. Drunk and laughing and driving fast with a blousy girl. Pasco was having a good day.

But when Maude showed me Pasco's photograph I knew Black Jack Beau was lying.

Pasco Pete had ten years on Maude and a nose as big as a shoe. He was five feet two in his stocking feet and he wasn't just broke, he looked broke. All he had left in the world was three teeth, his own boots and a sweat-stained hat full of sass. The story would have made more sense if the busty girl had been crying.

The investigation led me to spend long days and nights in a mean little bar in Gower Gulch called the Watering Hole. Retired cowpokes sat in there sipping sour hooch all day long as they waited for casting directors to ring them on the public telephone and call them in for background scenes in cowboy pictures.

These people were famous but they were not stars. They were the ocean that the big fish moved in, hangers-on and backgrounders. The movie colony is made up of people with burning ambition and these people were warming their hands on that fire. Most were broke and working to make rent like the rest of the world. They'd never get a title credit even if movie-goers knew their faces well.

Pasco had been a real cowboy in his youth. He'd worked out in Texas, spent three years driving steers and sleeping under the stars, until a bronc threw him so bad on the edge of a steep gully that he shattered both his legs. He was lucky they found him at all, double lucky to survive, but his legs were different lengths afterward and his lungs weakened so he came out to California to convalesce. By the time he was halfway better the ranch he'd been working on had been broken up and the time was past. There was nowhere to go back to. Pasco still had all the skills though. He could ride like the devil on wheels, lasso and shoot with the best of them.

His fellow drinkers at the Watering Hole were all real cowboys too. They came to the bar in their old work clothes. That way, when the casting call came, they had their own costumes on already and saved the production time and money. It made them more bookable. Within their society the biggest toads in the puddle had trailed a chuck wagon for at least one season. Pasco wasn't in that group but Black Jack was. He was almost royalty. When the telephone in the booth rang they all sat up and looked at it, eyes glittering, until it was answered and they heard the call was not for them. The glitter was hope and you only missed it once you'd seen it.

That bar was tragic and then wild and then tragic again, two sides of the same coin. Spending time in there made me ponder questions a man in his prime should not be asking, like what was the point of anything and did anyone really need teeth.

I got talking to Black Jack Beau. He was smart, saw that the movie work wouldn't go on forever. He could feel it drying up. He'd saved up and bought a warehouse over on Vine that he leased out for storage. I went over for a look around and that was where I found Pasco Pete. He'd been dumped in an alley behind the warehouse and what was left of him was supporting a large family of rats. The smell led me to him and the cops took over from there.

Turns out Black Jack Beau never liked Pasco Pete. When he heard Pasco had been answering the telephone and taking other boys' roles it got too much for him. He was cursing up a strip and issuing threats for all to hear, declaring Pasco Pete a varmint who deserved to be taught a lesson. The stakes were so low they made dirt look tall but this breach of native etiquette led to Black Jack Beau serving up justice in traditional ol'-west style: luring Pasco Pete into the alley and beating him to death with a tyre iron. He hadn't seen Pasco driving on Alameda because Pasco was already dead. Black Jack Beau was lying like a rug.

Maybe Pasco Pete was a varmint, maybe he deserved to be beaten to death and left to bloat and stink in an alley, but he was the love of Baby Maude's life. She was sitting on her buckled-up porch when I told her Pete was gone. She covered her face with both hands and rocked for a while and I heard her say, 'Now I'm gonna die alone.'

That flattened me.

I couldn't take her money even though I needed it. All I could do was convince her to put her pistols away, stay home and give the cops a chance to close the case and enjoy the comfort in knowing what happened to her dear old man.

I was glad when Black Jack Beau was arrested. I'd have liked it more if anyone but Lieutenant Moochie Ruud had got to bring him in. The press boys were all over the neat little story and Ruud was the hero of the day, even made them stop the car a half block away from the front door of the Central Police Station so he could walk Black Jack in single handed, taking it nice and slow so they could take his picture. I hate Moochie Ruud.

It was the neatness of it all that bothered me. I couldn't shake off the sound of Baby Maude keening on that porch. We all die alone. It does no good to think about it.

So that morning I was in the office making liberal use of a cheap bottle to help me unknow that. My feet were up, my tie was off, and I scowled at the dust motes slow-dancing in the hot oily air.

When the phone rang out, loud and cheerful, I wanted to fight it.

2.

She cleared her throat before she spoke,

'Good morning. May I speak with Mr Marlowe?' Her voice was cracked, like she smoked Cubans and stayed up late laughing at dirty jokes.

'This is Marlowe.'

'Mr *Philip* Marlowe?' she asked.

I glanced at the clock. It was exactly eleven a.m., as if she had been waiting by the phone for an appointed hour, following someone else's orders to the letter.

'What, d'you think we're a troupe of brothers? There is only me. Who's calling?'

'Oh,' she stalled. 'My name isn't important.'

'It is to me.'

'I'm phoning on behalf of someone else, Mr Marlowe. My name is of no significance.'

The tone of the voice was a lot more fun than the words from the mouth. It was an intriguing contrast. 'What is it, lady?'

An indignant huff tickled my ear. It felt kind of nice.

'I'll thank you not to call me "lady" like some cheap hoodlum in a gangster movie.'

I dropped my feet from the desk and found myself smiling, 'Ma'am, I can but apologize. I was informal to the brink of discourteous.'

I may have affected a small bow here. I really didn't care what happened next.

'It was a rather abrupt change in tone, I must say.'

'I was just warming up before. Tell me your name and trouble or I'm hanging up.'

She sucked in a breath. 'Well, you just get straight to the point, don't you?'

'Interesting that you didn't hang up.' I lit a cigarette, 'Why did you call me?'

'I was given your number by a certain party who thought you might be of assistance with regard to certain –'

'You want help with something?'

'I do.' For the briefest of moments, like a half blink, her voice cracked and she sounded very scared. She cleared her throat again, so vigorous and loud that I wondered if I heard right.

I sat up, 'How can I help?'

'It is my understanding, Mr Marlowe,' she was back on her pomp, 'that you are a licensed private detective? Would that be correct?'

'Licensed, registered, ticketed and everything. I even supply my own shoes.'

'Yes, humour,' she said flatly. 'That's a joke, obviously. Although I'm not laughing.'

She wasn't being mean. She was stating an observation.

'I wasn't trying to make you laugh. I was cheering myself along.'

'Why did you need cheering up?'

I blinked and saw a grain sack writhe in a back alley. 'Gnarling sorrow has less power to bite the man that mocks at it and sets it light.'

'Is that Whitman?'

'Shakespeare.'

'Well, get you, professor.' She left a small pause that might have meant yes, or no, or come over here and kiss me right now.

Then she cleared her throat and got back to the script, 'It is the understanding of the party for whom I speak that you are a discreet operator. That's important to them.'

I didn't know what the-party-for-whom-she-spoke understood or didn't understand. I took a mouthful of whiskey and didn't say anything for a while. She listened to it carefully. She took that to mean I could sneak cats into church in my pants.

'Very good, Mr Marlowe,' she said, sounding as if she was smiling, possibly wryly.

I imagined her as tall but not too tall, slim but not too slim, maybe a redhead. Maybe a little drunk or was that me? She probably wasn't any of those things but it lifted my mood to imagine her so.

'Well, Mr Marlowe, this is a matter of some urgency. We would like to have you come over here and speak person to person. Are you available right now?'

'No.'

'Later this afternoon, then?'

'No, I mean I'm not coming.'

'You don't visit your clients?'

'I sometimes do but you won't give me your name. I don't need work enough to pay a nameless stranger a house call on an unspecified matter.'

She stalled, 'Huh. I see. Well, I wish you would reconsider. Is that your definitive position?'

Definitely not drunk.

'It's not my position, lady. No one will come and see you without a name and some idea of the case. If we did that stick-up men would never have to leave the house. They'd just telephone and have us come over.'

'Oh, I hadn't thought of that . . .'

'Could be a bad fit anyway. Save us both time if you give me an idea of the problem. I don't do divorce stuff.'

'Oh, Mr Marlowe,' she sneered. 'It has nothing to do with divorce "stuff", as you call it.'

'Okay. Well, I'm not Psychic Betty, the Marvel of the Age, so right now this isn't any kind of stuff.'

'It's about a missing person. We're missing a person . . .'

I wasn't going to take it. Pasco Pete started as a missing person and I'm not superstitious but it was too soon.

'Aw, gee, I'm sorry. I'm booked up all week. Maybe all month.'

'The party for whom I speak would very much like to speak with you.'

'Just can't fit it into my schedule.' I flipped over some paper on the desk, sounding as if I was flipping through a diary. She seemed like a good kid. I didn't want to be snappy about it.

'Won't you come? Won't you come, Mr Marlowe?'

'Look, sister, I don't know your story and you don't know mine. Let's leave it there.'

'We'd so like to see you up here at the Montgomery Mansion.'

I sat up. I reached up to straighten the necktie I wasn't wearing. Suddenly I was as curious as a dead cat. There are offices downtown full of expensive lawyers whose whole job it is to stop Montgomerys having to know people like me. How my name came up was worth finding out.

I gave her a half-cocked lie about a secretary I didn't have showing me an office diary I didn't keep. I flicked a blank page in my blank diary. Well, what do you know, turns out I could make it after all. She didn't buy it but, as I say, she was a nice kid. She didn't want to be snappy about it either.

I said I could swing by in an hour or so. She said, well that would be just fine, thank you. If I pulled in at the main gates on Montgomery Avenue the gateman would come out and open them for me and direct me from there.

'Take Sunset past Selma, beyond the Dancers nightspot. Once you pass there take a sharp right —'

'I know where the mansion is, ma'am.'

'Oh, you know where it is?'

'Everyone knows where it is.'

She crooned that she would see me presently and hung up without saying goodbye.

The Dancers was a nightclub for the wilder kind, all fast money and never mind how. They drank as if it was Prohibition Eve again.

I didn't need landmark directions anyway. I knew where I was going.

3.

The Montgomerys' money was so old there was a rumour that some of it still had Moses' teeth marks on it. They'd got into the oil business early and owned big fields in the south of the city. All the derricks down in Inglewood were theirs. Old money has a way of multiplying.

Everyone had heard of the Montgomerys but only a handful of people could pick them out of a line-up. That is a special kind of rich. If anything interesting had ever happened to them it didn't make the gossip pages. They kept to themselves, didn't attend public functions or anything so vulgar as movie premieres. They only met with their own kind, other old-money families from back east.

Their estate was high in Beverly Hills, visible for stretches of Santa Monica, fenced off and protected by a private army. The land inside was as green as Robin Hood's britches on the first day of shooting. However dusty and dry or smoggy the city was, up at the Montgomery Estate the grass glowed with colour and moisture, the trees were lush and shady, the fruit was always ripe and plentiful. They had their own water supply up there, their own vineyard, their own stables and a fire station with three brand new engines. They probably had their own moon up there.

It was a mythic place. No one got in. We mortals stood at the foot of the mountain and gazed up at our Gods from the dusty doors of bars and diners, from sun-drenched train stops and muggy store fronts. We looked up and watched their grass grow, imagined the dew rising on the Montgomerys' Elysian Fields as the grit and the dust scratched our faces and we crossed off another day.

Someone had passed my name on to those Gods and told them I could be trusted to hold my nose. That didn't help me narrow it down. There was a lot I didn't tell but it was mostly about people like Baby Maude, Greek barbers who'd lost sons to Vegas or Pasadena housewives' bookie debts.

I gargled mouthwash to cover the tang of whiskey and despair, changed into my second-best suit and a fresh shirt. The suit was new and a little louder than I generally went for but, whoever that was on the phone, she deserved a chance not to fall in love with me. Everybody does and most of them take it.

Downstairs, I stepped outside. It was hotter than hell in July.

Thick heat hung over the city like an oiled rag. Sun and shade had sliced up the street, forcing people to cower, backs flattened to buildings like suicides on ledges.

I opened every window in the Olds, pulling out into the street, glad of the mild stir in the air. By the time I was drawing up to the Dancers I toyed with the idea of not taking the turn, but speeding up and driving west until my car was full of ocean.

I should have but I didn't. I took the turn.

I followed the road on for half a mile, until the houses fell away. Steep hills rose on either side, dirt and scrub, the urgent fizzing of the cicadas as loud as eggs in hot oil.

The mouth of the Montgomery driveway was floored in a herringbone of yellow bricks facing tall metal gates, the initials 'CM' worked into the iron: Chadwick Montgomery, patriarch and holder of the family bankbook. The gates were black, fifteen feet high and ending in spikes, chained shut with a big padlock. They looked hostile. Beyond them an immaculate strip of road led uphill, curved sharply to the right, and disappeared from view.

Before the gates stood a small guard house designed to look like a toy castle. It was cute. It had a little turret and tiny windows, a heavy oak door studded with iron to stop marauding Germanic tribes kicking it in. Unlike the restaurants shaped like chilli bowls or hats or giant shoes or any of the other buildings made to look like other things in this town, this wasn't made of plasterboard and tar paper. It was brick and mortar. It had glass in the little windows, a set of stairs up the side to the roof. A car had rammed the corner of the wall though, chipped out a brick or two, because it had been patched up with slightly lighter stone.

I stopped the car.

The studded door opened but no one came out. A figure moved inside. I raised a hand. They must have my name on a list somewhere, a list of people they could unchain the gate for. I expected a clipboard and a snotty attitude but as the doorman stepped out into a shaft of blinding sunshine and looked at me, he gave me a big smile. I beamed back. He tipped his chin hello and sauntered on over as if he'd never been in a hurry in his life.

'Mr Philip Marlowe,' he drawled, in case I had forgotten my name.

'Mr James Donoghue,' I said, in case he had forgotten his.

'How you doing?'

'Sure. You?'

'Always.' He refreshed his lazy smile and looked over to the gates. 'Hot.' Jimmy was pretty astute.

'Going to get hotter,' I said, because I was too.

They called him Jimmy the One. The Montgomerys wouldn't know that. They'd call him James and dressed him in a grey woollen monkey suit with the family crest embroidered on his breast, made him wear an insulting bellhop pillbox hat with a chinstrap like an organ grinder's monkey. Even the dumb outfit couldn't take away from Jimmy because Jimmy was regal. If they'd made Jimmy wear a barrel with straps you'd find yourself wondering if maybe you should buy a barrel with straps this season. He made a bad servant. Whatever it was he had, he had so much of it that it bordered on insolent.

Jimmy the One was six foot four, blond, blue eyed with a jawline you could open cans with, but it wasn't just that he was good looking. Jimmy had a lot more going for him than that.

Every so often someone would scout him for the movies. They'd see him somewhere, on the street, at a soda fountain, and think no one else had ever noticed him. They'd approach and say they were going to make him a star. Jimmy always went along with it. They'd buy him clothes and dress him up and take him places to show him off, maybe get him cast in something small. But they always found out, sometimes fast, sometimes slow, that Jimmy had more backstory than any studio could hide. It wasn't just his past. He wouldn't stop going to the sorts of bars the gutter press loved to expose.

Jimmy was a daisy. He wasn't unique in that regard, not in this town, but what was special about Jimmy was that he didn't care who knew it. That's why they called him The One. He wasn't going to lie. He wasn't even sorry and if you had a problem with that he'd punch the jaw right off your face. Jimmy was who he was and that was all. He was loyal to himself. Jimmy was on Jimmy's side. Nothing could convince the man to take the side of the world, neither money nor status nor life immortal. In this town it was like finding an honest man in City Hall.

Every time I met Jimmy I felt better about life. I think a lot of people did but most didn't know why. Some of them fell in love with him, men and women. There was always a big mess around him.

Jimmy's last position had come to a natural end. Coincidentally, this happened just after I found him in a cheap motel in Tijuana with the eldest son of the very rich family he worked for. The guys had been debating international matters for almost a week but had aggravated the local cops with their fighting which, in Tijuana, meant it was Olympic. I brought them both back alive and never mentioned it again. I didn't care who knew about the other guy, I kept it quiet so that Jimmy the One could get another job. He called me again, just once, when he was jailed for masquerading at a private party up at Silver Lakes. They'd found him wearing shorts and a feather boa, serving drinks to a room full of men. I knew the cop who booked him, knew he had a side piece and offered to tell his wife. Jimmy got let out.

'Did you give the big house my name?'

Jimmy squinted over the roof of the car, 'I did.'

I followed his gaze up the driveway, 'Heads up, Jimmy? What do they want?'

Jimmy pressed his lips together to stop himself smiling, 'They'll tell you when you get up there. I only know about a half of it anyway. She'll tell you.'

'Who is she?'

'Miss Anneliese Lyle.'

'Housekeeper or girlfriend?'

Jimmy looked away and lifted one shoulder in a shrug. Then he left it there.

'Should I trust her?'

He lifted the other shoulder to match it, 'Who knows anyone?'

It was a good question. 'Don't they have teams of staff? Why call in outside help?'

He squinted at the gates, 'They don't know who to trust. Someone told them you try to do the right thing.' He meant it nice but it sounded like it would cost me in the end.

'They said you'd tell me where to go.'

He slapped the car roof lazily, 'Go on up that road straight ahead, it zigzags around a bunch, just keep following it up until you get to the front door.'

'You going to let me through,' I said. 'Or should I just ram the gates?'

Jimmy's shoulders dropped. He looked over at the gate. It wasn't terribly far away but it was across a brick oven. The heat shimmied up from the bricks, warping the trees and the grass inside.

He sighed and made a slow-motion break for it, taking out a key as he moseyed over, unlocked a fat padlock, took the hasp off, bent down to lift the ground bolt, swung the gate all the way open and bent down again to secure the bolt into the hole. He straightened up, took a moment to eye his route to the other gate. He set off. I hoped he had sandwiches with him. Heat radiated from the roof of my car like a broiler. If Jimmy took much longer my hair might melt.

He made it to the other side and opened that gate too, secured it and then stood up, raising a hand at the driveway like a magician presenting a lady he'd sawed in half.

I pulled the Olds forward and told Jimmy I'd see him. He slapped the side of the car as an afterthought.

4.

The Montgomerys wanted visitors to know they had money so bad they should have had signs made.

The driveway turned right and into a tunnel of jacaranda trees in full bloom. I stalled the car and sat there for a minute or an hour, I don't know how long I was there. The trees were old and big and gnarled. The delicate flowers were spectacular tiny purple trumpets, just an inch or so, translucent, and the light filtering through them turned the world lilac and sweetened the filthy air.

I never wanted to stop looking down that road. It was food for the soul. If there was a bludgeoned cowpoke under each of those trees, even the hairless, bloody-mouthed baby rats would look beautiful.

I restarted the car and drove on taking it slow, breathing deep the sweet smell and the soft light.

At the other end, the road doubled back and lifted me on a steep level with the heads of the trees. This stretch went further round the side of the hill, to the back of a whitewashed cluster of stables with a paddock beyond. Turning back again it crossed a false hill and a turn-off to a small vineyard.

The estate was built not so very long ago, at a time when almost every house north of Sunset had stables. Any old millionaire could ride their horse down the Beverly Hills Bridle Path, all the way down Sunset Boulevard straight to the Pacific Ocean. Now the city had filled up and spread out, occupying all those wide empty spaces with cheap buildings and oil drills, parking lots and warehouses. But this driveway was a trip back in time.

I took the hill slow and the city dropped away below, taking the bitter edge of the heat with it. All the filthy intensity fell away. I took the last turn to where the road led straight to the ocean. A gentle breeze slipped in through the windows on either side, slithered under my cuffs, filled my shirt and pushed all the sticky heat up and out of my collar. I decided that I might never leave this hill.

The city looked very far away, all the difficult details blurred by distance.

The final turn took me around a shielding wall of popsicle cedar trees to the forecourt of the Montgomery place where a soft pattering fountain sprayed cool water in through the car window. The mansion was an L shape with the front door in the crease of the elbow. It was a nice family home if your family was everybody in Kansas. The windows were small and many and a heavy roof hung over it all like a furrowed brow.

A low row of garages stood at the side. The doors were open and identical black Packards winked and gleamed in the shade, big as trains but better kept, perfectly waxed and ready to serve, glinting side by side. I parked my dusty Olds, got out and went up the steps to the front door.

A bell rang inside, a soft echo in a big room. Footsteps, regular, even, coming in a straight line from a long way away.

The door opened and cool air wafted out and chucked me under the chin.

He was dressed in a formal morning suit, tails and a shirt so starched it could have been made from paper. What hair he still had was gelled back on his head, thin, like pencil scratches.

We had met before. I knew him as Errol Cooper. He was an actor and a good one too, maybe too good. He did background parts and could have made a career of it but for one thing and another. We'd always gotten on just fine but now his disgusted gaze skittered over my face and suit and loud patterned tie. The deep turn-ups on my pants upset him so much he couldn't seem to tear his eyes off them.

'You just have to ask,' I said. 'They do it right there for you in the store.'

The Bronx in Cooper made his cheek twitch but the actor in him caught it, threw it to the ground and stood on its neck.

I told you he was good.

'Please come in, Mr Marlowe.' You could have etched glass with his British accent. I was expected, he said, and stepped back to let me in.

A sudden drone behind me, shrill and high, made me turn to look. A small green Plymouth two-seater appeared from behind the garages. The sound of the engine was grating, an insect broadcasting a warning. It was a dusty old car, not waxed and clean and dried with warm towels, not a millionaire's car. A member of the staff would have used a servants' exit. It was a visitor like me.

I watched the roof slide down the hill like butter off a hot knife.

'Who's that?'

'Sir?'

'Driving that nippy little number, who was that?'

Errol blinked belligerently, watching the space on the horizon vacated by the little green roof. He was interested in whoever was driving that car too. By now the Plymouth was nothing but a hot purr rolling up the side of the hill. Cooper suddenly remembered himself, looked at me and offered a revolted smile.

'Won't you come in?' he said, keeping me on the step, giving me the option to scram.

'Sure, bub.'

I stepped into a hallway that was eighteen-carat cold and I took my hat off.

It was a nice room. High and square and cool, a floor of black and white checkers. In the middle a circular table held a display of flowers so fat and pleased with themselves they looked fake. They weren't. Cool air flowed softly through brass vents low down in the marble walls. Beyond the table a white marble staircase led up to a balcony and double doors, one of them ajar.

'Take a seat.' He pointed me to a jagged chair with a high back.

I sat on it. He stared at me and curled his lip. I crossed my legs and swung my foot cheerfully.

'Touch *nothing*,' he narrowed his eyes. 'Nothing.'

'You're more fun than a swimsuit full of squirrels, Cooper.'

If he smiled at that it was only on the inside. He stood over me, stretching up to his full six feet. 'Am I?'

I stood up, I had two inches over him and made use of it. 'Are you scared I'll tell them you're an actor?'

He stepped away and lost the war. 'They already know I was once an actor.'

'Then what's your beef?'

He didn't know.

'They ask you to fight everyone below the rank of colonel who comes through here?'

'Mr Marlowe, I apologize.' He gave a small bow. 'Please forgive me if I appeared impolite.'

I sat back down, 'Don't worry about it.' I flapped a hand in front of him and looked away.

He didn't move.

I looked back and found him staring at me. His eyes were narrow, his lips bloodless.

'I shall return for you very shortly,' he said and turned and walked away through an open arch. He left me with the sweat on my back turning to ice.

Errol Cooper hated me all of a sudden. It was strange. We'd always gotten on just fine when we were drinking in the same bars or standing together at the horses. Couple of times we were in the same card game. I didn't remember any ill will at the end of it.

Something must have happened when I was out of the room. He must have heard something about me. There wasn't much to hear. I'd hurt people. I'd taken things of disputed provenance, usually paper cash, but nothing big, and never without reason.

I looked up. Next to me, on a thin one-legged plinth stood a strange broken vase.

There were plinths next to chairs all around the room. One held a marble horse's head with a broken face. The one next to me had a potbellied vase in orange and black with a badly busted handle.

I was examining it when I became aware of movement up on the balcony. Small eyes watching me through the wooden banister. A kid. His hands clung tightly to the finials, knuckles white. Below them two skinny little legs in shorts and white socks. He couldn't have been more than four or five but was dressed like a retired admiral, in a navy blazer over a button-down white shirt and grey shorts with a seam pressed down the front.

I looked at him. He looked back at me, his gaze was unwavering. He watched me as if he'd never seen a person before. Then he blinked and dropped down to his haunches, fitted his skinny little legs through the banisters and let them swing. His hair was black, parted on the side and flattened with a watered comb. He stared at me without much interest. He was chewing something. It wasn't gum. It seemed like something he wasn't allowed to chew and he was enjoying it.

'Got a name?'

He chewed. He looked me up and down. He huffed a laugh through his nose. First Cooper and now a kid. Seemed like open season on me.

'I'll call you Piggy Poltroon – okay if I call you that?'

Starting an argument with someone who couldn't have reached my chin on a stool wasn't my finest moment but it didn't matter. He didn't go for it anyway. This kid, this little kid, he didn't get angry. His mouth smiled but his eyes didn't join in. He laughed a flat bark like a bitter old man. It was as if he could see me trying to fight him and that amused him. It felt like he didn't know any other kids.

He stiffened suddenly, pulled his legs in, jumped up and was gone before I heard Cooper's feet tippy tapping back towards me.

Cooper arrived at the door with the haunted look of a man who'd just been shouted at. I stood up but he said, 'Not quite ready for you yet. If you wouldn't mind waiting for another moment.'

I sat back down. His eye kept flicking to the broken vase next to me. It had a narrow neck and ballooned out fat in the middle with a black band, orange on the bottom and the neck. The black band depicted stick men and horses doing things.

I glanced at the missing handle, 'Dance party?'

Cooper's cheek did the twitch thing again. He seemed nervous.

'Have you been sent in here to make sure I don't touch that?'

I could tell from his expression that he had.

'Is that what I seem like? A man with a hankering to mess with a vase?'

'The vase is rather fragile. Mr Montgomery is anxious for its safety. It is a new acquisition.'

'Worth a lot?'

'Extremely valuable. One of a kind.'

'Next to a door is a pretty dumb place to keep it. He should put it somewhere safe.'

'Mr Montgomery particularly enjoys having his new acquisitions on show around the house.'

'Brash. I keep mine at the bank.' I pointed at the stick men, 'What's the story in these funny papers?'

Cooper tipped back on his heels, 'The vase depicts the drunk satyr Silenus being cared for by King Midas. On the obverse the God Pan grants King Midas his wish in reward. You know the story?'

'Heard a rumour. Midas wishes that everything he touches turn to gold. Goes south. Midas kills his family and starves.'

'That's about the sum of it. Midas gets exactly what he wants but it brings him no joy.'

'Greek myths don't do it for me,' I said, since we were being friendly. 'Stuff happens for no reason and then other people arrive and some other stuff happens. Personally, I like wrestling pictures.'

He raised a cheek at me. It wasn't a wink as much as a twitch caused by a deep-down wish that something awful would happen to me. I stood up.

'Cooper, what have I done to you?'

He reeled away from me. 'I can't imagine what you mean, sir.'

'Since I walked in here you've been giving me the stink eye. Why?'

Cooper opened his mouth to say something but a woman appeared at the open door behind him.

Miss Anneliese Lyle wasn't a redhead, she was a bottle blonde but it suited her. She was tall and slim and so streamlined she looked like a different species entirely, as if an architect got a woman and shaved off all the good bits. Her skin was flawless fondant, her pale lips wide and sensual. She wore a burgundy day suit, jacket buttoned tight, and a white blouse tied high at the neck.

Her green eyes met mine. Something shifted in me. Maybe something broke or grew, I don't know, but I was left with the impression that I would never be the same again. I think a lot of men felt that way when she looked at them.

'Now, Cooper!' she whispered, then slid sideways behind the door jamb and vanished.

Cooper held out a hand to the open arch, inviting me to follow her while shielding the valuable object with his body.

I passed him, 'You gonna marry that vase?'

Once he was sure the threat had passed and I couldn't go rogue and turn and lunge for it he murmured back in a thick Bronx accent, 'I'll marry your face and my fist.'

I stopped. He nearly banged into the back of me. I turned and he already looked as if he regretted breaking cover.

'Oh, hey, Errol, how you been?'

His cheeks reddened. Must be a sweet gig up here. He didn't

want to lose it. Must pay decent. Can't blame a man for wanting a job but I can blame a man for threatening me.

He bobbed his chin at the arch, ordering me forward. I nodded back towards the vase and grinned. He shook his head. I took a phoney step towards it. He gave out a little panicked cry.

'This vase . . . it just draws me in . . .' I grinned, 'I can see why it's so expensive.' But then I fell back and turned to the arch and walked away. 'What a nice vase!'

Cooper's face expressed the relief he couldn't bring himself to voice. He stepped in front of me and led me through. He was glad I hadn't smashed it but he didn't like me any better.

I muttered at his back, 'Don't know what I did to fire up your pyre.'

He wasn't going to tell me.

He nodded and dipped his chin down as he led me out, into an open-air courtyard with a water feature in the middle and a lot of burning sky above. A colonnade ran all the way around the sides. It was hot but air was moving, carrying spray from the fountain in the middle, and it made the temperature tolerable. The whispered hush of water filled the void.

Cooper led me through a large open door and into a long dark corridor lined with heavy paintings. Miss Lyle was in an all-fire hurry, walking fast on low heels, swinging her arms. I leaned around Errol and watched her walk. It was a nice walk. Piston-like legs. Even step. Smooth calves. Suddenly, without turning, she lurched left and was swallowed up by a wall.

I heard a door click shut.

Cooper stopped outside the door she'd gone through and turned so his shoulder was square to it. He coughed, got back into character, tugged the front of his jacket straight and tidy and smoothed his thinning hair. Whoever was in there noticed flaws and wasn't shy about bringing them up.

He didn't look at me as he whispered, 'I apologize if I've been less than convivial, Marlowe. Miss Lyle, you see . . .'

'It's all jake to the angels, Cooper.'

Big of me but he didn't acknowledge it. He turned away and opened the door. He walked into the room just as though he was stepping on to the stage at Carnegie Hall.

'A Mr Philip Marlowe to see you, sir.'

He ushered me into a library the size of Union Station.

5.

It was one of those museum pieces that get shipped over from Europe and reassembled in the wrong climate, wrong setting, for the wrong people.

The bookshelves were full but the wood panels were coming away from their frames, the parquet floor was warped and lumpy. In the middle of the room a map-reading table dipped at one corner and a drawer was jammed open. The elaborate carved ceiling above us didn't look too stable either, as if it might all cave in on our heads at any moment.

At the far end of the room behind a black desk sat a chair that should have been on an altar somewhere. A big altar. In an old church. With giant priests. I've rented bungalows it would dwarf. And in that throne sat Mr Chadwick Montgomery, Esquire.

He was dying.

He had been a big man once, his skin remembered that, but he was shrunk inside it and the skin hung grey on his face, loose around the eyes, showing the red inner lining. His hands sat on the desk like unemployed hams.

Next to him stood a drip stand. The fluid bag was full and new. Each time a drop fell from the bag to the tube it caught the light and flashed a cheerful spark of light across the room. Drip-drip-drip, the seconds of his life trickled away.

Montgomery raised a white linen cloth to dab the side of his mouth. 'Closer.'

I ambled over but it wasn't easy: the parquet on the floor was uneven, too valuable to sand smooth, maybe, but it was hard to amble on. I had to concentrate. Each step felt like a moment closer to a fall.

It was hard to see because of the light flooding in behind his shoulder through a big stained-glass window poached from somewhere. It was very old, more lead than glass, and all the colours had faded to shades of yellow and grey, the colour of time. When you squinted at it all the panels added up to a picture of men in long dresses with swords and pointy toes.

I arrived at a wing-back chair in front of the desk and Montgomery indicated with a glance that I should sit.

Despite the heat he wore a heavy brocade robe with a velvet collar and embroidered with gold pomegranates. Up close I could see that his colouring was all the wrong way round: his lips were blue and his eyes were red.

I didn't much like this. I didn't like these people or this place built with other people's walls and floors and desks. I didn't like the feeling that I was the only audience member at a carefully staged play.

I did like looking at Anneliese Lyle though. She was standing by the side of Chadwick's chair, the bird-boned wonder girl with the cigar-wrecked voice. She was holding one of the wooden spikes at the corner of his throne, squeezing it nervously.

Jimmy D. might not know if she was a girlfriend or secretary but even from all the way across the desk with a strong light behind her, I knew. Lyle was standing too close to Montgomery for it all to be business. She pressed her hip against the side of his chair, balancing on one foot. Her arms were open, her mouth soft, a posture that declared loud and clear that she had the run of this man.

'I am Chadwick Montgomery and this is my personal secretary, Miss Anneliese Lyle.'

She looked at me with those green eyes again. I don't know what she saw in my whiskey-tinged brown eyes. Whatever it was she liked it.

'We spoke on the telephone, Mr Marlowe.'

I lit a cigarette, 'You called me.'

She pushed a brass cigar ashtray across the desk with her fingertips. 'I did,' she said.

The desk was so deep that she only got it halfway across. I had to get up out of my seat to reach for it. It had a holder for a box of matches in the middle and four fat rests for big cigars. Chadwick watched it cross in front of him with a yearning that was palpable.

'You smoke cigars, Mr Montgomery?'

'Used to.'

As my fingers took the edge I looked down at the desk top. Tucked underneath the blotter with a fresh sheet of paper in it was the corner of a green business card, the same colour as the Plymouth I had seen leaving.

I pulled the ashtray over to myself.

Anneliese smelled of lemons and mornings on the beach. There was some element of her, a robust healthiness that was almost obscene. A sick man would have been drawn to that. A bad man would resent it.

Her fingertips lingered on the desk top, the nails painted the same shade of wine as her suit. The white cuffs of her blouse sat a perfect half inch proud where it had ridden up when she pushed the ashtray over and I could see that her wrist was bruised. Three bruises in a row on the bone. The marks were old, yellow and green, the size of a big man's fingertips in just the place where he might grab and squeeze.

She saw me looking and whipped her hand back, pulled the cuff down to hide them and looked at Chadwick Montgomery's head. She was nervous.

I sat back down, flicked my ash into the mausoleum to cigar smoking.

'Why am I here?'

She gave a tight-lipped smile. He tried to smile too but something hurt and made him flinch.

'You *do* just get to the point, don't you?'

Their grins hardened. They had discussed what I said on the phone. They were together. I was the schmo.

I flicked non-existent ash from my cigarette to stop myself getting up and walking out. I wanted to know why I was here.

Montgomery began to talk in a low rumble that commanded attention. He took breaths in the middle of his sentences like a man who never expected to be interrupted, a man used to being listened to. As he spoke he looked over my head, projecting his voice as if addressing an army. He thanked me for coming all the way up here on such short notice, and in this heat. As I could doubtless see, he was a man of not insubstantial means. He got what he wanted, when he wanted it. But make no mistake: this was not simply because he was rich. He knew the governor personally. He knew the congressmen and senators and all the police chiefs in the whole of California. He wanted to make it clear that he was connected all the way up to Washington and beyond.

He looked at me to see if it had landed. Telling me about that kind of power was like describing a kite to a fish. Even if you could make them understand what a kite was it wouldn't impact their life very much. He seemed to want a reaction from this fish, though.

'Good for you,' I said, and tapped my cigarette again.

My smoke trail hit his nose. I saw him crane toward it.

I had something he couldn't have.

I took a deep drag. I held it. I blew a warm cloud of delicious tobacco smoke toward him. The clean white smoke formed a flat and widening circle, stopped by the warm air, widening where it stood. He watched it form a shield between us, willing it to his nose. The smoke didn't make it to him. It seeped north, south, east and west but nothing went to him. He looked at me coldly through the lifting fog.

Then he was telling me about the room. Everything was old and from someplace else. The floors were French, the walls and ceiling were English, the stained-glass window came from a

Flemish cathedral. Miss Lyle advised him but he had the experience and understood history in a way that not many men did. He was a Yale man, don't you know. As he told me this I smoked and nodded as if I cared, raising my eyebrows, looking at all the broken, stolen things.

But I was watching.

When Lyle looked up at the carved ceiling I saw a red flare under her ear. She had bruises on her neck as well. Bruises on a wrist might come from holding a hand and suffering sudden pain or a shock. Not too many people reached for another person's neck to steady themselves. That was deliberate. That was done for a purpose.

I nodded as if six-hundred-year-old stained glass was hot news and then got down to business, 'So: what did you want to see me about?'

Lyle stepped in, 'Firstly, confidentiality is of the essence. Do you have references we can contact, Mr Marlowe?'

I smiled, 'No.'

She smiled back, 'Then how do we know we can trust you?'

'You don't.'

She was a little thrilled by that. He wasn't. 'This is not the way we usually conduct business.'

I sighed so hard I ruffled my parting and stubbed my cigarette out.

'Look: this free museum tour is nice and all but I'm a working man. I get paid forty bucks a day plus expenses. This has already taken up my morning. I'm twenty bucks down and you've told me nothing apart from you know everyone and own a bunch of stuff. Let's stop pretending I begged to come up here to hear about your new floor. You called me. Out of the blue. At my office. You asked me to come up here. I didn't want to but I came here.'

Her eyebrows asked her boss what he thought. He didn't think much. He lowered his eyes to a drawer in the desk.

Elegant as a fan dancer, Lyle used both hands to lift a delicate gold chain from her neck and lifted it over her head. It had a little key on it, an old bent one with a clover-leaf end. She held my eyes as she used it to unlock the top drawer on the desk, took out a cheque book and slapped it open on the desk top. She wrote in it, slid it over to Montgomery to sign, then tore off a cheque and held it out to me.

This was when I should have turned and walked away. If I had, Manny Perez would still be alive. Maybe Pavel Viscom would be too, I don't know. But I didn't walk. I just sat there, holding a cheque for a thousand dollars, knowing I should leave. I don't know why I didn't leave. It was hot. She smelled of lemons. Why does anyone do anything?

'No,' I put the cheque back on the table and shoved it over to their side. 'I get forty a day, up front, plus expenses afterwards.'

Montgomery smirked, 'We know how much you charge, Mr Marlowe. We're offering you substantially more than that.'

'I'm refusing,' I said.

'Why? Surely, if it's a commercial proposition, we're free to offer you more than you asked?'

He liked this. I didn't.

'Sure. You can offer it and I can refuse to take it.'

'Why would anyone refuse more?'

'My rates are set. They remind me who I am. If I take more than that and you ask me to dance the hoochie-coo I'm liable to be in two minds about it. This way I can tell you to blow. I don't dance. I'm a cheap man with a bad car who gets into trouble and finds things out for people who can't do it themselves. You want me to find something out?'

'Yes,' he said. 'That's why you're here.'

'Wrong, Mr Montgomery. I'm here to find out how you got my name. I know that now. And I'm here to see these grounds from the inside. I've done that now. Nice jacarandas, by the way.'

'You like them?'

I nodded. 'Very much. They almost made it worth my coming up here and listening to you talk about your English ceiling.'

'My ceiling is incomparable.'

I looked up at it. He had a point. 'Okay. That was dessert. The jacarandas were the main course.'

He nodded, remembering something that made him happy. 'I planted those thirty years ago.'

Montgomery smiled down at the cheque I didn't want.

'Once upon a time I would have the staff set up a table under them. We would ride these hills for hours and then gather there for luncheon. My happiest memories. Lunches with my wife, Arriane.' His rheumy eyes were lost to the memory of those long-ago days when he was young and healthy and happy. He took a deep breath, rolled his shoulders back and his body seemed to fill his skin for a moment. He was young and his wife was alive and he would ride and eat and see the trees in all their gawdy glory. Then, as sudden as death, he was old again. The drip in his fluid bag winked the sun at me. 'Most unfortunately, Arriane was afflicted with a brain fever. She spent her last eight years in a sanatorium. Never recovered. They tried everything.'

'Mr Montgomery, Miss Lyle, there are large agencies downtown, office blocks with entire floors of lawyers and investigators who can find out what you need to know. They'll give you references and they handle all sorts of jobs. Give me a pen and paper. Off the top of my head, I can give you the names of three reputable agencies who are just as discreet as I am. They'll sign undertakings to keep whatever they find out confidential. This isn't for me.'

Montgomery looked at me with a glint of a smile. 'Mr Marlowe, am I hearing you right? Are you *refusing* to work for me?'

'Look I've been here all of five minutes and it's already going sour. You seem like people with something worrying you and fighting with a smart aleck PI in a cheap suit can only add to your troubles. Let's throw in the towel before that happens. Give me a pen and some paper. I'll give you the names.'

'You're a man of honour?' said Montgomery.

'Well, let's not go nuts. But you want a big agency, trust me.'

Lyle looked worried. 'We don't want a big agency. We want a one-man operation.'

'Why?'

'It's not just private,' she said. 'It's delicate.'

Her voice cracked as it had on the telephone. She looked scared. I hoped they hadn't killed someone.

'Tell me what it is or I'll leave.'

Montgomery leaned forward and flattened his big hands on the desk. He rocked forward. After a couple of false starts, he levered himself out of the chair and a checked blanket slithered from his lap to the ground. It hurt him to stand, I could see that. He steadied himself with one hand and held the other out to me.

'Give me your word and we'll forgo the references.'

I shook it. It was a big hand.

He lowered himself halfway and fell the rest. It had taken effort to get up. I appreciated it.

'What's the problem?'

He opened the drawer immediately beneath his hand, a slim drawer lined in baize. He took out a photograph.

'This is my daughter, Christine. We call her Chrissie. She is my only child. My heir.'

Chrissie Montgomery had her father's thin lips and wide eyes. It was a formal portrait of an unhappy young woman, more handsome than pretty. She sat side on, turning to the lens, showing off her long slim neck. Her black hair was pulled up in a complicated set more suited to an older woman. Her shoulders were bare and bony. Around her neck, resting on her clavicle, sat four ropes of lustrous pearls. Matching earrings hung heavy from her earlobes.

The image had been carefully posed and lit. Chrissie looked straight into the lens, eyes hooded. Her top lip was raised, twisted in disgust, an expression that hayseed movie stars like to pass off as sophistication but Chrissie's eyes looked sad. She reminded me of the boy in the hallway.

'The picture was taken just after her husband died. They had been married just eight months when she was widowed.'

'How did he die?'

'Crashed his plane into a hillside. Fog.'

'Easy mistake to make,' I said.

'It was for Robbie St John. He was an exceptionally stupid boy. It's a wonder he lived that long.' He sighed, 'But we chose him for his family not his brains.' He took a deep breath. 'Would you like a drink?'

I asked for a scotch and soda and Lyle slunk off to see if they had such a thing.

Montgomery waited until the door shut behind her. 'My daughter is missing. She is twenty-two, a strong-willed girl, capricious, like her mother. I want to know she's all right.'

'Is she staying with friends?'

'None that I know. She spends time . . . *in the city.*' He looked down to his left as if the city was there and giving off a bad smell. 'I didn't know that until she left. I don't know who she was spending time with or where she was going. She had been *meeting* people.'

'When did she go missing?'

'Two weeks ago. We had a party to celebrate her second engagement. Next morning she was absent at breakfast. I didn't notice, she often sleeps late. She'd had rather a lot to drink at the party. She was absent all day. Finally, one of the gardeners said he'd seen her walking down the formal drive carrying a small suitcase. She went out through the main gates. This was verified by others. Some articles were missing from her room: a necklace her mother gave her, some books she favoured, some clothes. She walked out. Didn't take a car or a driver. She's missing and I'm worried about her. I want to know where she is, how she is.'

'She left. Any reason she'd do that?'

He sighed, 'Chrissie is an only child. Her mother passed several years ago, then her husband, very suddenly. I'm afraid she may feel . . . What do you know about my family history, Mr Marlowe?'

I said I didn't know anything about them and he believed me.

'We Montgomerys are of old Carolinian heritage, my ancestor was one of the original Lord Proprietors.'

That meant nothing to me but he seemed delighted by it.

'Our family have old ways of doing things, we move among certain circles, specific types of people, do you see?'

I thought of Jimmy D. and Baby Maude. We all move in certain circles. I nodded and lit another cigarette.

'We all like to spend time with people who are like ourselves, similar background, interests, not everyone can manage that. In our case we can. It means that our world gets smaller and smaller. It can become stifling. The young rankle at those limitations. I understand that. They don't always see the value in tradition. They buck against the rules. Unbeknown to me she had been spending time in town, meeting people, low-born people. Who knows who they are. They could be Catholics or Jews or blacks. They could be *anyone*.'

He smiled at me, saw that it didn't take, and dropped it.

'Did she want to get married again?'

He shrugged as if I'd asked if God was a gas, 'She agreed to it. You may have seen the recent engagement announcement in the society pages?'

'Not the first page I turn to.'

'Well, she is now betrothed to Bruce MacIntosh of the Savannah MacIntoshes . . .' He trailed away, a faint smile tugging his thin mouth this way and that. I guessed the Savannah family were a deal. 'My daughter stood for photographs. She mingled on the MacIntosh boy's arm. She seemed very much resigned to the match but the next day she suddenly went missing.'

I tapped my cigarette. 'She's not missing. She left.'

'She is missing to me. Chrissie is my heir, Mr Marlowe. She stands to inherit all of this. She may not care for English ceilings but plenty of other people do. That makes her very vulnerable.' He waved a patrician hand around his marvellous room. 'She's a biddable girl. It may not have been her idea. Someone may have convinced her to leave. They may have some hold over her, I don't know, but she's not some mere clerkess who leaves home and forgets to call. You see Chrissie is not just a Montgomery. She's *the* Montgomery.'

Lyle came back with the scotch on a small tray, the ice hitting the side of the cut crystal glass with a high excitable tink. I took it and sipped. It was good. As good as any clerkess who left home and forgot to call.

I finished my drink and stood up.

'Mr Montgomery, this isn't for me.' I stubbed my cigarette out in the ashtray, snapping it in half. 'I don't think you're telling me the whole story and that's fair enough. It's your story to tell and I won't try to chisel it out of you. I shook your hand and you have my word: I won't mention this to anyone. If she's twenty-two then she left. She's entitled to walk and so am I.'

I was halfway across the room when Anneliese Lyle called after me: 'She has a son.'

I stopped.

'By Robbie St John. Chadwick the fourth.'

I turned back, 'She didn't take him with her?'

Montgomery shook his head. 'He's still here. All alone. We don't know what to tell him.'

'He's four years old,' said Lyle. 'He's already an angry little boy. We have to try to find her so that we can tell him we tried. When he grows up we have to have something to tell him, do you see? We have to try.'

I looked at them, the great beauty and the dying man in his room of broken things. They didn't think I would find Christine and, even if by some miracle I did stumble across her, they didn't think I could bring her home. They were glad she was gone. That's why they wanted me to look for her. They thought I was a small man. They thought I wouldn't be any trouble at all.

The light winked from Chadwick Montgomery's drip, ticking off the seconds until he wasn't here anymore.

'I may need some money for expenses.'

Lyle's eye contact could have heated Chicago for a week. 'That will not be a problem.' She went back into her drawer and pulled out a brick of notes, counting out half an inch.

'You both need to know that I can only find the truth.'

'Yes, of course,' she said casually and handed me the dough. 'For incidentals.'

'Incidentals,' said Chadwick Montgomery the third.

I took it and then we all smiled around the place as if everyone was going to get everything they wanted.

6.

Jimmy slid down next to my open window. 'Hey.'

'Jimmy.'

'Hm.'

'Saw them up there.'

'Go okay?'

'Sure. Cooler up there.'

'Hot down here.'

'Think?'

'Hmm.'

All this banter was exhausting.

'So,' said Jimmy. 'You see why I gave them your name?'

'No. I still don't know why you did that. I'm not sure I want this job, Jim. I didn't like them. Chrissie a friend of yours?'

Jimmy pressed his lips together to kill a smile. 'Not really.'

'You know Cooper?'

'The butler? Not 'til I came here.'

'You say my name in front of him?'

'Sure. Gave it to Lyle while he was in the car with her. He doesn't like you.'

'I guessed.'

Jimmy grinned, 'Why is that?'

'Search me. I swear he used to.'

Jimmy tipped his monkey hat to the side. 'Well, he seems like a good enough guy. Plenty of good guys, though, no?'

'I wouldn't really know, Jimmy, and I don't know how dis-criminating you are.'

He snickered at that and then the heat stole the mood. We both sighed and looked out across the road to the thin bushes on the hillside over the way. The air was so dry you could almost see it crackle.

No cars came by on the road. They didn't happen down here, not unless they were visiting the Montgomery Mansion and only then if they were coming in by the main gates. There'd be other routes in and out of the estate, dirt roads without over-hanging jacarandas, tucked away to save the Montgomery clan the horror of witnessing a delivery.

But Chadwick had been very clear: Christine Montgomery walked down the drive with her suitcase and vanished.

'Who'd you call, Jim?'

He gave a smirk and reached into his sleeve and took out a torn piece of paper. He held it out to me between his forefinger and middle finger.

I took it.

It told me to look for Manny Perez at the Carmelita Cab Company.

'Why you shy about saying?'

He reached under his chinstrap and scratched his neck, nar-rowed his eyes and shrugged a little. Then he told me.

They had come down here and asked him where she went. He said he didn't know, that she got out using her own key for the chain. But that wasn't true. He saw her and she was standing inside the gates, holding a little suitcase and crying. He let her out but she didn't know how to get anywhere. She hadn't thought it through, not really. He took her into the gatehouse and called the Carmelita Cab Company to come and get her.

'She wanted to get away. That was as far as she'd planned.'

He pointed over at the patched-up stonework on his tiny castle. 'She crashed the night before. Banged up one of the Packards pretty bad. Had to take her into the gatehouse and give her coffee.'

'Isn't brandy more traditional for a shock?'

'She'd had plenty already. Probably why she crashed in the first place. It was the night before she left.'

'Before her engagement party or after?'

'Before.'

She'd been drinking and crying, he said, he didn't know why but he knew the urge to run. They were asking around the staff and he gave them my number so that Chrissie might have the option of not coming back even if she was found. He knew I'd do the right thing.

'I don't think they want her back. They're just worried about her being kidnapped and ransomed.'

He nodded back up the hill, 'What were they like?'

'I think my second-best suit intimidated them.'

Jimmy looked down at me, 'Marlowe, that is a bad suit.'

'It was on a discount. You're wearing a hat with a chinstrap.'

'I am.' He slumped in the heat and pulled his hat off over his face, scratched his hair hard making it stand up. 'She's all right, Chrissie.'

'You know her?'

He was vague, oh, he said, no, just from the crash night and seeing her around here but he had that soft smile that I'd seen him give before. Jimmy knew a lot of things that he never said out loud. Habit.

Anyone who knew his life understood the shoulder twitch, the shy smile, the glance at a door. He lived in a world that didn't articulate itself for fear of being arrested or hassled or stabbed by a panicky man who scared himself to death when he noticed another man's height or nice hands. It was a world in shadow. You had to know it was there to see it, in basement bars and private tea parties, in the back of bookstores and private gatherings all over the city, high and low, good and bad.

'Maybe I won't find her.'

He rolled his head and held up a hand, 'Somebody will. I'd like it to be you.'

'They got someone else looking for her?'

He flinched at the gate. Or winked. Or both. A bead of sweat rolled down his cheek from his hairline and dropped off his jaw.

'Someone driving a green Plymouth?'

He dabbed his face with his open palm. 'The Plymouth didn't ask for the name of the cab company. Didn't think to stop and ask me anything, just drove off.'

I thought of the big number on the cheque Lyle had offered me.

The Plymouth driver would be in possession of just such a fat cheque. They'd be ambitious, up and coming, full of ideas, brimming with contacts, hell bent on pleasing their rich new employer and growing their business. But they wouldn't know the city the way I knew it, they wouldn't know all the byways and low bars because if they did I'd have met them already. Unless I had.

'How old was the Plymouth driver?'

'Twenty-five? Thirty? Hard to see her face under the big hat.'

The woman. Of course they had given the job to a woman. And if she was good enough to get recommended for this job it would only be a woman with a lot of contacts, a woman with a long top lip and a nose that turned up so slightly at the end you had to see her from the side to notice.

'Redhead?'

Jimmy nodded, pinched a drip of sweat off his nose and sniffed.

'If it's who I think it is, she's all right.'

'That kind of money stops people being all right.' He glanced resentfully at the gates. 'They pay for what they want.'

'Why do you care about Chrissie? Is she nice?'

'There's none of them nice.'

'Why do you care what happens to her, then?'

He wasn't going to tell me. But he did care. Jimmy Donoghue wasn't soft hearted. He came back from Tijuana with enough money to keep him in style for a year. He promised never to see the other guy again. Could be the love had burned itself off already or maybe it was never there but Jimmy was no mug.

I told him to go back in the gatehouse and cool off. He fitted his hat back on and rolled away from the car, banged gently on the roof with his fist and peeled off to the open door.

He didn't look back.

7.

The Carmelita Cab Company was run out of a back lane off Donehy. The shop looked onto the back door of Hank's Tavern, across an alley that smelled of gasoline and beer. I liked it. It smelled honest.

The garage door stood open and a tall white-haired man in grease-stained overalls was standing by a yellow DeSoto, the side bonnet propped open, looking worried and cleaning his hands on a rag. His name was Eduardo, if his overalls were to be believed.

I said I was looking for a driver called Manny Perez. Eduardo could neither speak nor understand English until I gave him a Lincoln. Then a miracle happened: his right eyebrow rose and in perfect, nay eloquent, English, he told me that Manny Perez was currently out on a call. He'd be back in half an hour, an hour tops because the shifts changed over then and he had to bring the cab back to the garage before he took the trolley home. Would I like to attach a financial incentive for him passing my regards onto the aforementioned Mr Perez?

I smiled. Angelinos try to make Spanish speakers feel small all the time, there was no harm in a little comeback.

Eduardo's right eyebrow was still in the on position. I flapped some small bills at him and said I would very much appreciate him passing on my respectful felicitations and inviting Mr Perez to engage in a refreshment at my expense across the alley in Hank's.

Eduardo looked across at the open door and his face dropped, 'Manny can't go in there.'

I looked over at the back entrance to Hank's. Boxes of empty beer bottles were stacked outside the door and it was dark inside. Across the room, the front door was open and I could see right through to cars cruising past on Santa Monica and stopping at the lights outside. It didn't look like a place with a strict dress code.

'Colour bar?'

'No.'

'Debt?'

'Say . . .' Eduardo rubbed his hands hard on the cloth as if he was trying to get something off that only he could see. 'Manny'll call to you from the door. I have to warn you though he can't talk about our passengers with you. We're a small company in the wrong place for Spanish-speaking drivers, this is a hard business. Last thing we need is all these white people telling each other not to call Carmelita.'

'Okay.'

His eyes read my face, 'It's about Mary?'

I didn't know who Mary was but it seemed he'd rather it was about her than anything else. I looked away.

Eduardo's eyes widened and he nodded sadly. 'She divorcing him?'

'No, but he might need the money I want to give him. Send him over if you can.'

'Okay. Sure. I'll send him over.'

He waved me away with the oily rag.

I stepped in the back door of Hank's. The floor was sticky, the clientele rough and the beer cold. Whoever Hank was he'd thought of everything: they had drink and stools and kept the front and back doors propped open for a cross breeze. It smelled of beer and stale cigarettes. I had found heaven.

I ordered a beer from a barman who looked as if he could have a sideline fighting bears. The beer glass was toy-like in his hand when he put it down in front of me. A car passed outside and the sun flashed off the window onto my beer. It turned the condensation into diamonds racing down the side.

It felt magical being in there, in my discount suit, out of the afternoon heat. There were a few of us, about ten, and we all savoured the privilege of standing still, drinking and smoking. Even the small man with two swollen black eyes and a wired-up jaw, sitting alone at a table and sipping his beer through a straw, looked content.

A red trolley car rumbled by on the tracks outside and a curli-cue of dust riding a breeze staggered in the door. We all watched it do a little dance in a sunshine spotlight and still, as if it suddenly became aware of being watched, and drop to the floor. We looked around at each other, delighted as kids at Christmas. We few, we happy few, who got to see that. Until the barman's voice cut through the peace.

'GET OUT OF HERE!' He was shouting at the open back door.

'I'm not in.'

'DON'T COME IN HERE.'

Manny Perez was five foot four of throbbing hangover. He clasped his hands in front of him, head bowed as if in prayer. He was in his work uniform, a wilted red bowtie over a white button-down transparent with sweat, baggy eyes tinged yellow. He was ill, sweating in patches that don't usually operate independently: on his nose, the backs of hands, his knees. It was as if his organs knew the jig was up and were trying to get out of there.

'. . . pedir un favor . . . ?'

'Never, Perez! Never again!'

Perez muttered something but the barman didn't want to hear it. He stomped toward him, a warning to scat and then saw the panda-eyed man with the smashed-up jaw on his feet, inch-ing along the wall toward the front door.

'NO! WALTER! He's not coming in. Go sit back down.'

Walter looked at his escape, mapped the open ground between Perez and the open door and then slunk back behind the table for cover.

'GET THE HELL AWAY FROM HERE, PEREZ.'

Perez backed away carefully into the brittle sunshine. He moved stiffly, holding himself as if a sudden jerk might make him throw up or pass out. But he didn't leave. He mumbled something about meeting a man.

I threw some coins on the bar and owned up that it was me he was looking for and followed him out.

The sun was blistering now. Perez tugged my sleeve to pull me into the shade at the side of the building. Whatever had happened in there, Perez was awful sorry about it.

I know a thing or two about what drink does to a man. Some men get giggly when they take drink, some sing. They seem different but they're not. Drink's done nothing more than loosen their collar. But Perez was a different breed and I'd met men like him before.

Down in the gutter there's a special kind of drunk.

There's a man who will follow drink fifty fathoms down, knowing they have the air to get to the sea bed but not enough to get back up. Looking into Manny Perez's eyes I saw that he was one of those drunks. It was a rare thing to witness, like the blooming of those flowers that happens in the dead of night, once every thirty years, under a full moon.

Perez was a drunk who would reassure other drunks that their drinking isn't so bad. Other drunks saw him and swore they'd take a cure if they got as bad as him. But they'd never get as bad as Perez because he was a moving target and getting worse all the time. He'd be dead or missing or in an asylum before they did.

Perez was looking over my shoulder, keeping his back to the wall as if someone was after him and he whispered, 'Mary send you?'

I shook my head.

'She didn't send you?'

'No. I lied to Eduardo. I want to know about a fare.'

Manny shook his head. He couldn't talk about that. I showed him some notes and he hesitated. Then he glanced up at the garage behind me and shook his head again.

'Eduardo is a cousin of mine, it's his business. They don't like us up here, and business is bad. It's a bad business.' His voice sounded like a cast-iron bath being dragged along a road behind a car, a grating and dark and rich sound. 'Eduardo, he's a good man, I owe him a lot of money and he didn't give me no trouble, instead he gave me a job to work it off. He's a good man despite his past. I can't get him in more trouble with these people up in here, you understand?'

We looked at each other.

'His past?'

'Old news, old news, boys fighting boys, but now he's a good man, on the level, doing business here with these cabs. He asked me not to talk about the clients, I can't talk about them.'

'Okay.' I thanked him very much for coming to find me anyway and I peeled off some notes.

'Sure, no problem,' he said, folding the money away in his hip pocket.

I said he seemed to be feeling it today and he was.

I said I'd walk him to the trolley.

Out on Santa Monica the heat was oiling up from the ground. Dust whipped past us on a spiteful breeze. As we waited on the sidewalk for the lights to let him cross to the trolley stop it rattled towards us in the distance and he wiped his face with a trembling hand.

Boy, I said, I sure didn't envy him taking that trolley all the way, what with it being so clammy and crowded. We could see it was busy, lots of people standing, craning at the windows and hanging out of the open door for the air.

Yup, he said, sweating and panting at the thought.

Say, my car was just in the next street, I'd be happy to drop him somewhere if he wanted.

Oh, sure, he said, that would be fine if I didn't mind.

No, I didn't mind. I didn't mind a bit.

We both knew we were going to a bar. He'd have me pull over and invite me in because I'd given him enough to get started but not enough for a skin full.

But, of the two of us, only Manny knew who I was about to meet. That small, shaking, sorry man was the meanest drunk I've ever met.

8.

It was an old story that Perez told me as we drove down Sunset. He grew up in the Chavez Ravine, in one of the little villages at the top. His family were poor but happy, his pops ran a lunch counter over by the docks, made enough of a living for them to have a decent life, which was something because Perez was the youngest of eighteen children. They were a close family but turned on him because he married out, married an Irish woman he met at mass. They didn't know her, they didn't like her, they didn't understand her culture but Manny loved her. She was feisty. Even after they married, even after the kids started coming, she made sure she kept her job. She'd been brought over from the old country by a rich family as a nurse to their son who wasn't right, and they paid her well because she was a big lady and strict and the kid liked her. She trusted no one. She paid her own way. She'd given him seven kids in six years but even then his family couldn't take to her. They didn't understand why he didn't just slap it out of her.

'I try,' he said, 'but Mary's big and she Irish. She broke my nose.'

I caught his eye and we both laughed. Hell, I was half in love with his old lady myself.

'Irish women . . .' I said, as if it meant anything at all.

'For sure,' said Manny and we both laughed again. 'Here, man, pull in here. You wanna drink?'

I could be persuaded, I said and parked outside Lefties Bar.

It was a low brick building on the corner of Selma and Sunset, one of those low-class hang outs in a good area just around the corner from a big engineering shop. As we stepped out into the street a dusty two-door black Ford Coupe rolled past us. The reason it caught my eye is that it's a strange shape for an automobile, big body and a little cabin, especially when the back seat is locked away, and this one had an almost full set of brilliant white-wall wheel trims: back left trim was missing. Maybe they were saving up to complete the set.

Manny didn't notice it. Manny was staring at the entrance to the bar as if he'd just spotted Banquo's ghost inside, smoking a cheroot and playing *She's a Latin from Manhattan* on the saw. He was wavering.

'You don't want a drink?'

He tried to shake his head. He might not want one but his body did. A sweat sprang up on his face. His hands began to shake. Suddenly stopping here with him didn't feel fair, like putting a kitten in a pen with a gator.

I nodded him to the car, 'I'll take you home if you want.'

Manny put his head down and balled his fists, rolled his shoulders to the door. I bowled in after him.

Lefties was a working man's hang out, a sawdust and spit place with mean little windows high in the wall to stop wives looking in and to keep the sun out. Inside the door, the carpet of sawdust memorialized the footsteps of the men coming in and out like the diagrams of new dances. Everything was clean and neat and all business. The drinkers were a mix, Latin and white, all blue collar guys. Lone labourers came in to grab a beer on their way home, or else to neck some shots of rye on the way to work. They drank, ate a handful of peanuts from the bowl on the counter, said hi and then moved on.

Manny chose a booth. I didn't understand why, he seemed more like a bar pigeon to me. He asked for a large whiskey and I got us both the same and brought them to the table. I put his on the table in front of him, slid into the seat opposite and put a bowl of peanuts down.

He didn't touch his drink, just eyed it nervously, hands on his knees, as if it was a dagger he could see before him and he was terrified of what he might do. I tried drawing him out with questions to get him in the habit of talking.

Mary loved Manny but she had an Irish woman's horror of drink. She had it in her head that Manny drank a little too much. She prayed with her church group for him to stop drinking. Then they started coming to the house the whole time to do a novena about him. She brought her spinster sister over from the old country to mind the children. She hardly needed him at all and she certainly didn't like him. Then she moved the family away from his family and friends, to a different parish. Pico Union was the sort of area where Manny, drunk or sober, would never feel comfortable. She said the children would have more life chances, coming from a good parish like that. She meant a white parish. Manny didn't say it but he knew. His wife had left him and taken the kids but it seemed like she'd forgotten to tell him.

I drank and asked him why he didn't leave her.

'It's forbidden in our faith. We don't divorce. But that place, is all lawns and white people. I pass my kids' school and they call the cops on me.'

Here was a man defeated by life. He looked small and defeated. He looked at his glass of untouched whiskey, 'Cervantes says, "God who sends the wound, sends the medicine." You know Cervantes?'

'Sure, I do. "Truth will rise above falsehood as oil above water." '

Manny smiled and, for the briefest moment, I saw a glimpse of the soulful Latin man a fierce Irish girl fell for. 'Does your Irish wife like Cervantes?'

'I read him to her when we met. She loves him, of course, because the word is life in Ireland. Same in Mexico. Is the art of the poor: the materials are free. She fell in love with me because I know Lorca. You know Lorca?'

I said I didn't.

'Lorca is a poet. I tell my wife his poem: "For love of you, the air, it hurts, and my heart, and my hat, they hurt me." This is Lorca. She is Irish.'

I smiled, 'I might use that sometime.'

He smiled back but then slumped in his chair so suddenly it looked as if his shoulder bones had melted. He whispered, 'My wife is faithful, she is kind, she is a beautiful soul who deserves better than me. I was lucky to know her, even.'

We both nodded at the table. I asked him to say the line of poetry again and he did and we rolled it around in our heads and savoured it like a good Scotch.

I was seeing myself in Manny Perez but the fellow feeling was not reciprocated. Manny was preoccupied with an over-whelming obsession and when he looked at me his eyes narrowed meanly because he saw nothing but a patsy who'd pay for his drink, which reminded him that he had a drink in front of him and he looked down at the glass. He stared hard at it, concentrating, willing it into his mouth.

He raised a hand toward the glass but was shaking, the tremor getting more pronounced as his hand approached the glass. He pulled the hand back to sit on his lap again and stared at the glass, formulating a plan of attack.

He brought both hands up this time, one on either side of the glass. I think he was planning to clamp the glass between them but the shakes were too bad. He got his hands halfway there and retreated. He tried moving the hands faster but that didn't work. He licked his lower lip, his breathing uneasy. He was getting tearful.

'Want some help?' I said.

He gave a scant nod. I lifted the glass up and he manoeu-vred his mouth to the edge. I poured a little in, like feeding a convalescent.

Manny Perez sucked it in. He closed his mouth, shut his eyes and rolled his tongue around inside his mouth. He swallowed and sat very still to see if it would stay down. I could tell from his twitching that it could have gone either way. Then it went down. He had stopped sweating.

Perez arched his back. He raised his steady hands to the table. He opened his eyes. It was instantaneous: here was a different man. He smiled to himself, a slow smirk, and lifted the rest of the drink to his mouth and, almost casually, downed it.

I finished mine and got us two more large ones. He drank his straight down and then stared at mine like a starving man eyeing a wheelbarrow full of chops. I pushed it across. He drank it as though I'd bet him he couldn't and he needed the money.

Manny was happy now. Whatever pain he'd wrestled with all day was gone. He knew why he was alive and who he loved and he knew they were well and he was doing right by them.

That incarnation lasted until his empty glass hit the table again. Then he looked around and I knew he was wondering where the next one was. Now a nameless worry wormed around in his eyes. Maybe he was remembering why he had resisted drinking all day long, why his wife prayed all the time, why she begged him to stop. I got another two. He let me have a sip of mine before he commandeered it.

The insight didn't last. He necked it with his eyes wide open and I saw the Manny Perez his wife wanted to move away from.

Manny was taller now. Filled out. As if he'd been born a quart down. He was looking around the bar and not enjoying what he was seeing. I thought of the man back at Hank's, Walter, drinking through a straw. It made sense.

I palmed him some notes and said Jimmy the One gave me his name. I wanted to know about a fare he picked up at the gates of the Montgomery Mansion a few days ago. Perez looked at the money in his hand. It was already damp and already not enough. I offered to double it if he told me where she went.

He remembered Chrissie. She'd tipped him twenty dollars on a dollar-fifty ride, which was an awful good way to get yourself remembered. He got her outside Jimmy's gatehouse over there on Montgomery. She had a little suitcase with her. She asked him to take her on up to Union Station to catch the train to Chicago. To Chicago.

If Perez hadn't been a decent man underneath, a man who regretted letting Eduardo down, he might not have repeated himself, but he was and he did and it was a tell. He was holding back.

The cast had changed in the bar. It was mostly Latins now, in grey overalls, friendly and warm. They all worked at an engineering joint around the corner, they told us, their shift started work in twenty minutes.

Manny Perez, the sorriest man in the world, looked up at one of them, peeled his lips back and said something in Spanish. It was a clipped sentence, a short statement that I didn't understand.

The entire room stilled. Everyone in there looked at him. Then they looked at me. Then they looked at him.

'What did you say?'

'Nothing.' Perez smiled the sickly smile of a man who couldn't help himself.

The shift boys finished their drinks hurriedly and got out of there but three men were whispering at the side of the bar. They didn't seem to be going to work. They were wearing baggy pants and sports coats. They seemed young.

Manny didn't look at them. 'Get me another drink.'

I glanced over to the trio and saw a flash of blade.

I stood up. 'Let's go someplace else.'

'Hell no! We's just getting warm!'

'I'm leaving. You can come or not.'

I slid out of the booth, staying between Manny and the blade, not looking back but knowing he was behind me.

Out on the street I glanced back and saw Perez, a mean-mouthed man with clenched fists swaggering after me.

Back in the car he said, 'You, man, I show you where I drink with men. Real men go drink up in here. It's real men drink.'

I like trouble. I like fighting. I like adventures but I didn't like

56

this. Manny felt like a man who wanted to die tonight and I didn't much want to die that night or any night soon. It's a rule I have, trying not to die, but I knew he was just one or two more shots from blacking out and when he did he'd tell me everything.

He directed me eight blocks over, to a busy street that smelled of rotting cabbage and tired men.

This bar had no name. It barely had a door. It was a cellar below a slumped one-storey wooden shack at the end of a row of crumbling tenements.

The entrance was a dark opening that yawned like an invitation to sin. Ripped bills were posted on the outside of the shack. Trails of cigarette smoke seeping into the street at ankle level.

'Here. We go down. This way.'

I looked down wooden steps so steep and worn you had to take them one at a time and sideways. Down there the ground was raw soil. Manny went first and beckoned to me to follow. He looked excited. I went down. The walls inside were running damp and plastered over with Spanish newspapers, haphazard, yellowing as they sucked up the moisture and smoke. The room smelled of earth and eggs.

It was busy, almost full. Some men wore greasy overalls, some were dressed in worn-out suits that used to fit someone else. No one in there looked like they'd come to celebrate a promotion in the bank. It was serious drinking in here, vocational. Hollowed-out eyes followed us down the ladder. I was the only non-Mexican in there and I was wearing a suit.

The room stilled and silence fell. Every eye swivelled toward us.

Manny Perez addressed the room, said something about him not being Tonto and me not being policia. Reading the faces around us, it didn't seem to have taken. Manny took the five dollar bill out, 'Hombre bribe me fi' dollar. I'ma drink it.'

That seemed to do it. The suspicion eased but the atmosphere didn't.

We parked up at the bar. It wasn't really a bar. It was a shelf with ashtrays on it. There was only one stool and a toothless man was sitting on that, so drunk that he was staying upright by force of will alone.

Behind it a man in a dirty white apron was guarding two bottles of liquor. They were sitting on a small table behind him, one clear, one yellow. Men would shove their glasses out to him and he'd take their money before filling them up again. When the bottle ran dry he threw it into a pile in the corner and called over to a boy who ran up the ladder and came back moments later with a fresh one. Then service would resume.

There wasn't much talking in the bar. This was a serious place where drinking was a religious practice, a temple to staying topped up. Men drank until they hit the sweet spot and left. More men would come down the ladder. The bottle would finish and be replaced. The men would pay.

The bad news was that most everyone here already knew Manny Perez and had a measure of him. They stayed back from us. One man watched from the far corner, standing straight to take in the sight of Manny Perez, back at this bar, and the foolish gringo in the discount suit he'd dragged along with him. He raised his glass to me and gave me a pitying smile, as if I couldn't know what was going to happen when Manny got liquored up.

But I did know. I was counting on it.

Before we even got our order Manny was feeling better. He wiped his mouth with his sleeve and pointed to the clear bottle of tequila.

The barman kept his eyes on me as he poured two shots. He looked my suit up and down. I'd found the one place in town where I looked fancy. That didn't endear me to it.

'You pay,' said Manny meanly.

'I'm paying?'

He narrowed his eyes to knife slits, '*You* bring *me*, ese.'

It didn't seem worth fighting about. Chadwick was paying anyway. I dropped some money, finished my drink and put my glass down for another tequila. It was rough but doing the job. The barman gave me a refill. I could see why Manny liked this drink. It was abrasive but only until it got halfway down. Now that I had a second one in my hand I could feel the first one warming my knees. I lifted the glass to my mouth and saw Manny: he was downing his fourth, his hand moving as smoothly as a tram on an oiled track. The look on his face would have broken his mother's heart. Eyes hooded with spite and brimming with remembered slights. He scanned the room for someone to take it out on. He settled on me.

'What you want with me, bubu?'

'Drink.'

'You want me to drink?' He wasn't buying that. No one wanted Manny to drink. Even Manny didn't want Manny to drink. 'Who you?'

I lifted the glass to my mouth, drained it and turned to him, taking a step closer, squaring up for a dance. He raised his face to look me in the eye. Even crazy-drunk Manny Perez could see I was a foot taller than him and less drunk. He decided to let it go.

I ordered him another and he shrugged as if he didn't care either way.

'Manny, I could just leave.'

He didn't want that. He didn't want that a lot.

So we drank and stood there, hating each other. He downed three for each one I had. I sipped and I watched his mood shift like sand in a storm, now angry, now sad, now sentimental. He didn't say much. It was soothing to watch. It made me feel like a winner.

Somehow an hour or so had passed. The heat cascading down the stairs seemed to soften. It began to feel like going outside might not be the worst idea.

The barman changed. This one was younger and moved faster but wore the same apron as the last guy: the stains were all in the same places.

Manny was by now fantastically drunk and suddenly we arrived at my station: I knew the blackout point when I saw it.

There was an absence in his eyes. Still moving, still lifting the glass to his mouth and swallowing, but the essence of him, the putting things together and recall, all of that was gone. I could have auctioned him for parts and he'd have gone along with it.

'Tell me about the dame at the Montgomery place.'

'Yah.' He drank. 'Union Station. Chicago. Train. Dropped. Tip. Twenty dollars tip. Ne'er fo'get her. Ha!'

'Where did she go?'

'Seen her next day. Hill Street. Walking.' Drink. Refill.

'Suitcase?'

'Nah.' Drink. 'Sae'n clothes though. Same same.' Drink.

'Sure it was her?'

'Who?' Drink. Refill.

'Twenty dollar tip, huh?'

Big smile. Drink. 'Twenty! Man, I seen her. Next day. Getting off the littl' funicular they got up there.'

'Wearing what?'

'What?'

'Twenty dollar. Next day, on the funicular, what was she wearing?'

'Oh! White blouse, yes? Black skirt, legs — man! New hat though. Cheap hat.'

'Kind of cheap hat?'

'Big *tonta* hat. Straw. Cheap, get them ever'where, know the sort.' He held his hands out to demonstrate. It seemed to be very wide. 'Next day.'

'Morning or evening?'

'Ha?'

'Twenty dollar tip. You saw her the next day. In the morning?'

'Sure. Morning. Hill Street. Getting off the littl' funicular they got up there, man. HA!' He slammed his open palm on the bar top and it made a sound so loud everyone in the room jumped and looked.

The current wearer of the sacred apron shot me a look. It didn't mean get him to do it again.

I wanted to ask Manny more questions but they were really the same question: could he be sure, was it really her, how did he know. I stopped myself because the moods Manny was floating in and out of turned on a dime.

I said we were leaving as if it was his idea, we'd already discussed it and we were going on someplace else, some place better.

He finished his last drink, looked up at the ceiling and screamed something in Spanish that shocked the other men in the room. Had any of the listeners in the bar been wearing pearls, they'd have clutched them. The barman's mouth dropped open. It was a parting phrase, a vulgar summation of a desire to leave so strong that the speaker would have happily committed a certain crime upon a co-sanguineous person of the same gender if it meant they could leave the present company. It sounded like a line of poetry: the rhythm was perfect, the balance of consonants and vowels perfect, but you knew it couldn't be a poem because no one would ever write sentiments that terrible down on paper, much less fit them into a poem and, if they did, no one would publish it.

It was a good thing Manny was so small. He needed a lot of help up the ladder. I was almost at the top, a hand under his arm, when he tipped back and closed his eyes, committing to wherever gravity wanted to take him, but fellow drinkers had anticipated it and shoved as I pulled. They wanted him the hell out of there.

In the street the heat and the smog and the sun and the day slapped my face hard.

The LAPD are tough on drunks and worse on Mexicans. I drove him over to Pico and left him sitting on the edge of the sidewalk. Halfway home I called in at a diner for coffee and a grilled cheese. It tasted of tequila. I ordered more coffee and that did too. I kept thinking about Manny Perez and his wife Mary and the mean, mean look in his eye.

I hoped Mary was a big woman. I hoped she never stopped slapping back.

9.

A ragged dawn was breaking over Bunker Hill. Street lights snapped off along Olive as I watched an angry sun rise over the city. I parked on a street that was broad and wide. Blocks of crumbling apartments lined it, muscling up against small houses and empty lots. I was watching the entrance to the funicular. It was running half empty at this hour in the morning.

Bunker Hill was high and overlooked the ordered civic buildings of downtown. It was there before them though, its steep dirt cliffs still threatened to spill down over the traffic below. It had been a grand address once, full of haughty clapperboard villas with parquet floors, more room than anyone could possibly need and shady porches where the winners and well-to-dos could retire of an evening to sip iced drinks on swing seats and watch the rest of us scramble around on the valley floor. The roads were lined with broad trees and fine benches. To capitalize on the glamour of the area, named apartment blocks grew up in the spaces around these villas: the Zelda, the Winnewaska, the Stanley.

But the old money and gracious living had moved on decades ago.

The grand villas were rotted to their roots. Rooms were rented out singly now to people at rock bottom or those about to get there. Parquet floors and wooden walls peeled apart, uncoupling slowly as if embarrassed by a long-forgotten passion. The population was old and saddened. Even the newer apartment buildings had a regretful air. Here and there sidewalks and tarmacadam ran out for no good reason and the roads turned to bare dirt. Some buildings had already been torn down because they were unsafe and sliding down the hill, leaving vacant lots that served as a place to dump clapped-out cars.

The Angels Flight funicular had been built when the area was at its height. It spanned the steepest part of the drop to downtown and was often busier on the way up than the way down. Chrissie had been seen getting off at the bottom, which meant she had to get on at the top. I figured I'd get up here early and watch from the car, wait and see if roaring drunk Manny Perez was telling the truth.

I watched the tired old hill wake in waves that morning. A smattering of office workers, men in overalls and shop girls gathered at the queue to the funicular. One little wooden carriage left just as one arrived, the door opened and it sucked them all in from the street and whisked them away. This went on for a while but the overalls were slowly replaced with men in suits and hats, men reading newspapers, carrying their paper bag lunches. There was some variation: once an old woman in a deep cloche hat struggled with her trolley and everyone helped her. Another time a tall skinny girl in a blinding white blouse carried a tiny dog and everyone wanted to pet it. Mostly though people were robotic in their early morning routine, barely looking at each other, their minds already on the day ahead.

I expected to glimpse someone who might or might not be Chrissie in the crowd and wonder all day if my tired eyes had imagined her, to come back later and look for a second sighting. That's not how it happened at all.

I noticed Chrissie Montgomery the moment she stepped out of her front door. She came from a small wooden house in my eye line. She used her own key to lock the door behind her from a wooden porch that sloped downhill as if it owed money to the rest of the house and was trying to welch on it.

The house was on a very steep hill with an onion dome roof that sagged like a beret on a drunk woman. It was a mini version of the big villas further up the hill, a limerick to their epic poems. It slumped, every line untrue, with two large bay windows, one above the other. The top one was cracked and mended with yellowing tape.

Chrissie stepped into the street, fit her sun hat on and walked down to the queue, waited, helped a woman with a baby and dog get a seat and then standing, holding the strap handle, disappeared below the lip of the hill.

She was tall and slim, had her father's height and big hands. The hat she wore was a big flat plate of straw, a cheap, silly hat that wouldn't last but was fun to wear. The bitter haughtiness from the formal portrait was gone. She looked like a younger self.

I noticed her, anyone watching for her would have, because Chrissie was the only person in the street not just rolling through motions she had performed a million times. She wasn't tired or bored. She was fully and completely present and it made her stand out. The quality of her clothes added to that because, apart from the crazy hat, nothing was over-washed, nothing a cheap version of something else. A white silk blouse tied high at the neck rippled on her back over grey wide-leg slacks and flat shoes.

Chrissie Montgomery was easier to find than an optimist in a casino. It had taken me less than twenty-four hours and if I could find her then others could too, bad people, or even good people. Someone in a green Plymouth could find her and they might not care that Chrissie had chosen to leave.

That thousand dollar bonus might be reason enough to turn her in.

10.

I stepped up the front porch and knocked on the pebbled glass. Subsidence must have jammed the door shut a couple of times: wide triangles had been shaved off the top and bottom of the door to keep the horizon of the window true. It was disorientating. A shadow widened in the window. A body was coming this way, walking heavily.

The door opened an inch. A shifty eye looked me over. 'Whaddaya want?'

'Good morning. I'm Buddy Asner, Investigations Department of –'

'Keep the racket down!' she hissed. 'I have shift workers sleeping upstairs.'

'Sorry, ma'am,' I whispered. 'I'm with the Mason Brothers' Aerodrome Insurance Company, Investigations Department. I wonder if I might ask you some questions about one of your tenants?'

She shut the door firmly but loitered behind the window.

I spoke to the glass, 'There is a cash bonus for aiding our investigation.'

She hissed back, 'How much?'

'Ten dollars.'

The door opened again. The eye narrowed. 'When is this? In two years, after you've finished up, and then it's ten dollars in tokens for a laundromat in Glendale?'

'No, ma'am. It's ten dollars in cash, right now, before I vacate your abode.'

She wasn't sure. 'And exactly how long will it take for you to "vacate" my "abode"?'

'Trainers tell us to make it a maximum of twenty minutes.'

The door opened wide. The eye belonged to a shapely woman with an orange headscarf wrapped around her rollers and a cigarette hanging from her mouth. Her house dress had seen better and cleaner days. Her slippers didn't fit her, they were too big, a man's slippers, and it made her shuffle. She didn't seem to have eyelashes on her tiny eyes. If she did, they were hiding. She was fifty and not one bit sorry about it.

I slid into the hall and shut the door behind me.

She murmured as if we were backstage during a play, 'Show me that ten dollars you were talking about.'

I duly did so. She liked looking at it. She licked her lips and touched her headscarf as if she was thinking of inviting it on a day cruise.

'What do I have to do?'

'Well, ma'am, just answer some questions.'

'About what?'

'About tenants and tenancies.'

'Not about religion?'

'No.'

'Okay. Come on in. But no religion.' She squinted at me, unsure that I'd stick to that, and then beckoned me down the corridor to the kitchen.

The house was clean and sparse, the wooden floors and table scrubbed raw and smelling of Lysol. The back door was open to a dirt yard and a big ginger cat loitered, half in, half out.

She whispered an apology for the smell, 'I leave a little bowl of white vinegar out but it takes a while. Have to keep everything clean around here because of the r— well, *pests*. Lots a' pests.'

She gave me a cup of burned-up coffee from a pot on the stove, topped up with an inch of cream. When I said yes to sugar she added five and used a paper napkin as a coaster for my cup. 'Drink that up, sonny. It'll put a bit of meat on you.'

She winked at me.

I almost winked back but figured insurance men probably didn't do that. 'And how may I address you?'

'Why, I'm Mrs Helen Sophia Dudek. Helen. Call me Helen.'

I sipped the coffee. It was unexpectedly delicious. When I told her so she swiped at me with a dishcloth and ordered me to go on.

I lifted my briefcase to my knee and took out a notepad and pen, 'I take it that you are the lady of the house, Helen? This is your house?'

'It most certainly is,' she said proudly and then remembered what the house looked like. 'My poor dead husband Willy bought this house for me. It's mine for as long as it stands.' She kicked at a skirting board that was coming away from the wall. 'Place is falling down the hill. One day I'll wake up and get out of bed on Broadway.'

'And you let out some rooms in this establishment?'

She wasn't sure about that question. 'Are you from the government?'

'No.' I hugged my briefcase. 'I am here on a matter which may be of substantial benefit to a certain young lady staying in your house. A widow. A young widow who is entitled to a substantial payment of a policy that I suspect she is unaware of.'

She clutched her heart. 'Joan.'

'Joan?' I said.

'You mean Joan Baudelaire? That poor young thing. Just moved here a week ago, a widow, bless her heart. His airplane crashed into a mountain.'

'Joan is using her maiden name.' I clicked my fingers. 'That's why we couldn't find her. Is she the reason we're whispering?'

'No, no, that's my dear Evelyn. She's been with me for two years. She works nights. Joan works days.'

'I see. Good. Well, we are Joan's poor husband's life insurance firm and the case has lately been settled. We pay out on a sliding scale, contingent on level of hardship, as it were, but we have to get it right. Hence our fund for ad hoc information on the financial circumstances of our beneficiaries.'

She wasn't sold yet. 'I still get ten dollars?'

'Oh yes, a flat rate fee regardless of outcome to the payee.'

'I'll tell you all about Joan, that poor kid.'

'So, Helen, here's what's happened. Miss Baudelaire's husband died in an accident and the insurance firm didn't want to pay out. We at Mason Brothers think that's a raw deal.'

'It *is* a raw deal. These insurance companies –'

'Oh, I know. Well, it is quite a lot of money, because of the way he died. They're very reluctant. If they get wind that we've found Joan here then they'll come here and offer her a tenth of what she's due to settle the case.'

Helen gasped. 'They wouldn't dare! Those sons of b– guns!'

'I know.'

'They'd chisel the glass eye from a blind man's head.'

'I know, Helen. They're very bad. They are fighting us tooth and nail. I need you to promise me now, if someone else comes to the door asking for Joan you won't tell them she's here. I don't know how broke she is . . .'

'Oh, she's got nothing. Just a little suitcase and a job. Like dear Evelyn. She brought Joan by and asked me to give her a room. Said Joan was a widow. Like me.'

'Well, you're good to help her.'

'Oh, I took a deposit.' She cringed at that. 'Not to be greedy but, in case something gets broke, you know?' Helen didn't know she had one of the richest women in America staying in her house.

'You seem like a nice lady. On the level.'

'Unlike the house.' She laughed at that. The cat left in disgust.

'They old friends, Evelyn and Joan?'

'No. They barely know each other but littl' Evelyn likes to

save people. Always bringing back waifs and strays. I think she found Joan at work. Maybe Joan was crying in there or something. Evelyn is a putz for stray dogs. She got those big eyes. She's a sweetheart. From Oklahoma originally. Her family write from all over, guess they must have moved. She'll tell you New York because of all the hate people out here have for Okies, but she's an Okie.' Dudek was smiling as she whispered all of this. The fondness was real.

'Evelyn been with you long?'

'Two years.'

'She out late every night?'

'Most. Hard worker.'

'We all got to make a living, Helen. I'll bet this is a swell house for young Joan. You said Joan had a job. Where does she work?'

'Down in that old Bradbury Building. Some art gallery they have up in there. The Art of Now, it's called. She showed me a book of the pictures they're selling. I don't know. Looked like garbage but what do I know . . .'

She was trying to see what I had written down in the pad, reading it upside down.

I let her read it as I finished my coffee. I had jotted her name and address, Joan's name and 'Bradbury Building'. The paper napkin was stuck to the bottom of my sugar-sticky cup. I peeled it off and looked at the image printed on the corner. It was a black smudge of two people dancing.

'What's this?'

'Oh! I got a box of them from Evelyn. The crate got left out and they all got wet. They let Evelyn take them, it's all above board.' Dudek looked as guilty as if she'd stolen the Lindberg baby.

'Is this a picture of two dancers?'

She didn't look at it, 'Oh yes, the bar. It's the Dancers. That's where Evelyn works. She's the hatcheck girl up there. They know she took 'em. You can call and ask if you need to.'

Made sense. Chrissie and Evelyn met there. The hatcheck

booth was small and away from the floor of the bar. It was quiet. They'd be around the same age.

'I don't mind about napkins, Helen, I'm just asking because my manager took me in there once but I can't quite recall where it is.'

Helen described the location on Sunset and I pretended to struggle to remember. 'Is it nice?'

'Meh. High end. Evelyn likes it well enough but Evelyn likes everything. She's sunny, you know? That's why she gets those tips.'

'I think maybe I saw her there. She a cute little redhead?'

'Blonde. A sweet little thing. Dimple on her chin.'

I put the napkin back down, 'Anyway.' I opened the briefcase and put the pad inside and stood up. 'I don't want to get up any false hopes so I'd be glad if you didn't tell Joan I was here. In fact, Mrs Dudek,' I smiled, 'I have to ask: would you mind if I write to my employers about you?'

'Tell 'em what?'

'That you have formally undertaken not to reveal the whereabouts of this young widow to any other callers nor my calling here to any other party, up to and including Miss Baudelaire herself?'

'Why would you tell them that? I already said I wouldn't say nothing.'

I reached into my wallet and took out the ten dollars, laying it on the table, 'Because, Mrs Dudek, such an undertaking, submitted in writing, in the proper form, automatically triggers the issuing of a further one hundred dollars to the party so mentioned.'

Mrs Dudek said oh! She didn't mind. She didn't mind one bit if I did that! Then she saw me out to the door. The ginger cat was sitting in the hall somehow. Must have found another way in.

'Mr Asner, it was my very great pleasure to meet you. Please don't write that I had my rollers in.'

'Mrs Dudek, had you met me in a ball gown, you could not have been more gracious.'

She tittered at that one. The ginger cat watched us, revolted.

'Please don't say anything to anyone. For Joan's sake.'

'Well, you tell them I won't say anything. You be sure to do that.'

'I will, Mrs Dudek.'

She mimed locking her lips and throwing the key over her shoulder. I stepped down off the porch, making a mental note to send her a hundred dollars.

If Chadwick Montgomery was paying my expenses, everyone I took a shine to was getting a bite.

11.

I pulled over outside the Bradbury Building. It was square, wide as a city block, squat as a toad. Fire escapes snaking up the outside and the big stones and small windows gave it weight and heft. It was blackened but red brick peeked out from a mourning veil of soot. Half the store fronts were papered over. Bums dawdled in the shadows, slumped to sleep it off or looking out at the day, worried. No one knew how long this spell would last.

The heat of the day was rising. It was climbing out of the sewers. It was creeping out of the stones. Cracks in the sidewalk flowered open to let out heat-warmed dust that lurked in the air, ready to catch children by the throat, smother babies or hold a cushion over Grammie's face. It was early, not yet noon, but the memory of yesterday's sandy heat made everyone dread it, like the sound of a second cough in an empty house at two a.m.

The heat was good for me. It would be harder for Chrissie to wonder who I was and why I was asking questions when half her mind was on the beach or the tub at Mrs Dudek's.

I got out of the car and stepped into a dried-out newspaper discarded at the kerb. Illness. Murder. Corruption. Foreign wars. Could have been from any time in human history.

Outside the doorway two bums were either fighting or dancing, moving so slowly it was hard to tell. One of them, barely five feet tall, had a heavy tan face of indeterminate age. The other wore wide-legged pants with frayed suspenders over a ripped shirt. He had a boxer's nose, a jockey's height and maybe someone else's knees: it was hard to see under his baggy pants.

The main entrance was set back from the street. I stopped in the shade of it, lit a cigarette and watched them wrestle awhile. Boxer Nose was strong, shoving Tan this way and that, making caveman grunts. Tan didn't seem to have any agenda that I could see, other than resisting Boxer Nose's shoves. He put his heart into it though, baring his yellow teeth and adding another rip to Boxer Nose's shirt. It became hypnotic, this shoving match conducted with great passion, but I had promises to keep and miles to go.

I went on inside.

The building had seen better days. The tiled floor was missing some teeth and masking tape was holding some other bits in place. The walls were chipped and the thick brown paintwork flashed white primer.

An elderly doorman sagged at his desk. No wonder. His uniform was dark blue. His hair was a shock of white, cropped close, glittering like light snowfall on a muddy hill. The brittle daylight did his face no favours. He looked like a headache in a suit.

On the desk in front of him sat a newspaper folded to the crossword. He had pencilled in one word and then licked his finger to rub it out. *Pensive.* He glowered at me as I walked in.

I watched him consider standing up and demanding to know my business here, but he was defeated by the heat. He stayed where he was, flapped his hand at me, beckoning me over to him. I took my time. No one tells me what to do.

'Ahoy hoy,' I said, flashing him a business card. 'Roger Allan. I'm from *Art Collector Monthly*, out of Chicago. I'm looking for –' I checked my notebook. It's the little things that set me apart. 'What's the name of this art gallery you boys have in here . . . ?'

'The Art of Now?'

'The Art of Now Gallery, yes, that's it. Do you have to call up?'

'I don't think so. You can just go in and look. It's like a store. Might not be open though because of the heat up there.' He pointed inside the door. 'It's five degrees hotter inside that door than it is outside, it gets worse the higher up you get and they're on the top floor. I'll call up for you, save you going up there for nothing.'

He reached over to the telephone and dialled three digits. I could hear it ringing out on the other end.

He looked me up and down, sighed, gazed yearningly at the street outside.

'Feeling it?'

He nodded as if his dog had died, attempted a smile. 'Bad.' The phone rang out in his ear but I could hear it as well, a distant tinny echo rattling around a wide-open space.

The doorman laid a swollen hand on his chest, 'They make me wear this uniform. Part of the job. Keeps the bums out.' He looked out through the door at Fred and Ginger on the sidewalk. They were slowing down. Boxer Nose was losing interest.

'They should get you a lighter uniform.'

He said, 'I should get me another job, brother.'

The ringing stopped and a woman's voice answered, a velvet purr, 'Good morning, Mr Farlow.'

He called her honey and explained that there was someone here wanting to look at the pictures. Okay to send him up? She wasn't too hot up there, was she?

She whittered on the other end, I didn't catch what she said but it made him smile and nod and he finished with, 'Okay sweetie, be sure and open all those windows as well.' He hung up, looked at me and remembered how hot he was.

'Top floor.' He glanced vaguely upwards. 'Take the elevator, second door on the left.'

I thanked him.

I opened the door and stepped into a narrow brick corridor. The building opened up above me, floor after floor of elegant blackened iron railings and yellow wood undersides. A glass ceiling over the gallery throbbed with white light and the heat dropped heavy into the narrow passageway. It was like walking into a pharoah's tomb.

The sound of typewriters and heavy machines clattered from

wall to wall but it was a soft cacophony, edgeless, faceless, a dream of busyness.

A man materialized from deep shadow on the first-floor balcony. He leaned over the railing, resting his bare arms on the handrail. His shirt sleeves were folded up to the elbows, held there with steel suspenders. He peered down at me. I took off my hat and showed him my face. He smiled and waved me away.

'Sorry,' he said, 'thought you were someone . . .' Then he stepped back and was eaten by the shadow again.

I was no one.

This no one stepped into the elevator. The operator was sitting on a stool, sweating like a politician in a confessional. He stood up slowly when I got in and gave me a look as if we were at the tail end of a day-long argument. I asked for the top floor. He sighed and rolled his eyes as if I'd asked him to carry me up there.

'I'm not picking on you,' I said, 'I just need to get up there.'

'You'll see,' he said, 'you'll see.'

He turned the crank to shut the door. He pressed the button and slumped against the side as the cage rose. We passed through a funnel of tiles and ornamental iron, floor by floor, the temperature rising by the second. By the time we got to the top floor I could see what he meant.

'You see?' he breathed, sweat dripping off his chin.

'Oh yes,' I said, taking my hat off to dab my brow. 'I see.'

He opened the door and I stepped out into the Sahara.

If someone was trying to represent a hangover through architecture, this was it. My eyes hurt from the glare. My head throbbed at the back. My throat hurt. I felt sick. I got over to the wall and flattened my hands on it, drinking in the cold from the tiles. I looked along the balcony to a sign.

The Art of Now sign had been painted by someone who couldn't make up his mind between red and black or backwards and forwards. It looked like the alphabet was learning to tango.

But below that sign stood Chrissie Montgomery, smiling and waiting for me.

12.

From a mile away along the balcony, Chrissie Montgomery gave me a little wave and showed me her teeth. I showed her mine. I suppose back in monkey times the showing of teeth was a peace sign but it didn't really mean that anymore. A smile could mean anything from 'Let peace be unconfined' to 'I'm planning to rip your face off'. It's all in the delivery.

I walked over to her, fixing to find out what she meant by it.

The heat up here was too much for her as well. Two urgent red dots sat high on her cheeks just under her ice-blue eyes. She dabbed her cheeks with a genteelly folded kerchief.

She was taller than she looked from a distance. Five ten or eleven, I only had inches on her. She was skinny and gawky but elegant still. Her black hair was oiled back from her pale, bony face. She'd added a lick of kohl to her eyes, a brush of clear red to her lips. Her white blouse was tied with a bow on her long neck, her wide pants were tight-waisted, secured with a small black belt, and she was wearing flat brogues, black. Even this far away I could tell they were good leather.

'Good morning,' she said sweetly. 'Won't you come in?'

She motioned me through a door to a blast of wind. Three big black fans were sitting in a row below the window, running high. All of the windows were open. I stood for a moment, breathing.

Chrissie Montgomery was behind me enjoying it too. 'Ah, the

fans. Stand there as long as you need to. We're not exactly overrun.'

I looked down into the long narrow room. Small windows ran along one wall but the wall facing them had raw plyboard stuck on it. Seats and benches were scattered around the room and they were made of cheap plyboard too, all unpainted and unfinished. Along the wall hung small paintings in elaborate frames.

'I'm Roger Allan, correspondent for *Art Collector Monthly*. Perhaps you know our publication?' I didn't know our publication. It was on a business card I'd come across but I'd never found the magazine on sale. From her blank expression I could tell that Chrissie Montgomery hadn't seen it either.

'Of course! Of course, I do, Mr Allan. Joan Baudelaire, gallery assistant here.'

'Well, how do?' I bowed a little and a smile tickled the back of her eyes.

'I do very well, Mr Allan. Thank you for inquiring.'

I held my hand out and hers brushed into mine. She shook twice and let go. My hand felt strangely wonderful. I looked at it. Traces of powder sat in my palm.

'It's so terribly warm up here,' she said, 'I powder my hands before anyone comes in otherwise . . .' She cast her eyes down like a stripper about to burst the final balloon, 'Moist . . .' She gave me a look that wasn't shy but not seductive either.

It was an honest, unembarrassed look. A straight gaze. If she was any other young woman I'd have been surprised by that but I knew she was Chrissie Montgomery, that she'd been married and widowed and was about to be married again, that she had a son and a fortune that would make Rockefeller's eyes water. She was young but she'd lived a lot of lives already.

'So: *Collector Monthly*? You're interested in investment pieces?'

'Of course.'

'Well, I can see why you've come. Ours is the show to cover, isn't it?'

I supposed it was. She liked that.

'Allow me to give you an information sheet.'

She handed me a piece of creamy paper typed with a couple of paragraphs about an artist they were showing. He was called Pavel Viscom, he was from Europe. Had a lot of exhibitions there but this was his first in the US and the first since his death.

'Just how did Viscom die?'

'He was beaten to death over politics. Dreadful how unsafe Europe is. Won't you come in?'

We were already in but she tilted her head and waited for an answer.

'Sure,' I said, and waited to see what would happen.

She walked further into the room, inviting me to look at the art on the wall. Behind the desk sat two three-feet-square wooden crates full of wood shavings, lids off, the shavings slipping onto the floor.

'We've allowed some buyers to take their paintings away immediately. When the Los Angeles Museum buys two pictures and wants to display them right away, one simply doesn't quibble.'

'Quite.'

'Viscom,' she said, 'was a genius. These works are flying off the wall faster than we can put them up. Look.' She pointed to a daub.

It made no sense to me. The painting was framed in gold as if it was something but it was bits of a German magazine article covered in red paint with black paint smooshed over it.

Chrissie looked at me and smiled appreciatively. 'Extraordinary, isn't it?'

'It certainly is something,' I said.

'He has fundamentally challenged how we think of visual representation.'

We shuffled sideways and looked at the next few pictures. It was all garbage. A cartoonish painting of a broken violin with newspaper collages in one corner. Another was bits of wood glued messily on top of each other and painted over. A small one with a cup on a table that seemed to be turning inside-out at the same time as turning outside-in. Then a terrible painting of a crying woman with five noses, wearing a hat.

I didn't know how long it would be before I pointed out that the Emperor couldn't paint. The worse the pictures got the more ecstatic she was. We looked until I couldn't take it anymore.

'Miss Baudelaire, don't you ever look at these and think – well, you know?'

She looked at me and a laugh bubbled up from her belly and fizzed in her eyes.

'Yes.' She barked a hoot. 'Yes, Mr Allan, yes I do. But we both know that in our business it's often not about the art itself so much as the story behind the art.'

'Of course.'

'So far we have sold major works of his to several very discerning individual collections, two museums – the Los Angeles Museum is the only one I'm authorized to name at the moment. But, as you no doubt appreciate, this is when the money can be made on these marvellous works. This gallery is the trustee for the estate and it will be very well managed. Your readers will want to get in on the ground floor.' She gave me a sickly smile, embarrassed by the hard sell.

I didn't think Roger Allan was the type to comfort her. I gave her a sceptical smile. 'I think you flatter your profession, Miss Baudelaire, assuming management can add that much value. It's the sheer quality of the work after all.'

She shook her head, 'Well, Vincent Van Gogh only sold one painting in his lifetime. He's doing rather well now and it's only because his sister-in-law was left all of his paintings when her husband died and she needed the money. She was so clever about it and no one thought too much of him before she managed the estate so brilliantly. And it's working. Mr Viscom's works have already quadrupled in value.'

'Is this the first show of his work outside of Europe?'

'Yes. He had never sold a single work here until Zimmerman

put this show on. He'd been invited but . . .' She went off on a ramble about how Zimmerman had managed the sales after his death. Well and profitably was the gist of it.

I interrupted, 'It's art without the messiness of the artist.'

'Exactly! Just so. And with Peggy Zimmerman being so rich she can decide not to sell until the market is favourable and commission articles and biographies that create a favourable mythos around him. Good things to know if you're thinking of purchasing. Or recommending that to your readers.'

'What is his *mythos*?'

'Well, he was a genius and he was murdered, which is important. I mean who is Van Gogh without his sad history? A painter of pretty pictures. Master of colour. He isn't even emblematic of an art movement whereas Viscom was a leader, a bon vivant and a political martyr, beaten to death by the Viennese anti-Nazis.'

'He was a Nazi?'

'Yes.'

'Isn't Miss Zimmerman Jewish?'

She drew a breath in through her nose and stood tall. 'Why, yes. The whole family are Jewish.'

She was expecting me to start something. She'd had this fight before. I surprised her.

'Well, it was brave of her to be over there just now, with the Nazi party everywhere.'

She warmed to me. 'Miss Zimmerman is very brave but I hear the Nazis only bother the poor Jews in the ghettos, not rich Jews so much. And, as you know, the Zimmermans, well, you've heard . . .'

I had heard of them. The family were even richer than the Montgomerys but more storied. They had endured so much personal tragedy that maybe even the Nazis shed an occasional tear for them. When they weren't dying in terrible house fires they were being paralyzed in racing car crashes, on boats, they died of gout, of cancer, were bed bound with infant polio and had horse-riding accidents. They sued each other all the time. And they bought art. Jonathan Zimmerman, a generation above Peggy, had built a museum in New York to house his classic art collection.

The Montgomerys did not mix with Jews. They did not employ Jews. Their country clubs excluded Jews. No one would talk about who the Zimmermans were seen with or employing. Christine Montgomery had found the perfect hide.

'I don't like Nazis,' I said. 'Too much singing.'

'Neither do I,' she said cagily. 'Not even the American ones. But the opposition are pretty awful too. They beat Viscom to death.' She looked at the painting of the woman with five noses. 'His identity papers were in his pocket. They were covered in blood, his face . . .' She cringed. 'He was so handsome in life, it's very sad. That's a photograph of our Mr Viscom,' she drew my attention to the framed newspaper article I'd noticed earlier on the wall behind the desk.

It was from a French newspaper and carried a large photo of a bald fifty-year-old man. He was clear-eyed and square jawed, wearing an open-necked shirt and smoking a large calabash pipe, grinning as if he'd gotten away with something. His teeth were very straight and worn but topped by undescended canines sticking out of his upper gums like tiny tusks. Further into the article was a smaller photograph of two strange-looking women at a dock, Peggy Zimmerman and her daughter. Both women looked dumpy and annoyed, dressed in heavy mink coats and sunglasses.

'Is she a good boss?'

'We've only spoken on the telephone so far. They've been in Europe the whole time I've been here. I'm meeting Miss Zimmerman for dinner tomorrow evening, in fact. First time. I'm greatly looking forward to it. She's rather Bohemian. We might go anywhere but I'm guessing it won't be a country club, they all exclude Jews. Would you care to see a price list for the works?'

'Very much, thank you.'

She loped over to a table to get it. She was happy. She thought it had gone well and she liked doing this.

She came back with the type-written sheet and I read it. I had to cover my mouth to stop myself laughing. If I had that kind of money I'd just buy New Mexico. The whole thing was a con act. No wonder the guy in the photo was grinning.

She saw me holding my mouth tight. 'I know it's so hard to choose.'

'Hmm!'

'If you had to recommend one to your readers, would you be leaning towards any one in particular?'

I pointed meekly to one particular shambles in a frame. If I had painted it I'd have laughed, given up art and burned it.

'Good choice,' she nodded at it.

I nodded at her.

She nodded back at me.

We looked back at the picture and smiles burst on both our faces at the exact same moment. We had to take a beat pause before we got back to talking.

I got my notebook out. 'What can you tell me about this one?'

'Sure,' she pointed at a small set of three figures, staring back at us with dancing eyes. 'This painting, *Bohemian Jail*, is from his early period, just after the Great War. You see how he's representing three dimensions on a two-dimensional plane? Because what is art to do now, in the age of photography? Perfect reproduction is just mechanical. Art must do something *more*. Viscom is the leader of a group of artists in Europe who are challenging the way we *see*. He drew from life. This was during a period of imprisonment. He was released when the Nazis walked into Vienna.'

'What was he in prison for?'

'Who knows? He lived well above his means and was always having fights, often with other artists. He seduced several of their wives.'

'That must have caused some fights,' I said, as if I was in the habit of wrestling other correspondents of *Art Collector Monthly*.

'Quite,' she said brightly.

She didn't know anything about that either. I wasn't the only one faking it. I looked at the price list again and said I couldn't decide

It was nice to watch her talk. She knew about this, cared about it and became animated when she did. She looked off into the distance, and her slender fingers fluttered around in front of her face, explaining and extolling, outlining and tracing time frames.

She talked me through the different pictures and, as she did, I wondered how she landed this job.

'Think about it,' she smiled. 'And come back as often as you need to. The exhibition is on for another month.'

She saw me to the door and along the balcony. We waved to each other through the iron mesh as the elevator slid down, my eyes level with her waist, her knees, her ankles, and then she was gone.

The next time we looked each other in the eye it would be over the body of a dead man.

13.

I found her address in the phone book but the green Plymouth was not parked out front. The Van Nuys Building at the corner of Seventh and Spring was colonnaded with clean windows and lumpy ornamentation, high and proud and solid in a way that screamed in the face of onlookers that they could trust the people in it. We will do the boring chores, the paperwork will be filed, the permissions will be granted, every document stamped in triplicate, notarized and filed. Don't even ask to see that stuff. All done for you, brother. Pay your bill.

It was so reassuring it set my teeth on edge.

I checked my wallet was still on me as I walked in and read the notice board. On the second floor, in a prime spot, were the offices of Anne Riordan Associates, her name etched on a brass strip in the list of companies. Next to the name a wooden slider told me they were open.

I touched my hat brim to the desk.

'Know where you're going?' demanded an unreasonably angry security man between puffs of the fresh cigarette he was lighting with the stub of his last one. He had an overspilling ashtray next to him and his garbage was lined with empty packets. He had done some work today.

'In here or in life?'

He didn't crack a light, 'In here. Do you know where you're heading?'

'Second floor.'

He waved me on to a fine set of opalescent marble stone steps with a cool-to-the-touch handrail.

All the fancy ran out on the first floor. The second flight of stairs was carpeted in cork to keep the noise down.

I found the office along a narrow corridor of doors. From behind each came the clatter of voices and typewriters. Anne's door was gold lettered, fresh and clean. It was a big office. They had three other doors all the way along.

I knocked and entered, stepping into a small reception area with four seats along a wall with mottled windows above them into the adjoining office. Shadows moved around inside.

A large desk faced me as I came through the door and the woman sitting at it had her blouse buttoned up wrong. She knew there was something wrong with it but hadn't yet identified the problem. Her hand came up and tried to smooth it. She smiled, puzzled, as if I'd dressed her. She had the air of someone who has been badly let down by life but was dang well making the best of it. Her thick pink lipstick was stamped on the end of the cigarettes in the ashtray that sat next to the switchboard panel.

'Hello, sir,' she said. 'May I help you this morning?' She attempted to follow it up with a smile but her head tipped to the side and her mouth twisted down at the edges. She looked an arm hair away from crying.

'You may.'

That cheered her up. 'Ah! May I inquire whom you are here to see?'

'Anne Riordan.'

'Whom may I say is calling upon her – Miss Riordan?' She'd got that wrong. She silently berated herself and looked at me to see if I was going to give her hell as well.

'Philip Marlowe.'

Silently rehearsing my name over and over, she pressed a button on a box with a red light that flashed as she spoke. The box crackled and then fell silent.

'Hi again, Audrey, I have a Mr Philip Marlowe here to see Miss Riordan?'

She smiled up at me as she said my name, as if I'd be delighted to hear it said out loud and in such auspicious circumstances. Then she left the smile there to go bad, let go of the button and folded her hands in front of her on the desk.

A bored woman's voice came back through the box. 'Miss Riordan is *out* of the office. She's out with a client. I told you this already, Mabel.'

Mabel pressed her button again. Crackle. 'Oh,' she said, to no purpose. She let the button go and watched it, waiting for an answer.

None came.

'Oh,' she said to me. She pressed the button again. Crackle. 'When is Miss Riordan expected back?'

'Can't say.' Crackle.

She smiled at me again. Things weren't going well for Mabel. I didn't expect her to last the week.

She pressed the button, 'Maybe in an hour or so . . . ?'

'Mabel! I'm right in the middle of something! She's off with Tiny Lanski. She won't be in again today. Get off the call box. Do your job and let me do mine.'

Just then the door opened into the office. Four women were working in one room, reading and typing and filing, all business and busy with cigarettes clamped between their teeth as they typed. A thick shelf of smoke hung in the bright office.

A woman in her sixties came out pulling a purse strap over her head. She wore a flowered pinny like a maid but had the air of a combat soldier about to take over a Gatling gun from a fallen comrade.

She didn't look up as she crossed to the door and left.

'Bye, now!' called Mabel to the door as it closed. 'Have a great time.'

'Yes, bye,' came the reply as the heavy door shut behind her. The glass rattled.

Mabel gave me a sick smile and a small sad grunt. 'I am *so* sorry.'

'Don't you worry, Mabel, I'll come back tomorrow.'

She tipped her head and pressed a hand to her ample chest, 'Would you, Mr Marlowe? We'd be so glad to see you again.'

'Can't wait.'

I wouldn't be back tomorrow. If Anne was with Tiny Lanski I knew where to find him. I wouldn't have put money on Mabel being there tomorrow either. I wished her well in her new position.

14.

Tiny Lanski owned a number of bars and night clubs around town, all high class with valet parking, but his office bar was called Whitey's. I knew I'd find them there.

Whitey's store front was painted black with house paint. The windows were high on the wall, small, mean. It was a signal that the bar was for serious people to do serious drinking. Tiny was a serious man.

The doorman was so muscled his neck was in danger of eating his head. His double-breasted suit declared his affiliations: Chicago black with a thick grey pinstripe. He opened the door for me, watching over my shoulder for car loads of gangsters with machine guns. I palmed him a note. He looked at it and gave it back to me.

'I'm good, fella,' he said as nicely as he could.

I was going to make a crack but he was already behind me, watching the street. I didn't know what he was watching for but I didn't want to be part of it.

Inside a civil burble of chat hummed through the dim room, caught in the perpetual twilight of a good bar.

Trouble didn't come to Whitey's. Trouble knew better.

Circular leather-seated booths lined the wall, high-backed for privacy to talk out important deals in an informal setting. Sitting on the tables in the middle was a smoking set: a box ashtray with cigars, cigarettes and cigarillos on offer and match books printed in gloss black with the name of the bar.

I'd been here many times. I waved and nodded to a couple of faces, slipped into a seat at the bar and ordered a whiskey straight from Tony Bass, the head barman. He made it, gliding from ice bucket to bottles and back to me, napkin down, glass delivered, a small bowl of peanuts appearing at my right hand, each movement fluid and smooth. Or maybe I just really wanted a drink.

'Tiny in?'

Bass didn't answer but glanced over at the back booth.

'Busy?'

He rolled his head to say he didn't know, maybe. Tony Bass didn't say much but you always knew what he meant.

'Thanks, Tony.'

I took my drink and napkin and slid off the chair. Two steps along the bar I looked into the booth. I didn't see Tiny though Tiny was there. All two hundred pounds of Tiny was there, one fat hand wrapped around a glass of seltzer, the other holding an unlit cigar. I didn't see him because I was looking at Anne Riordan and Anne Riordan was looking at me.

'Marlowe,' she said after a minute.

'Riordan.'

A smile broke on her face like sunrise after a cold night. 'Fancy meeting you here.'

'Yes.'

I smiled back. I had the impression that she didn't want to be grinning any more than I did, but it had been a while. Anne Riordan found me in a ditch once. She held me at gun point, brushed me down and took me to her house.

Anne was attractive. She knew she was and she wasn't scared about it. Her hair was set in waves to her shoulders and around her slim neck she wore a gold chain so fine it sat on her collarbones like dew settling on a rose petal.

'You're looking awfully tall, Marlowe, have you been growing again?'

'Unlikely, Miss Riordan. Have you been getting more beautiful?'

There was a time in our acquaintance when she would have blushed at a comment like that from me. Events had changed that dynamic. She was more confident than she used to be around me, less girlish.

'Yes, Mr Marlowe, I have been getting more beautiful. I've been having injections of monkey gland beauty serum and it's doing exactly what it says on the side of the barrel. Thank you for noticing.'

She had auburn hair and green eyes, skin the colour of heavy milk. It was a fine face, flawed in too many ways to count, but a face you could look at a long time and not want to stop.

She was dressed in a pale green two piece with a grey felt hat that had been untimely ripped from its mother's womb. The crown was the size of a thimble, the brim wide and scooped under the far side of her face, framing it.

We got kind of stuck, looking at each other, Anne and I.

'Youse two know each other?' This was Tiny. Tiny didn't have time for this.

'Sure,' said Anne and broke off, looking back at her drink.

'Marlowe, come sit, come sit,' said Tiny, waving Anne up the bench into the middle.

I sat down and took a sip.

'Youse work together?'

'No,' said Anne.

'No,' I said and drank again.

'I wanted to work for him but he wouldn't let me, on account of my being female.'

'That was not the reason, Anne.'

She whispered to Tiny, 'That was the reason.'

'I work alone.'

She whispered again, 'He doesn't trust a dame to do a job.'

'I trust a dame!' But my voice was high and sounded like a lie. Anne laughed at that.

She touched my forearm, I felt the warmth of her touch through my sleeve.

'Anyway,' she said. 'For whatever reason, he said no thanks and I set up on my own.'

'I'm a loner,' I told Lanski. I'd known him for ten years and this was more than he'd ever heard about me. He wasn't interested.

He blinked his puffy eyes and took a slug of seltzer. 'Maybes you two could work on my thing together?'

'No.' said Anne. 'Definitely not.'

'What you say, Marlowe?'

'I don't know what your thing is.'

'Hm,' Tiny nodded his big slug head.

Tiny was bald as a grapefruit but it suited him. He was an ex-boxer and all the muscle had turned to fat when he retired from the ring, most of it on his chest. He dressed with the care a foppish viscount might pay to his attire, immaculate in hand-made suits cut and tailored to his frame, shirts that fit his wide neck and cravats and ties that in no way echoed the redness of his puffy face.

He slid a ten dollar note over to me. I knew what it meant. It was a retainer, a way of placing me in his employ as a PI and giving him some guarantee of confidentiality. I put my hand on it and pulled it across the table top until it touched my drink. Then I pushed it back. It disappeared under his hand and he slipped it into his pocket.

My confidentiality was not a legally binding obligation now but Lanski was still a fighter and clung to his superstitions. He liked this ritual marking my loyalty.

'Yes, so I got all these clubs and whatnot, and on the floor all night we got cigarette goils there, going around to the tables and so on. Well, I'm being muscled in on by . . . parties from outa town . . . and I figured I could do with some support, *locally*, from, you know, straights: aldermen, newspaper people, cops or whatever. So I sees them all at the tables in these clubs I own and

I thinks to myself, 'It's all going on here,' at these clubs, chit chat and whatnot. Only I don't know about it. It's all come out under our noses only I can't get to it. So, I thinks, who can get me these morsels of information for me to, you know, *have*. So . . .' he waved his seltzer at Anne, 'cigarette goils.'

Anne caught my eye.

'Cigarette goils?' I said.

'Yes,' said Tiny, 'cigarette goils. Don't you make fun, now Marlowe, I know I don't talk right. My teeth've been punched more often than a Teamster foreman's time card.'

'But "goils", come on, it's not hard to say. Gi*r*ls.'

'Not hard for you.' He tried again, 'Go*i*ls.'

'Gi-*rls*,' said Anne, watching his mouth.

Tiny shut his eyes and moved his mouth, 'Gor-ills.' He opened them again and pointed at us both, 'Youse are lucky I like you.'

We were and we knew it.

'Okay, Mr Lanski,' said Anne, cupping her hand on his bulging forearm. She seemed to make a thing of touching forearms. 'I can do that for you.'

'Well, that would be wonderful, dear,' he said fondly. 'I knew your fatha, I respected your fatha but I *like* you.'

'And he liked you,' she said. 'Of all the men he arrested in Bay City, he told me you were the most well mannered.'

'He said I'd got the soul of a poet.'

She sighed. 'He said things like that all the time.'

'Well, it meant a lot to me. I was on the skids at the time. Nice thing to say to a fella.'

'Dad meant an awful lot to me, Mr Lanski, so thank you for reminding me of him.'

'Okay, come on now,' Lanski looked at the floor to tell us to scat, 'we all got jobs.'

Anne nodded as if this was a profound observation. Maybe it was. 'We do indeed. If you'll excuse us, I have some business to attend to with Mr Marlowe. I'd like to sit at the bar with him while we discuss something.'

'You're always welcome here, sweetie. You go do your business with Mr Marlowe.'

She stood up and kissed the top of his head. I had never seen anyone do that before. Lanski took it with a nod as we slid out of the booth. I found myself wondering if she'd done it before and, maybe, if she'd do it to me.

15.

Tony Bass had another drink ready for me, sitting on a napkin, ice fresh and crisp. He put one down for Anne. It was pale green with a red cherry in it.

'Did you pick your drink to match your outfit?'

'Yes,' she smiled at the notion. 'I always do that. Have to run home and change if I want a chocolate malt.'

I lit a cigarette, 'You still out in Bay City?'

'Sure. And I got a little beach house out at the Palisades now too. I spend a lot of time there. You should come and see it.'

She was telling me she was doing well.

'You still up in Hollywood?'

'Yep. I went to your office.'

She was pleased about that, 'You did?'

'I met Mabel.'

'Mabel.' She tutted. 'Give me strength. Watches too many movies. She's in a perpetual state of high emotion.'

'Why did you give her a job?'

'She can work all the machines, I don't know. She needed a job. I thought we'd be a squad of crazy gals, out serving up justice. Get a second room in your office and you're filling out forms all day and arranging holiday rotas.'

'I told you.'

'You did, Marlowe.' She speared the cherry with a cocktail stick. 'You surely did.'

She lifted the cherry out of the green drink, put it between her small white teeth and bit. The cherry split in half. A droplet of clear red fell on her chin. The whole event seemed to go on for an hour. I wished it was two hours.

'Let me get that.' I dabbed it off with my napkin. It brought me close to her.

She gave me a warning look not to kiss her. 'Don't you do that, Marlowe.'

'Don't do what?' My breath shifted the powder on her pretty little nose.

'Don't you do that . . .' But there was a smile behind her eyes and they rolled down my face to my lips. '. . . Marlowe.'

I looked at hers. She had no lipstick on and they were still moist where she'd licked the cherry juice off. 'You don't know what I was going to do.'

'Yes, I do. But I'm in work right now and I have to maintain my professional dignity. Smooching at a bar in the middle of the day would tend to undercut that, don't you think?'

'It would?'

'Maybe you're trying to undermine me. Maybe you'd like an office full of Mabels to feel responsible for.'

I winked and shot her with a finger gun, 'Pegged me.'

She sighed, 'It's hard for a woman. A guy can get drunk at nine in the morning, strip off to his combinations and run up Broadway. Everyone'll say he's having a bad day. A woman wears a hat wrong and she's dead in the water.'

I sat back. 'True. I wasn't going to kiss you, anyway.'

'Well, I like that. You were too.'

'No, I wasn't. I was going to ask you about the Montgomery case.'

'And you had to look at my mouth and half close your eyes to do that?'

'It's a very concerning case.'

She liked that, 'It is. It's concerning. What have you got so far?'

She lifted a silver cigarette case out of a side pocket in her jacket and held it in her hand, looking around for a match. I let her. Tony Bass was suddenly there with a flame in his hand and she took a light, thanked him and he slid away along the bar to a group of men.

'I could have done that for you,' I said.

'You weren't there. He was. What have you got?'

I took out my own cigarette, put it in my mouth and Anne gave me her cigarette to light it with. The end was moist. I held her eye as I did and then gave it back to her.

'Why?' I said. 'What have you got?'

'I can't tell you. That's between me and my client.'

'Doesn't it concern you that we've both been sent to find the same missing person and they didn't tell us someone else was on the case?'

She shrugged a slim shoulder, 'They're entitled. We might not be the only ones. There could be others.'

'We'd have seen them.'

She knew I was right. She hummed and smoked.

'Chrissie Montgomery isn't missing,' I said. 'She left.'

'I know,' she said. 'And I can see why. The minute I walked into that mansion I wanted to run away.'

'Have you found her yet?'

She almost laughed, 'Would I tell you?'

She wouldn't. Neither would I.

'That thousand dollar bonus must seem awful attractive to someone with your overheads.'

'D'you suppose?'

She didn't flinch or ask for details. They'd offered it to her as well. She played her cards close to her chest, I had to hand it to her.

'Anne, suppose she left to make a better life, would you turn her in for that bonus?'

'Why Marlowe, would you?'

We looked at each other steady but this time it wasn't fond. This time it was steely. I saw the core of iron in her.

Singing erupted around the corner of the bar, a boozehound was murdering 'Red Sails in the Sunset'.

Tony Bass turned his head and spoke softly, 'Leave.'

The singing stopped abruptly. The drunk man's friend bundled him out of the door, past the muscle-man doorman. A wave of heat from the street made itself known.

'Anne, did you discuss me with Lyle?'

'No. Why?'

'She didn't talk about me to you?'

'Why would we discuss you, Marlowe? She was giving me a job, not asking me to join her sorority.'

'Seems like you might have talked about me, is all.'

She sighed, unreasonably annoyed at that, 'Ugh, okay, champ.'

Anne and I drank our drinks. I finished mine and Tony Bass arrived with another. Anne looked at it.

'You don't think I should?'

'You do what you want.'

I didn't want to drink it but I wouldn't be told what to do by anyone. I held the glass, turning it around to give the impression that I was my own man.

'See, Anne, in this business we have to make calls sometimes –'

'Marlowe, I don't need you to tell me about this business. I don't need advice. I don't need you to help me. I asked you once and you said no. I won't ask again.'

I opened my mouth to speak but found I had nothing to say. She was right. She probably knew more about this business than I did now. Anne's father was a chief of police down in Bay City for seven years, a bull of a man, hated by the corrupt cops who got him sacked, sainted by the next generation. Anne could probably find out what the current Bay City chief had for lunch with one phone call and what the Governor had with two. It worried me that she had that office full of employees and that she was in here. If she was moving at this level, making deals with power brokers like Lanski, she had big plans for the future. She'd want to keep in with someone as connected as Montgomery and refusing to hand over Christine wouldn't endear her any.

I dropped some notes and pushed my untouched drink away across the bar, 'I'm saying that Chrissie Montgomery might have made a choice to leave and she might be entitled to that choice. She might be happy for once.'

'She might want to play at being a normal girl for a while, but Chrissie Montgomery isn't ordinary, Marlowe. We are who we are. She is who she is. Even if she denounces her family money she'll still be a mark. It doesn't stop it being true because she doesn't want it to be.'

'She might want a different life.'

'Who doesn't?' she said. 'I want to sit out at the beach contemplating my navel all day.'

'So you don't need the bonus. Maybe you're too busy to care about a thousand dollars. Too busy setting up a spy network of cigarette girls so that Tiny Lanski can blackmail elected officials.'

'Get lost, Marlowe. Those shirts are all on Chicago's dime and you know it. The cops have everyone tapped and they're spying on the rest of them. The game's already started and it wasn't started by cigarette girls. Lanski's just evening up the teams.'

'Well, I'm not on anyone's dime.'

I left her at the bar, sipping her drink and feeling sore.

On the way back to my car I argued with a man who stepped in front of me on the sidewalk. I argued with a car that broke a stop sign as I was walking in front of it. I had words with a paving stone that stuck up at one end.

I was sore too. A kind of sore I hadn't felt in a long time.

16.

The parking attendant at the Dancers took the key to my Olds as if I'd handed him a drowned puppy. He warmed up when I gave him an oversized tip. It was Montgomery money. I was glad every time I threw some of it away.

He must have signalled the doorman about it because he smiled and swept the door wide as I stepped up to it. I tucked more stained notes into his pocket. The hatcheck girl might have heard the rumours too, judging by the size of the smile she gave me as I handed over my hat. She gave me a stub and called me sir, smiled and nodded. She was so nice about it, so fresh and unjaded, I'd have taken her as new in the job.

'Are you Evelyn, by any chance?'

'I sure am!' She put her little fist on her hips, 'We met before?'

'Only the last time I was in here.'

'Well, *you* must have a great memory,' she smiled, 'most folks wouldn't remember a hatcheck girl.'

She placed my hat on a shelf, sitting it down as if it was the nicest one she'd ever seen and gave me my ticket. She was cute. Mrs Dudek was wrong though, her accent wasn't Okie, it was solid New York cut with something I couldn't quite place. She had thick blonde hair and a dimple on her chin you could have kept pencils in. I dropped some coins in the plate, thanked her and went on into the club.

Inside was all dim table lights and dark corners. It was the custom not to look around or examine the faces of fellow patrons. I wasn't looking. I knew that if I made myself seen she would find me.

Around a corner someone was bothering a piano, pleasant notes minus a tune. It created a soft landing for the burble of chat among the patrons. I walked to the end of the bar and took the corner where the light would hit me and anyone coming in through the door would see my face. I ordered an old fashioned, smoked and minded my business.

There were too many men in here and they all smelled of hard cash and loneliness. The women were all younger and better looking than the men, too interested in the dumb monologues the men were giving.

The atmosphere was loaded and soiling.

A couple sitting at a table behind me were having a fine time. Her words were being swallowed, she must have been facing away from me, but his voice carried. She was laughing mostly as he talked and teased and made cracks about famous people he claimed to know. Through a pall of drink his jokes must have sounded fluid and clever, word play and lies mostly. To soberer ears the banter clunked along with a frantic edge to it. They hit the same note so often, he joking, she laughing, that it got sad and tired and their timing went bad. She was leaving pauses after the punchline, then blowing up gales of laughter halfway through. He started repeating the punchline as if she didn't get it.

She ran out of fake laughs, 'Boy! You sure are funny!'

'Funny is as funny does!' he declared.

Her laugh had a tinny rattle now, sharp edged, like a comedian's wife planning her divorce during a live show. There was a whole language in the varying texture of her laugh, mocking sadness, sneering disgust. I imagined they'd end up punching each other to death when they got somewhere private.

But I had been drinking all day. It could have been my mood. I had drunk myself sober.

I ordered another to right the world by, thinking of all that was wrong with it, thinking about Pasco Pete. Something was up and I knew it. The case was too neat by a mile. Then a familiar voice crooned at me from the darkness.

'Mr Marlowe.'

She slid onto the stool across the corner from me and laid her purse on the bar. Our hands were almost touching.

Anneliese Lyle was dressed in a white satin evening gown and a matching scarf wrapped around her slim neck with both ends draped down her bare back between the shoulder blades. Her purse was white satin too. I guessed she wasn't planning on changing any tyres this evening.

'Miss Lyle.'

'You know my name. We have formally been introduced though, have we? I suppose you know what my drink is too?'

'I'm not that good. What would you like?'

'A gimlet.'

I ordered two.

'Ever had one before?'

'Some.'

The couple behind me were whispering. I think they were planning where to kill each other. She squeezed out a laugh that sounded like a death rattle and he talked over it. I couldn't listen to them any longer.

'Cigarette?'

Lyle took one and leaned into my lighted match. The lights above the bar hit her face in a way that would have restored the faith of most men. It fell softly on her brow and cheekbones, her eyelashes were untouched by mascara, the line of her lips a perfect Cupid's bow. She kissed the cigarette to life, pursed her lips into a perfect circle and blew a straight fluid flow of smoke that hit the back of the bar.

She sat back half an inch and looked more human, glanced sideways at me and mouthed a thank you.

The badly written dialogue behind me melted out of earshot. The smell of other men dissipated. Her beauty had the effect of making the soul-grinding mundane tolerable.

The drinks arrived. A wheeze of lime filled our corner of the bar. I watched Lyle lift her glass and drink so delicately that she didn't even leave a smudge of lipstick on the rim. Two thirds of the gimlet was gone though. It was the first graceless gesture I'd seen her make.

'Thirsty?'

'Very.'

She emptied the drink and I motioned to the bartender to give her another.

'You're not so very thirsty, I notice,' she said.

'I slaked my thirst before I got here.'

She silently mouthed the word 'slaked'. I knew she'd use that word tomorrow, possibly to Chadwick, and then pretend she'd always known it. She was an impermanent woman, a fiction. She took parts she observed from people she met and reproduced them. I wondered if her perfect chin was a skin job, if her slender waist was a corset, if her arms could really be that slim. The bruises on her wrist were invisible in the dim bar. Maybe they weren't real either.

'Where do you hail from, Miss Lyle?'

Her eyes narrowed meanly. 'What do you mean?'

'Which state were you born in?'

She raised the elegant shoulder nearest to me and a glimmer of amusement slid across her eyes like headlights over a hotel room ceiling, 'We moved around a lot. Where are you from?'

She was slippery. I liked that.

'California-Ohio-Montana,' I said.

'Oh, I've heard it's sublime in winter.'

I sipped my gimlet. It was sickly and reminded me of nights I'd rather forget, 'We have our summers though.'

'I heard that too. I believe they get everywhere?'

'Certainly they do, one fella I heard of, he was driving through a bunch of summers and they got all over his car. Next morning all that was left was two tyres and an axle.'

'Gosh! Ate all the way through?'

'All the way. Those summers. They'll do for you.'

'Was he insured?'

'That was the rub of it: his insurance had run out just the day before.'

'Good lord!'

'The Good Lord had nothing to do with it. He should have checked his policy.'

Delighted with ourselves, we snickered and I suddenly thought we sounded like the couple behind me. My mood took a nose dive.

'Say, Lyle, what happened to your neck?'

She didn't like that question, 'My neck?'

'The bruise on there and on your wrist. I take it that's why you're wearing a scarf.'

Her second drink arrived then and she covered her face with the glass. She tipped the fluid gently towards her perfect mouth. When she put it down the glass was empty. I motioned to the barkeep to bring her another.

'It's not safe up there, is it?'

She looked hard at me. 'Where is safe?'

'It's a matter of degrees, isn't it?'

'Is it? How did you know I'd be here?'

'I didn't. This is an accident. I drink here all the time.'

'No, you don't.' She instantly saw that she'd given herself away and snorted sadly.

'He's asleep now, isn't he?'

She nodded.

'Did you bring Chrissie here with you?'

'Once or twice. Poor kid. It wasn't her sort of place . . .'

I looked around at the moneyed drunks and the pleading eyes of the women, 'I'd have thought it was a pretty good fit.'

'Well, you're wrong.' She ordered another and lifted her purse, lowered a foot toward the floor, readying to leave. 'You will find her, won't you?'

'Do you want me to bring her back? You're more or less the same age. Seems like you two might be pals in some way. I figure she's had enough and left. She's entitled to leave Ohio-Montana if she wants to. We did.'

'She's not like you and I, Mr Marlowe. She's heir to an enormous fortune. She's not safe out here on the savannah, a big cat could feed off her for years. Chrissie can burn in hell for all I care but she'd take us all down with her. And then, because she's rich, someone will pull her out of the pile of smouldering bones, hose her down and set her on her way. Better to find her before she can hurt too many of us small things. She'll cause a lot of damage.'

'What's she like, as a person?'

Her third gimlet arrived and she sipped it. 'A romantic, God help us, always disappointed and angry, as all true romantics are, especially if they have a lot of money. Everyone meets her approval initially, but she turns on them after a short time. She wanted to marry Bruce MacIntosh then she didn't. I think she realized that before the party.'

She tipped her chin at a dark corner booth but dropped her eyes suddenly. When she looked back up she looked at me like a starving man seeing a crate of warm bread. She'd used that expression before. I think it was probably her best one.

'What happened to change her mind? Is there something wrong with Bruce MacIntosh?'

'You tell me. Seems decent enough if a little dull.'

'I don't know if you're any judge.'

She bobbed her perfect eyebrows, 'Hmm . . . well, I watched her that night at the party. I saw her realize that she couldn't go through with it. He gave her a diamond necklace. Three strands of diamonds, worth a fortune. Everyone was cooing at it in the big velvet box. I saw her look at it and realize that she wouldn't be able to make it work. It was obvious. Right there at the party.'

Her beautiful eyes tried to flick back to the corner booth again but she disciplined them. Whatever changed her opinion it hadn't happened at the party. I'd put money on it happening right there in the corner booth but Anneliese Lyle didn't want anyone to know that.

'What about her kid?'

'She doesn't like him. He's better off with the nannies. They like him and they'll probably stay longer than her anyway. She didn't see him too much even when they were living in the same house.'

'Why did you mention him then?'

'Chadwick has an idea that she's the ideal mother. She isn't. He doesn't know what a mother is supposed to be like. None of them do.'

'But you asked me to find her for the boy.'

'No, I didn't. I said we needed to try to find her so that we could tell him we tried. The kid will be a Montgomery whatever happens. I'm more concerned for her than I am about him.'

'You think someone has their claws into her?'

'If they don't already they will soon. She's a walking target.' She drained her medicine and slid off the stool. 'Heaven only knows what she'll get messed up in or used for.'

She picked up her purse.

'Why do you stay with him, Anneliese?'

She looked at me, lips parted, eyes steady and wolfish. 'Why would I leave?'

'He hits you.'

'Mr Marlowe, when you look like me everybody wants to hit and hurt you. At least Chadwick falls asleep at six o'clock and he's too weak to break anything. I let him hit me. If I need to fight back I can just pull his drip out.'

I saw a world of hurt in her eyes. A story from before. A memory of a fractured love who did break bones and stay up past six. Then she blinked and when she opened her eyes I was looking at a fortress wall.

'Not everyone wants to hurt you.'

She leaned over and kissed me on the mouth so softly that I wondered if it was happening. Then she pulled away, just an inch, and looked at my face as if she'd like to lick it.

'No divorce stuff? I think you're a romantic too, Mr Marlowe, that you're always rescuing damsels. I expect you're often disappointed and angry about it too. Those two go hand in hand. Pragmatists like me are always being punished by dismayed romantics. Not everyone wants to hit me immediately. But it always comes. They always want to break me, eventually. That's why I have to protect myself.'

'By standing next to the biggest animal on the reserve?'

'Exactly. You know those birds that stand on the backs of hippopotami? Only a fool would suppose they were driving it when they're eating fleas on its skin and staying away from its jaws.'

She took a step toward the door but stopped and turned back, mouthing to me over her perfect shoulder.

'Slaked.'

I ordered another drink, not because I wanted it, just because I couldn't go after her without looking desperate. Which isn't to say I wasn't desperate but I didn't feel the need to advertise the fact.

I overtipped the barman. 'The dame who just left, you know her?'

He nodded, seemed like he did. I had the impression he didn't like her very much. She used to sit in a corner seat, if his facial expressions and monosyllabic mumbling were credible, and she used to sit there with a skinny girl with a long neck and they'd hold hands under the table. In terms of personality type she might be properly filed under 'bag of poison' according to my server. I don't know if poison comes in bags or he was right. There seemed to be a personal angle to it. Maybe he was half in love with her. Plenty were. I gave him a final tip and strolled off into the night.

The parking attendant was missing in action. I waited for a while, watching the headlights of squiffy drivers weave their way up Sunset but he never came. I went back into the foyer and asked Evelyn. She rolled her eyes, apologized and led me to a wall cupboard full of car keys on numbered hooks.

'I'm not gonna lie, he's the laziest person I've ever met. Thinks he's too good to work. European aristocrat or something.'

She found my keys and gave them to me.

'I tipped him heavily on the way in.'

'That's your first mistake, mister.'

'What's my second mistake?'

'Tipping me heavily on the way out.'

I made that mistake gladly and she apologized for the parking attendant again. I told her forget it, I'd had jobs I was bad at too and we parted on shoulder-punching terms.

The car park was around the corner, a dark chasm between the steep hill behind and the back of the club. I was looking for the Olds when I saw it: big body, little cabin and an almost full set of brilliant white wall wheel trims but the back left trim was missing.

It was still dusty.

17.

Jimmy the One was standing outside when I drew up at the gates early next morning. He sloped over to my window and gave me a look.

'Marlowe.'

'Donoghue.'

'Bringing her in?'

'Would I be here alone if I was?'

He patted the roof of the car and smiled away from me.

'Who else did you tell about Carmelita Cabs?'

He looked up the hill, 'No one. A gardener saw us jawing out here. The big house sent someone down after you left the other day. Cooper. He asked me what I'd told you. I said you grilled me pretty bad but all I could tell you about was the crash before the party.'

'Thanks, Jim.'

'Sure, Marlowe, sure.'

'Are you going to let me in?'

'Sure.'

He peeled away but I called him back. 'Jimmy, I'm not the only one on this.'

'Yes, I know. She in a fix?'

I didn't know yet.

'Don't need to be rich for that to happen.' Jimmy grinned his million-dollar smile as if he was a fix people often got into.

He opened the gates and I drove through. I could see him in my rear view, shutting them after me as I turned the corner.

He was watching me, wondering if I was on his side this time. I didn't know myself yet.

The jacarandas had shed their flowers in the unseasonable heat but every fallen petal had been cleared away. The gnarled old branches remembered what they'd lost though. They bowed heavy, grieving the fleeting season.

The drive was less impressive this time. I knew about the faceless army keeping dead flowers off the road, the shadows cutting grass, removing any reminders of decay and failure and the temporality of life. These ghosts lined the driveway, heads bowed. To have all of this and overlook the people was like buying a peach and eating the stone.

The front door was opened by Cooper, who hated me even more now. He took my hat with one hand, didn't even call me by name, just ordered me to sit away from the broken vase he loved so much. Then he went away and came back and flicked a finger for me to follow him.

Out in the hallway I asked him, 'What's your deal, Cooper? How come you're all high-hat with me now?'

'Why don't you shut your head,' he snarled back in fluent Bronx.

We were outside the study door and he turned to look at me. It was the wrong face on the wrong day. I couldn't let it slide.

'You'd like to chew my ears off, wouldn't you?'

He leaned into me and murmured, 'Maybe I will one day, Marlowe.'

I punched him in the eye. He went down like the Lusitania.

I stepped over him, opened the door and walked into the study. They hadn't had time to set the scene for me. Chadwick Montgomery was pulling his robe closed and looked up, surprised that anyone had the nerve to walk into a room he was in. Anneliese Lyle was standing feet away from me, the light on her face this time instead of behind her head. She was using a compact to powder over a big bruise on her jaw. I had startled her.

'You're not supposed to be in here.'

Cooper had scrambled to his feet and came bowling in after me.

'I'm sorry, sir, I'm most dreadfully sorry —' Suddenly he was from merry old England again.

Chadwick looked at him, at the rapid swelling of his eye. He looked at me and tipped his head back and gave a wheezy laugh that made me sick to my stomach.

'That's quite all right, Cooper. Quite all right. Mr Marlowe, come in. Sit down. What can I do for you?'

I went over and sat down, lit a cigarette and asked him where I could find Bruce MacIntosh, Chrissie's fiancé. He didn't seem to care why I was asking. He was too thrilled by my socking Cooper.

He wrote the address down on the edge of the blotter and tore it off. He held it out.

'You know, it's not everyone I take to, Mr Marlowe but I must say, I'm rather taken with you.'

'Great. I have a solid lead on your daughter's whereabouts. Just need to tie up some loose ends before I give you what I've got.'

He opened the slim drawer in the desk and brought out a slim stack of fifties. He dropped them on the desk top as if they meant nothing to him. 'Expenses. There will be more . . .'

Anneliese Lyle slithered next to him. I saw now why they liked to arrange themselves in front of the big window. That soft back light sure hid a lot. The bruise on her jaw was barely visible. I took the money.

'I hear you two met for a drink last evening.'

Lyle stiffened.

'We were in the same bar,' I said. 'Is that the same thing?'

'Is it?'

Lyle was ashen. She hadn't told him so he must have eyes on

her. If I had to guess I'd have fingered the barman dropping a dime as soon as I left.

'Bars are public places, Mr Montgomery. If you're wearing pants and holding they'll mostly let you in.'

He hummed and his blue lips parted in a bitter smile. 'Is that so, Mr Marlowe?'

He held my eye and took Lyle's hand in his, tenderly at first. He stroked it, trailing his big liver-spotted hand over her fingers slowly as he came to the tips. Lyle stiffened. She knew what was coming. This had happened before. Montgomery watched my face as he squeezed her fingers tight together.

The knuckle bones ground tight against each other. Her fingertips paled to white.

Lyle had dealt with worse than this, she knew how to ride it, breathing in deep, looking at a spot on the far wall, steeling every muscle. She chose to be here. She came back for more. Maybe she wanted it. But I hated him. Not just for doing it but for making me watch. I hated him for being old and rich and having a drawer full of money to toss at me.

I left.

Cooper was outside the door holding a hand over his eye. He followed me down the corridor making sure I left without stealing all the vases. He needn't have bothered. I turned on the doorstep.

'You know he's knocking her around.'

'He knocks everyone around,' he said. 'I expect she'll get it bad tonight. He's dying. She's the only person he has the strength to hurt anymore.'

'And you work for him.' I couldn't think of anything more insulting to say.

'So do you, Marlowe.' He had a point.

'I'm rethinking my position,' I said and walked away.

'Well bully for you, Marlowe,' he called after me. 'I need this job. I got plans.'

I drove down the hill, glad to get back to the honest fug, down with the filth and the crowds and the drunks. In the drive down to the gates I saw no one. It was a ghost world with all the messy people with their sorrows and lies and smells erased. It was a charade of a life. It was a lie.

I drove over to Mrs Dudek's and told her that the company were so impressed with her they insisted she get two hundred dollars.

Mrs Dudek took the bills out of the envelope, squealing with delight when a small figure came downstairs to see what all the noise was about. Evelyn Hamilton in yellow silk pyjamas, tousle-haired and as cute as a bug in a beret. She was one of those girls who look as if they should skip everywhere. Mrs Dudek, mindful of her vow of silence, said a cousin had left her some money and showed it to her.

'Oh, Mrs Dudek, darling, how marvellous!'

She looked at me. She tipped her head. Her eyes widened. Evelyn the hatcheck girl recognized me as the big tipper who was rotten at some jobs. She didn't quite know why I was there and it worried her. But she smiled at me and held her landlady's arm protectively, 'And for this money you have to . . . ?'

'Nothing, dear, I don't have to do anything. It's a gift from my cousin.'

'Well, isn't that something, darling?' said Evelyn, standing daintily on one foot, her hand resting on Mrs Dudek's shoulder. 'It's almost incredible.'

'Isn't it?'

I smiled at her. She smiled at me, a thin sort of smile, her lips pressed together so tight they lost their colour. Her eyes were glaring me a warning that if I messed with Mrs Dudek then Evelyn Hamilton would hurt me in ways I could not imagine.

18.

Bruce MacIntosh's house was in Los Feliz, a wealthy area for a looser set. The houses were all big and set back from the road, far enough away to give the impression of being open but the windows are glimpsed behind strategic hedges and small walls, less formal than the Montgomery place. The house on Ambrose was set back far enough from the street to make you feel welcome but not expected to call.

It was the biggest house on the street, a vast white stucco Spanish colonial on the steepest part of the hillside. The series of buildings seemed jammed together incoherently, the red clay roofs of each lapping over one another like a lumpy blanket. The buildings were all tall and thin, all the windows big and arched, wide open like a chorus of screaming mouths.

I knocked on the door and it was answered by a butler in a lemon yellow sweater, a casual choice compared to Cooper. He might have been a friend of the family and took the trouble to smile at me and shake my hand. He welcomed me into a wide hall with a red tiled floor. He led me through to a vast living room and Bruce MacIntosh himself, reading a newspaper and smoking on a couch. He jumped up.

'Oh, hello,' said MacIntosh, and he shook my hand too. 'Yes, my soon-to-be father-in-law called ahead and told me to expect you. Won't you come on through to the garden?'

MacIntosh was a tall young man with a blond gaucho

moustache, yellow hair to match and a lot of pale freckles. They covered his face and hands, the back of his neck and even the rims of his ears. When he blinked I saw that he even had them on his eyelids. He wore a loose linen shirt and peasant pants, wide and cool, all white, and tan loafers with argyle socks. Two excitable russet Springer spaniels capered around his legs.

We walked through a large room bordering on the garden where a Spanish maid was arranging a table for lunch, two places. She wore a black uniform and a white apron.

'Thanks, Rosinna,' he rolled his 'r' and I didn't feel it was for my benefit. 'I'm taking this gentleman to the garden, then we'll take our meal.'

'Si señor,' she said without looking up.

He led me out of the door and down the steps to the grassy lawn outside and asked me what he could do for me.

'I'm looking for Chrissie, I think you know that.'

'Hmm.' He reached down to pet one of the dogs, running his fingers through its red forelock as it panted with joy.

'Did she say anything to you at the party?'

He flashed a smile at me, 'She said a lot of things. It was a special night.'

'Who all was at the party?'

'Ha!' that electric smile again. 'Everybody who's anybody really. The cream of California: half my Dartmouth class were there, oil money and the sailing set of course.'

'Any art dealers?'

'*Dealers*? Good Lord, no. Buyers, but no dealers. Nothing so vulgar.' He tittered at that, a self-deprecating kind of snort, and expected me to titter along with him. I didn't.

'Specifically, which buyers?'

The question stumped him, 'Hmm. No one springs to mind, not specifically, I mean they'd be more likely to buy than have actual businesses selling, is what I mean.'

'Who were your close friends at Dartmouth?'

His face tightened. 'I suppose . . . well it's so hard to choose one chum from so many . . . I don't know if they'd be happy to talk . . . They didn't know Chrissie anyway, really, not most of them. Why? Why are you asking about me?'

'Just asking.'

'Because I didn't disappear. She did.'

'She didn't disappear though, did she? She ran away.'

'Huh, of course,' he rubbed the dog's ears. 'And where did she go, do you suppose?'

'Chicago, looks like.'

That worried him. 'Chicago, eh? Awfully cold. Why would she choose Chicago?'

'Maybe she's in love with Bronko Nagurski, how do I know. She didn't say anything untoward that night, nothing sticks in your mind?'

'Nothing. Nothing at all. She was drunk when I got there though, that was new. And she seemed a little upset. I understood she'd had a prang in the Packard. Smashed into a wall.'

'Would that have accounted for her mood?'

He considered it. I think he wanted to lie but his conscience wouldn't let him, 'Not really. I passed the car on the way in. It wasn't that bad. Not really.'

'Was her son at the party?'

'Chadwick the fourth? Sure, he was brought in by Miss Lyle to see the party.'

'You talk to him?'

He raised an eyebrow, 'Have you talked to him? He's four, what's he going to say?'

He was not wrong. MacIntosh was not lying. He didn't seem to have a need. He was on the level.

'Chadwick the third is a character.'

He huffed. Sure is, he said, but we were back at a Dartmouth-chums wall again. He wasn't going to say anything indiscreet.

'Miss Lyle been with him long?'

'Oh, a year or so. Why are you asking?'

'General background. Thought perhaps she and Chrissie didn't get along.'

'They get along just fine. Miss Lyle came on board to help Chadwick with his museum pieces. Chrissie likes that sort of thing. They get along just fine.'

'Señor,' Rosinna stood at the top of the steps, arms folded softly in front of her. 'Luncheon's ready, señor.'

We went inside. The dogs tumbled and skidded around us as we sat down, one at each end of the table. In the middle was a pot roast, green beans and freshly cut green salad. It was too much food for two people and I had a feeling that the staff would be getting their meal after us. The meat was tender and came away easily on the fork but I wasn't hungry. I was trying to understand why Chrissie ran from this man. He might not be her type but he was decent and of the same social background. There was nothing special about him, nothing that would make a woman run away and burrow under Bunker Hill.

We finished eating and Rosinna brought us strong coffee in tiny cups with saucers and spoons to match.

'You know,' said MacIntosh. 'If there was one thing that bothered me about that night it was how drunk Chrissie was. She isn't known as a drinker. But that night she drank. Spirits. A lot of them. She got rather squiffy.'

'Maybe she was trying to keep up with you.'

'Oh no, Mr Marlowe, I'm teetotal. I don't drink at all.' He dabbed his mouth with his napkin, 'As a matter of honour I have to tell you that I did not feel she was completely safe with her father. He beats Miss Lyle in a rather unsavoury way. I've spoken to her about it . . .' He looked unhappily into his coffee.

'So have I.'

He was surprised I'd broached it, 'Did she say the same to you as she did to me, I wonder?'

'That she was used to being beaten?'

'That all men beat all women? Yes, she said that to me. I must say, if it were true that all men beat all women I think I'd have a lot less free time on my hands, what with the hitting and the miserable self-recrimination.'

He was likeable, MacIntosh. I didn't see us driving down to Tijuana for the weekend anytime soon but in his own world, by his own rules, he was all right.

'I think we both realized that night that it simply wouldn't work. We've known each other since we were very young. Two dauphins. It's easy to think you know each other when you really don't.' He sipped from his coffee cup. 'But maybe that's what marriage is.'

'Maybe.'

'If you do find Chrissie I wish you'd tell her that she's terribly welcome to come here if she needs to get out of the way. I know her father's house is . . . let's call it difficult. But if she needs a place to stay, I can have my sister come to chaperone. Chrissie does have friends.'

I left him playing with the dogs in the garden as Rosinna let me out.

If a marriage of convenience was your thing, Bruce MacIntosh wasn't the worst. He was straightforward husband material. He didn't seem like someone about to fly their biplane into the side of a mountain.

Chrissie wasn't just running away. She was running to something.

19.

Every sunset on Bunker Hill felt like it might be its last. It was a melancholy evening sort of place. The sun gave up and went home. As the shadows grew long on the broken-up sidewalks all the people and the cats and the rats sloped off to look for a safe corner to spend the night.

I waited for three cigarettes before I saw her leave the house alone. She was unmissable.

Chrissie Montgomery wore a red dress and carried a clutch purse in her white gloved hands. People in the street stopped to look as she passed by. It was the way she moved.

Her hips led her. She didn't watch the ground as she walked but kept her chin up and her eyes on the horizon. It was the walk of someone who didn't carry groceries or children or laundry, hadn't broken heels on paving stones a hundred times and gone hungry to have them mended.

It was obvious she was rich.

Even without seeing her face I knew she was someone. Even her cheap hat, worn to pass, was tipped at a classy angle. She stood a head taller than the other people in the queue, watching for the trolley, thrilled and interested, a tourist playing the part of the poor person and it stood out a mile. It was a wonder she hadn't been robbed already. Hell, I was half thinking about robbing her myself.

I followed her down to the queue for the trolley but stayed

back. I slid down the steps at the side, watching her in the lit trolley.

The funicular passes between broken-down tenements and patches of waste ground, doesn't cover a long area, but there's a set of steps underneath where it's dark and the thin yellow light only deepens the shadows.

Chrissie Montgomery sat by the front window as the carriage took off with a jolt.

I lowered my hat and ran down the steps, racing the flashes of light from the trolley windows passing down the high rails through the dark narrow passageway, passing windows, lit now, and fleeting sights of residents ending their day, leaving for work, slumping in chairs.

We were less than halfway down when I saw the regulars in the trolley gathering their things and getting up, anticipating their arrival at the bottom. Chrissie Montgomery was on her feet.

I got there first and arranged myself, tipped my hat to cover my face and turned away to hide my heavy breathing.

At the bottom of the hill the passengers filed out of the open door and dissipated into the crowd at the busy junction. Chrissie stood at the edge of the sidewalk, looking up the street for a taxi. She was going to meet Zimmerman. I was going to lose her but I knew she'd be going to a bar in one of the three swank hotels in the next two blocks.

Resigned, I turned away to a dusty shop window and watched her reflection. But Chrissie wasn't waiting for a cab. She was waiting for a break in the traffic. One came and she flattened a hand to her head to hold onto the hat and ran across the street.

I went after her.

She walked fast, with purpose, she knew where she was going.

A block down I thought we had arrived but she raised a hand to a man leaving the Bradbury, he reciprocated the gesture and watched, a little concerned, as she walked on, moving fast and lithe. By the time she threw a left along Main I knew Chrissie Montgomery was in deep trouble.

The richest woman in California was walking alone into the black heart of Skid Row.

From Third to Sixth along Main was full of missions and soup kitchens, strip joints and broken-down movie theatres where the films were a side hustle. The real business was the dark and the seats and somewhere to sleep for the price of admission. Posters of gangster and wrestling flicks, creased up and badly hung, glared out at passers-by, daring them to come into the yawning mouths of darkness. Bored ticket sellers sat behind glass in small booths, smoking and chewing gum, flicking through magazines as they suffered their public.

Chrissie passed a strip joint and dodged the grabbing paw of a half-crazed john on the door with a slick side step but she looked worried. She knew she was out of her depth.

This was bum town, sad town, lost town, a place of sad endings: end of the road, end of the line, Skid Row. Freight trains from all over America delivered fruit and flowers and flour and milk and all the lost men, cut loose, men and women and children chewed up and spewed out by the Depression.

It was the final stop for the terminally confused and hopeless, alcoholics running from trouble. They got here and found there was nowhere left to run. They'd gone all the way west they could and then they settled here, in rotting rooming hotels that charged by the week, getting by on free soup, queueing up for a piece of floor to sleep on at the missions, drinking and stealing and dying on the sidewalk. The city fathers didn't know what to do with the numbers arriving. They were the ungovernably chaotic, people from all over with needs and illnesses and problems. Itinerant salesmen and travellers stayed but never for longer than they needed to. Casualties of the European War, amputees and trembling shock victims gathered in cheap beer halls, begging from passers-by and each other.

This is what she was walking into the heart of. Anneliese Lyle was right. This was the savannah.

Drunks passed out on the sidewalk, food all down them,

trousers on their tenth owner, shoes with no soles. Men shouted at invisible foes, took swings at them, but through the middle of them, like Daniel in the lion's den, floated one of the richest heiresses in the city and she knew where she was going.

I wanted to turn back. No one wanted to be here, not at twilight, not in this heat, but I couldn't leave her here alone.

She crossed over and took a right, down Fifth, until she came to a large building on Crocker with a gaggle of drunks on a bench outside. They were passed out or passing out, slumped over each other. She walked across the face of the Alhambra Residential Hotel, one of the roughest residential hotels on Skid Row. Some men slept in the street rather than go in there. Others found they belonged and paid two bits to sleep on the floor.

Chrissie crossed the street from it and walked into the bright lobby of the Brody Hotel.

I stood across the street, my back to the big windows of the Alhambra Residential Hotel, expecting her to come straight back out. I smoked a cigarette. I caught the eye of Sunshine Aziz, the manageress of the Alhambra, sitting behind her desk, smoking a long black pipe and watching me with steady, black-kohled eyes.

But after a while, when Chrissie didn't come out and Sunshine Aziz wouldn't stop giving me the evil eye, I crossed the street and went into the lobby of the Brody Hotel.

20.

The mirrored foyer walls were foxed and yellow, cracked so often it looked like a pattern. It was a funhouse if all the fun was replaced with grime and sadness.

A skinny lad with greasy brown hair was slumped over the mirrored desk, squinting through thick glasses at a fat cowboy novel. On the cover a galloping cowboy was falling off his horse as an Indian brave watched in the background, arms crossed and watching, enjoying his rival having an accident. It made me think of Pasco Pete, as if today needed to get any worse.

He was enthralled and held the book with one hand while he worked a toothpick in his teeth with the other. He looked up as I came in, his eyes distorted by the thickness of his lenses into distant rumours.

'Yah?' he said, standing up and letting the fat novel frrrip itself shut as he shoved it under the counter.

It seemed an informal sort of place, the kind of hotel you could walk about in your shirtsleeves and possibly only that. I pointed to the stairs and the elevator at the back of the lobby, 'Dame in a red dress and hat?'

He looked me up and down, had me pegged as a tragic romantic. The thought made him smile and not in a kind way.

'Your wife?'

'Is she staying here?'

He stood straight and coughed to clear his throat, looked at the door out to the street, 'We are not at liberty to discuss visitors, sir. May I assist you with anything –'

I cut him short by putting notes on the counter.

He stared down as if he'd never seen two dollars in one place at the same time. 'Woah! Are you a rich movie star?'

'Yes. Are you a famous comedian who doesn't need two dollars?' I made to take my money back but he slapped his hand over the bills, sliding them back to his side as he shot me a look that would have soured milk. He crumpled the notes into a ball and shoved them into his pocket.

I asked him to show me the guest book and he did. She had signed as Joan Baudelaire.

'Who's she visiting?'

'Name of West.' He wanted to peg one on me, 'She your wife?'

I only gave him hope so I could snatch it away later, 'Maybe.'

His eyes raced around my face, looking for clues. He could see it wasn't personal. 'You a gumshoe?'

'I gave *you* the money, bub. I'll ask the questions.'

'Sure.'

'Where'd she go?'

'Room 109: one floor up. The corner room.' He looked up to the edge of the ceiling. 'If they left the drapes open you can watch them smooching from the street.'

'West is a man?'

Giving succour to others did not come instinctively to this kid which explained why he was working on the reception desk at the Brody. He looked around for a way out of being useful and caught sight of his own tiny eyes, multiplied a thousand times, peering back at him from the mirrored walls.

'Peter West.'

'Did he just turn up and ask for a room?'

'No. Some dame booked two rooms for three weeks.'

'Who? Her?' I looked up the stairs.

'No. I wasn't on but the day guy, Flaky Hondrat, he said she had legs into tomorrow.'

'She booked two rooms?'

'Right next to each other.'

'Someone travelling with him?'

'No. He brought crates with him. Cargo. Not clothes, wooden boxes. I had a little look-see in the middle of the night.'

'What's in the boxes?'

'Dunno. Tell you what, he don't belong at the Brody. He's got nice shoes. Good clothes. He's about a million years old and don't a-speak-a da English.'

'He's Italian?'

'No, German.'

'You were doing an Italian.'

Tiny Eyes didn't want to lose on points but he struggled to think of a comeback line. 'Sue me. He dresses all formal. Pocket square to match his tie. Makes him stand out around here . . .' He looked at the backs of the doors, the imagined sights of Skid Row, and braced himself. 'A couple a' bums tried to roll him one night and he beat them bloody with his cane. Tough ol' bird. One boy's ear was hanging off.'

'Cops come?'

He shook his head and the movement rippled around the mirrored room, 'Cops don't come down here without a paddy wagon and a press photographer, not unless somebody dies. That useful?'

He looked at the pocket I kept my wallet in but I wasn't going to pay him to take a guess. I didn't like the guy.

'I'll let you get back to the OK Corral,' I said and went back outside.

Across the road, I settled against a wall, keeping my eyes on the corner window. The lights were all on inside but the white drapes were drawn. Shapes were moving in there but it could have been one person or a party of twelve. The molten shadows gave few clues.

Night fell and evening sounds of the streets bounced off the high buildings, hoots and hollers and sad old songs. Sure, there were drunks there, sitting on the ground or shambling from bar to bar. There were ordinary people too, though. Suits and blouses, kids running errands, dragging the day out, trying not to go home. One man caught my eye. He was sleeping on the ground, right where the buildings ran out and the dirt was marked with patches of cracked concrete. He was wearing a suit and tie, curled up and sleeping, his hat placed carefully into the comma of his sleeping body. This man wasn't drunk or running from anything but bad luck. He'd run out of places to go. He could have been me but he wasn't me. Not today at least.

I tore my eyes off him, bringing them back to the corner window of a fleapit hotel where an heiress was meeting an old German with nice shoes.

I was none too happy about leaving her in there, none too happy about being here myself.

I waited, smoking, moving my spot sometimes so I didn't attract attention.

I was halfway through my fourth cigarette when a star exploded in the street. A white flash of light was followed by the sound of a shot. Reflexively, everyone in the street looked up to where the noise came from: corner, first floor, the Brody.

As if another light had been turned on, a sudden second flash, a second slap on the ears. The white light in the window turned red.

I bolted for the stairs.

21.

The clerk in the lobby was flattened to the mirrored wall looking left and right, gasping and cursing.

I ran up the stairs and turned to the corridor on my left. Thirty feet down, at the corner, an open door was spilling light into the dark corridor.

I ran towards it.

He was on his back, his stockinged feet toward the open door. He'd been shot twice with a small-calibre pistol, once through the heart, once through the jaw. It made holes, sprayed blood up the wall and the window, but caused little damage otherwise. He was just a man on his back. A man with holes in him.

A dead man.

Chrissie Montgomery was behind him, standing between the bed and the window. The blood dripped down the drapes behind her. She was frozen there, the dead man lying between her and the door out, her shaking hands hung limp by her side. Her eyes were open wide, as if she was trying to see more, see something else, something that would make this not real. Her breathing was shallow and jagged.

I looked down.

The man was Mussolini-jawed, in a silk smoking jacket over a dress shirt and pants. This was his room. Two glasses were set out on a small table next to a bottle of clear schnapps but they were clean and unused. He'd been expecting company. A suitcase sat on the floor with an empty string looped around the handle where the name tag should be.

On the dresser behind Chrissie an expensive wristwatch lay on its back, the leather strap still holding the shape of the wrist, like a two-legged spider, crouching.

'He's . . . shot.' She pointed at the body. 'Is he moving?'

She raised a hand at his chest. Blood was pumping lazily from his injured chest, darkening his shirt. He wasn't dead yet but the widening stain spreading under his body meant he would be any moment now.

I looked at his face. The eyes were open in surprise. I could see under his top lip two jagged canines on either side, undescended, little white nubs above the row of perfectly straight teeth. Pavel Viscom.

'Come here.' My voice set off a tremble through her body. She tried to speak but nothing came out. 'Come with me.'

She looked at me for the first time and blinked, confused, 'Mr Allan? From *Collector Monthly*?'

'Chrissie, I've been sent to look after you. Come with me.'

Dazed, she shook her head.

I reached over the bed, wrapped my hands around her skinny waist, dragged her across to me and stood her on her feet, then picked up her purse and hat from a chair.

From the distant city came the mournful wail of a cop car, heading our way.

I pushed Chrissie out of the room, turning her stiff shoulders away from the stairs to the lobby. She caliper-walked down the corridor to a corner. The window at the end was open out to a fire escape at the back of the building. We took the turn as the myopic gunslinger from the lobby arrived at the door to the room. He gasped, fell against the door and then ran, slamming off walls as he made his way downstairs.

I eased Chrissie out of the window, onto the fire escape, climbed out after her and pulled the window shut behind us.

The fire escape was already down. Someone had come down here moments before us.

We were twenty feet above a dark alley that smelled of spoiled milk and rats but it was dark and at least we were out of there. That was when the platform swayed beneath our combined weight. Iron bolts attaching the fire escape to the wall grated away from their moorings, dragging free a small shower of glinting sand that caught the light and twinkled like confetti.

Chrissie grabbed the railing.

I hurried down the ladder, jumping to the ground as Chrissie came down after me. At the bottom rung she got stuck, her skirt caught on a metal mesh. I picked her up and pulled her away, ripping the hem just a little. I shoved the ladder back up to the platform.

The siren was closer, three blocks away, then two.

A crowd had gathered across the street, staring up at the red window. Mothers in nightgowns and fathers in slippers, nosy grandparents and excited barkeeps, lone men, all pointing and saying what they knew, what they heard, when it happened.

I put my jacket over Chrissie's shoulders to cover her bloody blouse and led her over to join the crowd. I took my cigarettes out, lit two and gave her one.

'I don't want it . . .' she whispered.

'Take it,' I said. 'Smoke it and gawk.'

She did. We let the chatter wash over us. There were a lot of opinions in the crowd. A husband had killed a wife. It was a gang hit. All that Chicago trouble was coming down here. Three shots. Four dead. Italians. Irish. A French man beat up two locals earlier. Revenge killing. The Chinese.

A cop car arrived at the far corner and swung toward us, lighting the crowd with merciless twin beams. It screeched to a halt, rubber on hot tarmac and all four doors flew open.

Moochie Ruud, Lieutenant, stepped out onto the street, smirking at me.

He swaggered over. 'Mr Philip Marlowe,' he said, looking Chrissie up and down.

The crowd around us parted and turned to watch.

'Moochie Ruud,' I said. 'You the only cop in this city?'

'Don't call me Moochie.'

'That's what everyone calls you. How will we know who I'm talking about if I don't call you by your name?'

'Call me Lieutenant Ruud.'

'Okay, Moochie.'

He smirked and decided to let me have that one. 'The boys upstairs are pretty happy with how quick the Black Jack Beau case got rolled up. Looking at a promotion for that one.'

'The boys upstairs being your father-in-law and his brother?'

He didn't like that but the two uniforms flanking him did. They liked it plenty.

I hate Moochie Ruud. You can get a free drink in any cop bar in this city by saying that aloud. He married the brass's daughter, had the unearned stripes to prove it and a lip on him that would make a Quaker violent. Everyone around him felt sour about his promotion because he was about half as smart as he thought he was.

'Give me a cigarette, Marlowe.'

'You come all the way down here for a free smoke, Moochie?'

'Give it to me.'

I gave him one and lit it for him. He took a languorous draw and looked Chrissie Montgomery up and down carelessly. She let him, her slender shoulders sagging. Shock made her look drunk and miserable and messy. She'd mussed her hair climbing out of the window and ripped her hem on the ladder. She looked as cheap and shop worn as the rest of us now.

'Who's the broad?'

'A friend.'

He snorted on the exhale and gave himself a coughing fit. It lasted quite some time. When he recovered he said, 'What's your name, sweetheart?'

She whispered, 'Joan Baudelaire.'

'That your real name, honey?'

She shook her head sadly. If Ruud had looked at her and paid attention at all, he might have seen the spray of red on her collar. But he didn't. Ruud didn't look at anything carefully. Maybe his father-in-law paid someone to do that for him.

He smiled over at me like the boy who ate the whole thing. 'Didn't have you down as paying for it, Marlowe. Didn't see that coming at all.'

'Don't you have somewhere to be, Ruud?'

'Do I?'

'Did you come flying down to Skid Row for a free cigarette?'

He looked at his boys, two toughs in uniform hanging back, trying not to let the boss see them enjoying him being taken down.

'Yes,' he looked Chrissie up and down again, puzzled by her shocked and vacant eyes, thinking her drunk. 'You'll get yours, Marlowe.'

He turned away and got back into the car, looked at me from the open window and threw the lit cigarette out onto the road.

The uniforms got in. They pulled out, drove thirty feet to the front of the hotel and stopped again.

Big exit.

The mob of rubberneckers followed them around to the front of the Brody leaving us alone in the street.

Out of the alley behind the hotel crept a shadow, a small figure. It must have been down there, hiding. It must have seen everything. It bolted out to Ruud's discarded cigarette burning in the road, hand outstretched, ready to grab it. It stopped. It looked at me. A boy, no more than ten, dressed in the ragged clothes of a full-grown man. He looked at me, asking if I would beat him if he took it. I nodded him on. He bent down and picked it up, stuck it in his mouth and stood tall, hands on hips, puffing away like a railroad magnet.

I walked over. He had a scar above one eye. It looked as if someone had tried to rip his eyebrow off.

'Hey, sonny. Use five bucks?'

He squinted up at me through a cloud of smoke. 'Bub?'

I looked back at the alley, 'You down there all night?'

He looked back, 'Hmm?'

I peeled off a five-dollar note and handed it to him. He watched it as if it was a magic trick. 'See anyone come down the fire escape just before us?'

He looked at the money in his hand. He looked at me. I grinned and held out a twenty.

'Dame. Got in a car and skedaddled.'

'Car wouldn't happen to be a black Ford Coupe, two-seater, would it?'

He nodded and a smile dawned on his filthy face as if I'd guessed his card right.

He nodded.

'Happen to see if it had white wall tyres?'

He shook his head and shrugged, 'Nuh huh.'

I gave him the note but held the end of it as he tugged. 'Sonny, you didn't see nothing tonight, you hear?'

'I hear ya, Cap'n.' He puffed the cigarette and gave me a half grin. I let go of the note. I gave him my packet of cigarettes. He walked away, taking the middle of the road because he had a full five dollars and a pack of smokes. He was a king tonight and he'd do whatever he wanted.

He turned back in the middle of the street and saluted me.

22.

Chrissie was silent for the cab ride up to Franklin Avenue. She folded over her knees, her back curling slow as a leaf in an oven. I let her be, watching the night city pass by the window. I saw something fall from her face, drop to her dress, glint and spread. She was crying. It was good. It meant the shock was passing. Any day now she might blink.

'Who shot him, Chrissie?'

She started at my voice.

'Did you see her?'

Her eyes slid to the dark well of the cab and she wasn't in the rattling cab now, she was back in that corner room, watching someone coming through the door. She held her breath. Her eyes widened in horror and she jumped, blinking sharply, twice.

'Chrissie? You recognized her, didn't you? Was it Peggy Zimmerman?'

She glared at me, 'How do you know it wasn't me?'

'Hard to shoot around corners.'

She looked puzzled. I pointed at the bloody spray on her blouse. 'You had to be behind him when he was shot.'

She looked at it as if she had never seen the colour red before, touched it, rubbed her fingertips together. She covered her eyes with her clean hand. It was a fine hand, long-fingered, expressive. The face behind it was sobbing hard. I looked away and let her have her privacy.

The cab stopped outside the Hobart Arms and I paid the driver, being sure not to tip him twenty dollars. Enough people would remember seeing us tonight. We didn't need to add a cab driver to the list of witnesses.

The street was quiet. Some cars cruised past but I saw no one who gave me pause. No dusty coupes idling on the corner, no strangers smoking under street lamps.

Chrissie didn't need to be dragged anymore. She followed meekly as I led her through the building lobby and past the manager's office, upstairs to my apartment. I let us in and sat her on a chair.

'Rye?'

'Yes please.'

'I've only got the cheap stuff.'

'I like the cheap stuff.'

I poured us two fingers each and sat across from her. She held the glass with both hands as if it was warming her, lifted it to her mouth and drank as if she needed it. She grimaced as she swallowed and sighed afterwards.

'Cheaper than you're used to?'

She almost smiled. 'It's good.'

'That was quite a night.'

She sipped this time, 'How did you know I was there?'

'I followed you down from Bunker Hill.'

'Well, I must say, *Collector Monthly* is being unusually thorough . . .' She raised a sceptical eyebrow at me.

'I'm not really with *Collector Monthly*.'

'You don't say. I suppose someone asked you to follow me?'

'You suppose right.'

I took her glass and poured her another.

Now I could see her properly, when she wasn't in a gallery as hot as the Sahara or wearing a hat, I noticed it: she looked like Anneliese Lyle. It was striking. The hair color was different but the chin was the same. The long neck and fine nose read the same.

Anneliese was a slicker version of Chrissie, more cultivated to look like she did, but Chrissie was the original. She was who the mould was made from. I couldn't unsee it. The more I looked at her, sipping rye as if her life depended on it, trying not to tell me anything, the more uncanny the likeness became.

It happens.

Rich old men marry younger versions of ex-wives and often they look like their daughters. It's creepy but it doesn't mean anything. This was different. These women moved the same. They walked, hip first. Their tongues darted behind their teeth when they thought about saying something.

They weren't related, their colouring told you that, but Lyle had been chosen by Chadwick Montgomery because she looked so much like his daughter. Whether he knew it or Anneliese knew it, I had a feeling Chrissie knew, and that the bruises on Anneliese's neck were meant for her.

I could see why she felt trapped, why she might always feel trapped now. I sipped my drink and watched Chrissie working out the exits, where the door was and what she would need to do to get to it. I pushed my chair back, clearing her route.

'You can leave if you want. Go back to Mrs Dudek's.'

Her eyes flared in shock and she covered her face with the glass again.

'It won't be safe there now, though. That's why I brought you here.'

She sipped again, mapping her route to the door.

'Feel free to leave,' I repeated.

She considered it, she glanced out of the window at the lights in the street. Then she teared up. 'I have nowhere to go.' Her hair was sticking up and out now, whatever she had used to flatten it down had worn off. It was thick and black and had made up its mind to be curled but she didn't want it that way. She looked as wild as the small boy in the hallway at the Montgomery Mansion.

'How did you meet Mrs Dudek?'

'At the Dancers, the coatcheck girl, Evelyn. She found me

crying in the powder room and gave me her home address. She didn't know who I was but she said I could stay with her anytime. She took me in when I arrived at her door. You never hear of those people, do you? No prizes for everyday decency.'

I liked her at this point but that was about to change.

'Why not run away to a hotel?'

'They'd find me,' she said, dead eyed. 'They always find me.'

'Do you know the stiff at the Brody?' I asked.

'He looked so much like Pavel Viscom but Viscom's dead. I know he is. It was in the newspaper . . .'

I watched her realize that a paragraph low down on a front page wasn't a death certificate.

'Tell me what happened at the hotel.'

She shook her head.

'Chrissie, if you don't tell me I can't protect you from the cops. If they see Joan Baudelaire in the visitors' book they'll find you at the gallery and they'll grill you.'

She flashed me a scornful look, 'Mr Allan, I'm a Montgomery. If they work out I was down there I shall simply tell them who I am and they'll ask my father if they may speak with me. He'll say no.' She could have been wearing the pearls and posing for a portrait.

'Did you see the shooter?'

'No. It took me a long time to find the room, I went to the wrong floor. I didn't know the first number was the floor number, the bell hop always takes us to the room when we travel as a family. But I was on my own. So then I had to work my way down again until I found it and knocked and he let me in. We didn't know each other. He didn't speak English and we were trying to work out if I was in the wrong room. I thought there might be another booking under the name of "West", or maybe I was on the wrong floor again, but then the door was knocked. He held up a finger and looked out of the spy hole, and said, "Ah!" and he threw the door open. There was a flash so bright and a sound so loud that I was blinded for a moment. When I could see again he was on the floor. And then you were there.' She shook her head slow. Her eyes widened and brimmed with shocked remembering. Then she looked at me, remembered she was better than me and wasn't a bit happy about being here. 'Exactly who are you?'

'Your father asked me to find you.'

'Hm.' She looked around the small apartment, at my brown furniture and bedsheets sticking out of the wall on my unmade Murphy bed. She looked my clothes up and down, nothing she saw helped her any. 'I knew he'd send someone to find me but I don't . . .'

'They didn't want me to find you. They hired me because they think I'm a two-bit operation. They didn't expect me to manage much.'

'But you did. You going to hold me to ransom or something of that nature?'

'You can walk out of here if you want. I won't even get up. But you seem like you might need a bit of help.'

'I can't go back. I want to be free of them, of all of them, but I love my job.'

She'd had a job for a fortnight. Chimney sweeps could like their job for a fortnight.

I gave her another drink. She went slow on this one. She still didn't like me much.

'*Collector Monthly?*'

'A business card will do wonders. There's a trade in them. Go down to Tipi Halligan's on Central and she'll give you anything you need.'

'I'll bear that in mind. What's your real name?'

'Philip Marlowe.'

'Where did they find you?' She looked as if she expected to hear they found me stuck to Chadwick's sole after a hike through a barn full of pigs.

'Jimmy Donoghue passed on my name.'

'He did?'

'Sure.'

There was an absence in her. I couldn't place it. She wasn't drunk or on dope.

'You don't know who Jimmy is, do you?'

'No, I don't.'

'He's your gateman. He opens the gate at the bottom of the drive. He called the cab for you when you left.'

She shook her head, 'Oh, the tall one?'

'The handsome one.'

She remembered his face, registered that yes, he was handsome but it was a technical knowing. She couldn't see beyond the monkey suit. 'He was kind when I . . . in the Packard. It's impossible to remember all of the staff. When a lot of people work in your house . . .' she trailed off.

'You stop seeing them?'

'You have to. Otherwise it would be exhausting. You don't see them as people. And staff change all the time, you know how it is.'

'Yes, I got through three butlers last week. Jimmy asked me to be kind to you. Why would he do that?'

'The *gateman* asked you to be kind to *me*?'

'Yes. Have you met him before?'

'No. I don't think I have.' She tried to remember. 'Other than him calling a cab for me when I left and the crash the night before. He made me coffee.'

'He cares what happens to you. Why would that be?'

She smirked bitterly, 'Men. Being an heiress will make you attractive to most men.'

'They call him Jimmy the One. That ring any bells?'

It didn't. Not a one.

'Jimmy doesn't fall in love with women, if you get my drift.'

'Oh? Oh!' She laughed at that, at how silly that was, that decency and fellow feeling might extend beyond the boundaries of those who looked like you and lived like you and came from the same economic bracket as you. I wondered again why Jimmy cared. Maybe I was the fool here.

'How do you know this "Jimmy" person?'

I told her.

'Is that what you do, fix problems?'

'Sometimes.'

'Am I a problem you're trying to fix?'

'I don't know which problem I'm trying to fix right now. Taking you home is what I'm getting paid for but I'm not sure I want to do that.'

'Why?'

'Your father beats Lyle.'

She gave a disgusted laugh. 'My father does a lot of things. He's an important man from a long line of important men. They can do anything they want, hurt anyone they want.'

'You don't want to go back there?'

'I'll kill myself if they make me go back.'

'Why'd you leave? Something happen at the Dancers, before the engagement party?'

She laughed into her drink, a nasty little snicker, and when she looked up she was bitter beyond her years.

'Bruce, the man my father wants me to marry, he was brought into father's study the day before the party. I was brought in. D'you know what father said? "You can marry it, Bruce. You can breed with it. You can dress it up in diamonds but it'll still be mine." He was talking about me. My father owns a lot of important things, like me and Anneliese and those museum pieces he litters the house with. And then he sends you.'

'When the room door was knocked why did he open it –'

'Stop.' She held a hand up to me as if I was a chicken she was training.

I don't hit women. If I did she would have been wearing the building. I didn't want to be anywhere near these people anymore and Black Jack Beau felt like a month ago.

I got up, picked up my jacket and threw her purse at her. 'Move.'

She stood up on her foal legs, flattening her hair, self-conscious suddenly.

'Where are you taking me?'

'Back to Camelot.'

'You can't! You can't make me go back there!'

'Lady, if I have to fold you up and put you in your purse to get you out of my life I'll do it.'

'He beats her. He beats me. It's not safe there.'

'You speak to me like that again and you won't be safe here. I'm not related to you. I don't need to be near you. Get up.'

'I can't. Please? It's not safe.'

'In your mansion? With your son? Your father's dying, it'll all be over soon. Come on, princess. This place isn't for you.'

She looked around my modest apartment, at the worn divan and full ashtrays, at my cheap suit and fifty-cent haircut. She looked jealous. 'Camelot. Ha! Even Queen Guinevere made a break for it. Can't I stay just a little longer?'

She looked so scared and I'm a fool. 'Why d'you go to the Brody in the first place, Chrissie?'

She downed her drink and sighed. 'Peggy Zimmerman's just back from Europe. I was to meet them down there and take them for dinner —'

'Who's "them"?'

She shook her head again, 'Peggy and her daughter. I was to meet them. Well, I said I'd take her to the Jane Jones' Little Club.'

She glanced at me to see if I understood her.

I did.

Jane Jones' place was up on Sunset. It was a butches' bar, kittens-only. Men were allowed in for an exorbitant fee but only if they were card-carrying perverts and swore to keep their hands visible at all times. I'd seen them outside, gathered to talk away from the music, the butches dressed like men in slacks and suits and hats, like an army of short men. I saw them leaning over pretty girls, pressing them against the wall. Inverts. Jimmy's people. She was one of Jimmy's and he knew. Where he'd seen her, I don't know. Maybe at some bar, dancing close to slow old tunes, or laughing at a table, just being herself. I

remembered her father's horror that she might stoop to spending time with Jews.

'Who made this arrangement?'

'She did. She said she'd be booked under the name West at the
Brody. I asked for West and the manager sent me to that room.'

'The manager? You mean the guy with thick glasses who was
reading in the lobby?'

'Yes. Was he not the manager?'

'I doubt he was even the security guard, but I know who you
mean. Why doesn't she use her own name?'

'Too Jewish. Lots of places are exclusive.'

'The Brody isn't.'

'You know that?'

'I don't think they can afford to be but go on.'

'Well, he sent me up to the first floor, room 109. When I got
there the door was open a little. I knocked but there was no
answer. I could hear water running in the bathroom. I thought
Peggy might be washing her hands or something so I went inside
and called out to her but then the bathroom door opened and
that man came out. I recognized him. I thought he looked like
Pavel Viscom but I knew Viscom was dead. I thought he must be
his brother or something, but he was so pleased to see me. It was
strange. He tried to kiss me on the cheek but I pushed him away.
He seemed hurt by that. So, I was by the bed, I'd backed away to
the window and I was asking for Zimmerman. He knew the
name, I could see that much. He said the name back to me and
nodded but then I was still trapped there, it was a strange situa-
tion. He spoke German. He asked me who I was, I asked him
who he was. I asked him if he was Pavel Viscom and he was
confused, he kept looking at me, wouldn't answer, then he got a
photograph out from his wallet and said I wasn't who he was
expecting either. He showed me a photo of someone I – at least,
I *think* that's what he was saying. I don't speak German. I still
thought I was going to meet Peggy Zimmerman, that she'd be
in the suite, so I thought – I've gone to the wrong door, this is a

different person called West. That's when the door was knocked. We smiled at each other. He held his hands up at me, showed me his palms and he tilted his head as if he was saying "wait" or "sorry" or "we'll sort this out". I'm by the window and he is between me and the door but I feel safe. Then he turns to the door and opens it and he makes a noise, "Leib —" and he raises his hands but then there is a flash.'

She fell backwards into a seat as if the flash had happened just that moment behind her eyes.

'A shot: painfully loud. Then another. I shut my eyes and turn away. Then I hear the bang for that too. I hear him fall. I don't want to see but I have to see. I open them. Everything is red and he's hurt.'

She was seeing him now, looking at a spot on the floor where he fell. She was shocked and sad and hardly breathing. Her eyes glazed over. She was back in the room, watching. 'I couldn't see who was coming in. The closet was in the way. I couldn't stop looking at him. I know someone was there. They were moving around. But he was on his back and he had this —' she touched her temple with her fingertips, 'And it kept moving, the shirt was moving and I'm thinking — he isn't dead, it's moving . . .'

'Did the shooter speak?'

She had to think about it. 'No. They were moving around,' her left hand made vague movements to the side. 'Picking up things? Pulled the luggage tag from the suitcase, I remember that. Then — gone. Then you came.' She looked at me with pure, childlike affection that evaporated as suddenly as innocence.

'Could Peggy Zimmerman have been the shooter?'

'It wasn't her. It was someone younger.' She might not have seen them but she had a suspicion.

'Do you know them?'

But just then my front door was knocked, soft and low. Chrissie Montgomery leapt to her feet, flattening herself to the wall in horror.

But I knew the knock. I knew it was okay.

'A friend of mine,' I said. 'Sit down. Finish your drink.'

Chrissie sloped back to the chair. I opened the door to a pair of grey-blue eyes with flecks of gold and turned to see Chrissie's face. She didn't recognize Anne at all.

'Hello, handsome,' said Anne. 'Better get your skates on. The cops are looking for you.'

23.

Anne Riordan sailed into the centre of the room and looked down at Chrissie Montgomery.

There wasn't that much between them in age. Anne was ten or so years older and a hundred years smarter. There was a steadiness at the core of her that added to her neat figure and large eyes. Her hair was hidden under a brown hat that must have seemed ludicrous in the shop but looked classy on her: a man's Derby with green feathers standing tall at the back. It was brown, with a short brim, and sat on the side of her head at an angle that defied gravity. Maybe gravity saw her trying the hat on in the store and thought she looked so cute with it perched just above her ear like that that it would let her off, just this once.

'Hello Christine.'

Chrissie was startled to be spoken to. She thought Anne was here to see me and had gone back into her trance. She looked up at her, 'How do you know my name?'

'Your father hired me to watch out for you.'

Chrissie looked at me.

'He hired me too,' I said.

'You work together?'

'We're in competition with each other,' said Anne.

'You're a PI? But you're a woman.'

'Very astute. Yes, I asked Marlowe to take me on but he refused.' Anne enjoyed telling the story again. Me less so. 'I had no alternative than to set up on my own and now I run my own agency. I have four gals working as PIs, all licensed and registered with the city. We have three secretaries, a receptionist and two telephonists, all gals.'

Chrissie Montgomery had just witnessed a man being shot to death in a hotel room and that may have fogged her interest in how many administrative staff Anne's business employed.

'Say, Anne, what's your position there, in terms of tax liabilities. I'm sure Chrissie is dying to know.'

Anne slapped my arm. 'How are you, Marlowe?'

I patted her back, just gently, 'I'm jimdandy, Anne. How are you?'

'Broadly the same story: Jim's been dandying all over my day too.'

'He keeps busy. What are you doing here?'

'Came to see you.'

'About anything?'

Without moving we had somehow come to be inches from each other, standing too close, we were face to face, stuck in a bubble of time until one of us managed to break it off. If we didn't we'd either kiss or burst into flames. Could have gone either way.

To break us out of the moment, Anne reached up and took her hat off. They should have made a ballet out of it. She lifted both hands above her head and cupped the crown of the hat with her right hand. Her left hand rose behind her head and then, both rising in perfect unison, she pulled the hat pin out and lifted the hat off. That broke us up a little.

We both smiled at the rug until Anne did that gliding thing she did into the middle of the room. She held out her hand to Chrissie who stood up and shook it.

Anne sat down and kicked her shoes off and sighed up at me. 'Marlowe,' she said. 'I'm afraid I'm here with some pretty bad news.'

She looked at Chrissie. Chrissie looked back at her. Anne pointed to the bathroom, 'Give us a moment will you?'

Christine Montgomery couldn't quite believe it. 'Oh.'

'Yes,' said Anne. 'I'd like to talk in private, if you wouldn't mind.'

That was when I knew she wouldn't turn her in for a grand. Anne Riordan was still master of her own soul. Chrissie got up and sloped off like a third wheel. She locked herself in the bathroom and turned on the tap.

'Manny Perez got murdered last night. Word on the wire is someone driving an Olds was seen rolling him out onto someone's lawn. Word on the street where he died is that it wasn't an Olds at all, it was —'

'Let me guess — a Ford Coupe two-door with three white wall tyres?'

'Well, you ought to go on the stage as a wanderin' seer.'

'Do you think so, Anne?'

'I'd pay to see you.'

'How much?'

'Two sticks of gum and a shirt button.'

'Main button or cuff?'

She looked up at me and smiled. 'Collar.'

Some nights Anne Riordan is all I want to look at and this was one of those. It wasn't always mutual. She looked away.

'You know it's only a matter of time before the troops work out that you were drinking with him. It took me all of twenty minutes.'

'Someone has a plan and Perez was a small man who got in the way. Pretty careless way to treat the small man, speaking as a small man myself.'

'You don't think you're being set up?'

'Manny Perez was a fighter. I don't imagine the list of suspects will be short. In the brief time I'd spent with him he had annoyed a lot of different men and he often drank in bars so low the rats were wiping their feet on the way out. He managed to be the worst in them.'

She smoked thoughtfully. 'Well, doesn't look like a crime of passion. This was professional. He was lying on a lawn, on his back, probably asleep. Someone walked up and shot him in the heart once, once through the head, got in their car — Olds or Ford — and drove away. You're being set up. We need to get you both out of here until we can work out what's going on. CHRISTINE!' she shouted and Chrissie came out of the bathroom. 'We're getting you out of here until we can work out what's going on.'

'I can't go home,' said Chrissie. 'He wants to take me there but I can't go home.'

'Why not?' asked Anne.

'I'm not safe there.'

'You're not safe out here either, Chrissie.'

Having Anne in the room made me feel different. I didn't want to drop a piano on Chrissie for talking down to me any more. I wanted to rescue her. Hell, I wanted to rescue everyone while Anne watched me and made wisecracks about my suit.

'I know a place,' I said. 'Someone who owes me a favour.'

24.

We drove down to South Central. It was a moonless night, a deep velvet dark lay heavy over the city and the heat of the day nuzzled in the low basin, clinging close to the ground, but it was better now. The sun wasn't making it any worse.

Neighbours gathered on benches in the grand old avenues to smoke and enjoy the cooler evening air. They were in their shirt sleeves and loose pants, or house dresses, glad of the easement from the heat of the day. Streetlights were dim, soft and thin dogs barked in the distance and music from all the corners of the world floated from windows. A couple were screaming at each other inside a house and another couple, out walking their dog, canoodled on the street, as if the misery of the people inside added to their enjoyment of the world. It was a nice area.

Though the tall buildings of downtown glowed in the distance, a pivot on the heel would bring the eyes to the hills and the wild interior. The roads were wide, the place was safe and there didn't seem to be many building restrictions: shops were next to cabin houses with fenced-off junkyards in between.

Anne had let me take Chrissie away myself. She didn't know about the murder at Brody's yet but Moochie Ruud was a blabbermouth. The moment she met him he'd be sure to blurt it out if she took a breath and left a pause and it wouldn't be long until she put two and two together. She would not like me holding out on her.

Chrissie watched the streets pass by the window. She felt no comradeship with the old man sitting on a bench, smoking a pipe, or the old dog panting next to him. She looked around at the smashed windows and an abandoned car with a man asleep in the front seat like a chauffeur waiting for his master's call. To her it was strange and picturesque, a foreign land.

I drove on to an old wooden house with a rotten porch. The house stood on its own, its neighbour on one side had been torn down when it became too unsafe and flattened to make a dirt-floored car park. To the right the land wasn't even useable for parking cars. The dirt was drying out in the recent heat, all the tall weeds had dried up and broken or fallen over.

Wall Street was south of downtown on a flat plane of land. From here the San Gabriel mountain range was visible in the far blue distance. Maude said that was why she and Pasco Pete had moved here in the first place, so they could see the mountains calling to them and remember to leave while they had enough money. They meant to leave every year but never got around to it. That was why they didn't do any upkeep on their house. It wasn't falling down so much as melting.

Built of a temporary wood, it sucked in what rain fell and swelled and buckled and crumbled away. It was built into the dirt so it didn't even have a solid base. Now all the once-charming flaws and wrong angle-ness were causing the building to collapse in on itself. It seemed incredible that Maude was still living in it but she missed her Pete too much to just up and leave now she had the money. I had a feeling she was hoping she would die before she had to go.

'This can't be it,' said Chrissie, looking up the dirt drive.

The house was about one loud sneeze away from collapsing. The soil it was built on was falling away and the walls were going with it. The crawl space underneath was visible now, the wood rotting and grey. A bedroom at the very top of the house had an iron railing frieze in front of it that was hanging on by its fingernails.

I parked and we walked up to the porch. It was a high step up to the first plank. I reached down and helped Chrissie up, crossed over, and pulled the bell.

'Mr Marlowe?' It was an old witchy voice, high and cracked and strained. Baby Maude must have spotted us coming up the path.

'Maude, my friend is in trouble. Can she hide out for a couple of days?'

Miss Maude used her body weight to drag the reluctant front door open. 'Come on in, honey.'

The first thing through the door was a big photo of Pasco Pete, poster-sized, propped up on an easel. It was framed with black crepe and a wreath of paper flowers that hung jauntily over one corner. Maude must have brought it from the funeral service. It wasn't appropriate for a funeral and had drawn some remarks at the service but everyone agreed that it was no more inappropriate than a life cut short by a bitter rival with a tyre iron. Pasco had used the picture for casting and Maude loved it.

Pasco was pictured in a quick draw, legs wide, pointing his pistol at us, smoke billowing out of the barrel. He was dressed nice though: in matching beige suede chaps and waistcoat and a white cowboy hat. A tin star twinkled on his chest. He didn't look like a varmint, he didn't look broken down or anything but grand and giving life his all. It was how I'd like to be remembered if I'd been a cowboy bit-part player.

Chrissie was cautious of Maude at first and I couldn't blame her. Maude had her falsers out, a night cap on, and was dressed in a grey negligée so old Martha Washington would have asked for something more up-to-date. It hung heavy on her thin shoulders, dragging the neckline down to show her flat liver-spotted chest. The weight came from two small silver pistols in the front pockets one on either side. She'd been ready for us when we came to the door. Maude would always be ready and that's why I knew Chrissie would be safe here.

She looked Chrissie up and down. 'Who in the Sam Hill is this long strip of misery?'

That was the moment Chrissie took to Maude. I suppose being a Montgomery shields you. No one calls you names when you're as rich as God. She smiled down at Maude and offered her hand.

'Joan Baudelaire. And you are?'

Maude slapped her hand away, 'I'm the owner o' the house you're standing on, sweet cheeks, and it's one in the morning. You're lucky I didn't put a hole in you. You on the lam?'

I said she was and I figured Maude's house looked abandoned and she was so handy with the gun so Chrissie couldn't be much safer.

Maude grunted and said, okay then, come on into the body of the church.

Inside, the house was as baroque and unstable as Maude herself. The staircase straight ahead sloped to the side. Through a carved circular transom, the living room was crammed with knickknacks and ornaments, all leaning toward the front of the building. The flat top of the old upright piano perfectly articulated the thirty-degree slope of the floor.

I looked in, 'Miss Maude, I think it's gotten worse since last week.'

She looked in there with me. 'You might be right. I can't see it anymore. Anyway. You can hide up the stairs, honey. I can't make it up and everyone else is afraid. I'll leave your vittles on the stairs. I'm moving to Pasadena in a week so you've got until then.'

'Insurance cheque come through?'

'Yes and I bought a place,' she said heavily. 'We'll see. Might not be all bad.'

We followed her to the back of the house, a steadier place, and the kitchen with a big cast-iron blackened stove.

Maude sat us at the table and got out a bottle with no label on it. 'Thanks for coming to the service, Marlowe.'

I nodded. I didn't much want to talk about Pasco right now but she didn't seem to have anything else to talk about.

She rolled through a bunch of tired old lies about him to Chrissie, how he was a nice man and everybody liked him. From the haunted look in her eyes I guessed that she was trying to convince herself as much as her guest but Chrissie bought it, listening, pouring her a top up when her glass ran dry, laughing along at punchlines so worn through a mild breeze would've blown a hole in them.

It was kind the way she did it. She could see the good in Maude and not everyone could.

I left them drinking, looking to make a night of it. I hoped Chrissie would be company for the old girl.

25.

I caught a few hours' sleep on the divan in the office. I was feeling none too sparky when Moochie Ruud arrived with his uniforms, banging loudly on the pebbled glass, hitting it so hard he was liable to break it.

'Are you going to let me in, Marlowe, or am I going to get my men to kick the door in?' He'd been watching too many G-man movies.

'The door is open, Ruud. Just come on through.'

Ruud's messy shadow disappeared left. He tried the door further down the corridor, found it locked. I could hear him rattling the handle.

I lit a cigarette as he came back.

'Other door,' I said through the glass, already tired of him. 'The one with "Philip Marlowe, Investigations" written on it.'

This was the thing with Ruud: he was a small man in big shoes and it made him angry.

He couldn't just make a fool of himself sometimes and then be grateful when he didn't. He'd been promoted too fast so the rest of us had to reassure him that he hadn't. I can see a father-in-law giving his boy a hand up and I could see that Ruud had qualities that would make him good for the job, but Moochie didn't believe it. He'd do stupid things, humiliate himself and then the rest of the world had to make him feel all right about it.

He came through the open door ready for a fight.

'Everyone makes that mistake.'

'Don't give me that, Marlowe. You were seen all over town three nights ago with a cabby called Manny Perez. Then he turns up dead on a lawn off Pico and *then* you're at the Brody with some broad when a kraut gets killed with the same pistol —'

He'd already told me what I needed to know: he had no idea Chrissie Montgomery was at the Brody Hotel last night. He'd have led with that. And the myopic desk jockey hadn't shown him the Brody register either. Joan Baudelaire's name was signed in. Even Ruud would have made a connection with me if he'd seen it.

I pulled my jacket on. 'I was drinking with Perez and dropped him there. I drove away. But you know that already.'

His face told me he did know it but he didn't want to. I went low. I appealed to his ego.

'Ruud, I knew you'd find me here. I have information but for your ears only. Let's go get some coffee.'

'Just tell me.'

I glanced at his men. 'It's kind of confidential.' Then I leaned in and muttered, 'I need to speak to you alone, *if you know what I mean.*'

Ruud lapped it up. The only thing bigger than his ego was his snobbery.

He nodded in a heavy-is-the-head way. 'This better be good.'

'Would I waste your time?' I said, trying to think of some way to waste his time.

'Let's go to The Pantry.'

I didn't want to go to The Pantry. I didn't want to be seen there but I'd played all my cards.

The Pantry was a cop hang out, serving short orders all day and all night. It had wooden booths and counter service and the food was good if you liked salty oil. The griddles were behind an open hatch and you could see it was clean enough. It was always full of cops and crooks, a regular club house for men with too many opinions. They liked to peacock about in front of each other. A lot of rumours started there: which cop was in which club, who was getting promoted, who could be trusted, who not. They were all on the take to one degree or another. It was wrong but it was predictable. Moochie Ruud was the worrying kind: he needed gossip and fall guys to show his father-in-law he had his finger on the pulse. He was unpredictable and that made everyone uneasy around him.

We drove over to a car park full of black and whites.

Breakfast service was ending as we walked in. Ruud gladhanded a couple of uniforms on their way out, looking around for friends or ex-friends or soon to be ex-friends before settling with me in a booth.

Day or night the Pantry waitress was always called Gloria because the owners were too cheap to pay for another name tag.

Current Gloria came over and I asked for coffee. Moochie went for biscuits and gravy. In fact, double that up, will ya, Gloria hon?

'Four biscuits?'

'And gravy on all of them.'

As she wrote it down one of her stockings made a break for it and unravelled to her ankle. She didn't seem to notice.

Current Gloria, mighty holder of the name tag, had been a looker once but hard living and late nights had left their mark. Gloria remembered those days well though and so did her make-up routine. Her hair was dyed scarlet, set in waves that were the style ten years ago. She had drawn the Mae West lips she wished she had over the thin ones God gave her. Stuck in the middle of those lips was a cigarette, worn like a cocktail stick in a club sandwich.

Current Gloria was confident, though. Whatever Gloria thought she was hauling, somebody else agreed, she was dynamite to someone, you could tell by the way she swayed her hips.

Moochie Ruud didn't get that. He took in the confection of her mouth and condescended to call her 'young lady' before he turned back to talk to me.

Gloria was mad as a box of bees about that. She stabbed his order into her pad as if she was guessing his weight to pass on to a hang man. If Moochie's gravy didn't have at least a thumb in it I'd be disappointed.

'Tell me about Perez.'

I lit a cigarette, 'Well, as we both know, Manny Perez owed money all over town. Serious people have let it be known they were after him for it.'

Moochie nodded that he knew that. Of course, he knew it. It was all anyone was talking about.

'And we both know that those are not people you want to cross. Don't you think they're more likely to be responsible for a clean, daylight hit like that than me? I don't kill people if they don't try to kill me. I'm funny like that.'

Yes. He knew that too. He knew so much it was a wonder he bothered opening his eyes in the morning. The world had nothing to tell him.

He said it was great we were sharing information. What names had I heard?

I threw him a guard-dog steak, spun him a tale that would keep him busy and buy me some time: many years ago Manny had borrowed money from two brothers over in Boyle Heights, the Chavez brothers, he must have heard of them?

Sure, Moochie had heard of them, who hadn't?

Well, this money was due to be paid back, with interest. He got it to trade with, promised a high return for smuggling bales of Mary Jane in through his family on the border. But there was nothing to give back. Rumour had it Manny Perez had used it to buy a house over in Pico for the wife and a bunch of kids, bought it from a kraut called West. Paid cash. When the Chavez brothers heard it wasn't being spent to bring blue tea in from Mexico they put the squeeze on him. That might be why they killed him there, as a message to all those other aspiring homeowners. Manny knew hell was coming down, he was nervous that day, drinking like a man who knew it was over.

Moochie nodded along as if he already knew this but enjoyed having it confirmed from a second source.

His breakfast arrived, a great oval plate of salty cream and biscuits. Gloria hon put it down with a smirk. I didn't see a thumb in it but she'd got her own back somehow and she flashed me a smile as if I was in on it.

It was coming up for nine.

All around us the shift was changing. Diners folded up newspapers and signalled for the cheque. Cops were leaving to go into work and crooks were leaving to go to bed.

Moochie ate slowly. I could see him planning to go over to Boyle Heights later and ask around for the Chavez brothers. If he managed to find a set of brothers over in Boyle Heights whose surname wasn't Chavez I'd buy him his next breakfast.

He finished his food and sat back, took out his cigarettes and drew one from the packet with his lips.

'I didn't know you carried, Moochie.'

'Ha ha,' he took out a book of paper matches and tore off two. 'You want one?'

'No.'

He dropped the book on the table and lit the match with his thumbnail.

'So what you're saying is Perez was in with some Boyle Heights bad boys and they got him after you dropped him off. But here's what I don't get: how come no one saw them?'

'Maybe they did see them and just didn't know what they were seeing.'

'You telling me some Latin gangsters could be driving around Pico-Union in the middle of the afternoon, on a school day, and no one called the cops?'

'Hm, just telling you what I heard.' He had a point. I picked up Moochie's matchbook to keep my hands busy. 'Doesn't make it airtight.'

The matchbook was glossy, red, with yellow writing on it: *Coomes.* I turned it around in my hand, thinking about who would go unseen in that area at that time. All the men would be at work. It was a white area, middle class. A white woman in a Ford Coupe would fit right in.

'They have dancers there,' said Moochie.

'Where?'

'Coomes.'

Current Gloria came past and poured me a refill. I saw her eyes slide over to Moochie's empty plate, savouring the sight. She offered him more coffee like it was a reward.

Moochie batted her away. Gloria sashayed over to the counter and muttered something to the cook that cracked him up. I saw him look over at us, at Moochie, at Moochie's empty plate. I was glad I wasn't eating.

'So,' I said, 'Moochie, how come you were downtown last night?'

'A body. A murder. Got a call at a hotel there. Man shot twice, once in the heart, once in the head, through the jaw. There was a dame in there with him. High class apparently.'

'Really?'

'That's what I'm hearing. Street bums calling him "Pavel Viscom" but who knows with these guys.'

'Was it a robbery?'

'Yes. Musta got interrupted though. They only took his wallet. Now we don't know who he was.'

'His wallet?'

'Yes, he wasn't a bum.' He leaned over to me. 'No passport or identity papers on him but he was Austrian. The coroner showed me the label on his shirt. It was hand-made in Vienna, he said. Hand stitched. Very nice.'

'Were you trying it on?'

'Very funny. No, Coroner was showing me because the bullet hole in the shirt didn't match the hole in the chest.'

'Didn't match? How?'

Moochie was too full. He sighed as if it was an effort to explain. 'The hole in the body was there,' he touched his heart. 'The hole in the shirt was there.' He touched his navel. He lifted both hands as if surrendering. 'Money on it being a robbery. He opens the door, sees the piece, "give me all your money" says the bad guy. Hands up but he shoots him anyway. Panicky robber. What can you do...'

It was no robbery. The man's watch was left on the night stand. His hand-made shoes were tucked under the bed. It might have helped Moochie if I mentioned that but a lot of people were trying to help Moochie. That was Moochie's whole problem.

He let me pay as a 'gesture of friendship' to the department. Outside we said goodbye and Moochie got back in his car.

As I watched him drive away I wondered why he hadn't asked me what I was doing down by the Brody last night. He didn't ask anything much at all.

It seemed that someone very high up had already decided that the case should be as good as closed.

26.

Skid Row was fifty blocks of downtown and the very last stop on the Southern Pacific Railroad. For thirty years trains had stopped here and discharged their freight of single men looking for something different than what they had come from. Some came deliberately. Some by mistake. What they found were other men in the same frame of mind, all running, all untethered, and they got stuck here together, having fights, drinking, chasing money and meals and skirt.

The sun was high and goading, the air still crisp. The only places doing good business at this time of day were the Chinese laundries. Steam and the smell of carbolic soap and bleach wafted out into the street from the shop fronts all down Main. Men in white overalls dragged wheeled cages of clean linen tied in bundles, packed unfeasibly high, across the sidewalk to waiting trucks, lifted them easily and threw them onto the flatbeds where they were neatly stacked by other men. These were the sheets of the high-class hotels and the big houses up in Beverly Hills. These were the towels of effortless millionaires and hardscrabble movie moguls. Everyone sent their linen out. No one could get that kind of clean at home. Even the worst boss wouldn't ask their staff to use that much bleach.

It was preferable, though, to the other smells down here.

Baggy-faced men were being evicted from the floor of the Mission Halls.

I drove past the Brody, down toward the corner of San Pedro and Sixth, passing a tall office building that had been respectable once. It was where I had stood the night before, watching the Brody across the street. This was the Alhambra now, a residential hotel for single men who didn't mind sharing a bathroom with forty others. But not everyone could afford that. The manageress, Sunshine Aziz, was known for charging a quarter to let men sleep in the lobby. Not everyone got a chair but a slice of floor was better than a dark sidewalk to many. She made them leave during the day, these lobby men, sent them out to the day like errant children cluttering up a kitchen. They gathered in the shade under ripped awnings of stores and residential hotels, sharing cigarettes and working out how they were going to fill their day. Many, blinking hard, simply took the crosswalk to the doors of Frenchie's, a cheap beer hall due to open in an hour or so.

A Frenchman owned the hall once but no one remembered him. The current owner was a German called Adolph. I'd seen him breaking heads on tables and crack a man's fingers to get a knife out of his hand. I'd also seen him hold a drink to a sweating man's mouth to stop him descending into the DTs, feeding him slices of sausage and the soft inside of bread, caring for him like a baby until the danger passed. He said he wasn't being kind, he was only trying to stop the man dying in his beer hall, but I had my suspicions.

Adolph's beer hall had only two rules: no credit, no gun play.

I parked around the back and went in through the staff entrance. Two tramps were guarding crates of beer bottles inside, each sipping from an open bottle they'd taken in lieu of pay. They watched the alley behind me with mean eyes, ready to flatten invaders. I wasn't the only one who knew where the door was.

'Fellas,' I tipped my hat. 'Here to see Adolph.'

They shook their heads. They didn't know who I was asking for. 'Adolph. He owns this place? Big kraut.'

'Alan? Alan's in there.'

One pointed a dirty finger, swollen at the knuckles, to a doorway into the dark and cavernous hall. I stepped through.

Adolph was standing at the side of the room, arms crossed and resting on his big belly. He was dressed in his usual bar apron but had a crisp white bandana over his nose and mouth, like a pernickety bandit. The lights were on in the hall, bare dim bulbs straining to compete with the shock of white sunshine showing around the brim of giant wooden shutters blocking the day over big arched windows.

The hall was lined with eight rows of tables, benches on either side, all of bare wood. Each row was being scrubbed by one of his customers with a bandana over his mouth and nose, each sweating and using red raw hands to dip scrubbing brushes into pails of strong chlorine. The smell was nauseating.

He saw one of them do something he didn't like and hollered: 'Hoi! Ein bisschen gefehlt!'

The man he was shouting at didn't understand. He was thin as a string, eyes weak and hooded. He looked at the table and shrugged.

Adolph strode over to him, 'This part!' he stabbed the table with his finger. 'Do it on this part of here!'

Then he looked at the end of his finger and held it away from himself as if it might go off. He watched it, carefully dipping it in the pail, bringing it back out red. He looked at me.

'Marlowe! TB in here, we have,' as he walked over to me. 'Cover up your face.'

I took out a handkerchief and covered my mouth and he looked instantly sorry. 'Come outside.'

He ordered the skinny man to watch the others, make sure they didn't leave any parts unscrubbed, promising him an extra beer. Then he turned and led me out of the room to the back alley. I looked back. Skinny was taking his promotion seriously. He watched the others, hands on hips, eyes tight and mean in the gloom, watching for infractions.

Outside, Adolph pulled the bandana off under his chin and lit a cigarette. His fleshy face was flushed.

'Tuberkulose. Gah! But, thank God, only one case, we have,' he said under his breath. 'From Alhambra men, I think. Many of them are brand new here. We must be very careful of this. Many men are weak on the chest.'

I lit a cigarette myself but it tasted of chlorine.

He watched me. 'Why you come down to this place?'

'Pavel Viscom.'

Adolph's lips twisted in disgust. He lifted his bandana to his mouth and spat into it. 'He's here. A week. At the Brody Hotel but he won't stay longer. A man was killed there last night. When they hear about Viscom they'll think he did it. He's a bad, bad man.'

'Viscom isn't a suspect. Viscom's the stiff.'

He liked that news, 'So?'

'Yes.'

'Dead twice, this man: he died in Europe a few months ago also.'

'What do you suppose happened there?'

'Ah, Viscom is a rascal. He would have to die to get out of debts or trouble. This was him all the time. He has these scandals all the time in Vienna. Then he appears, alive and staying down the street from me. Incredible. He got shot?'

'Twice.'

'Twice, yah? Good. Didn't die with the first shot. Excellent. I hope he suffered.'

'You didn't like him, Adolph?'

'Viscom is pretty famous, you know. In the newspaper in Vienna. Has antics. Is an artist well-known. He beat one of my boys with his stick. I hear everything. Happened outside the hotel. He was staying there. When they describe and say German speaks, vampire teeth, I say "Pavel Viscom". Then I see him inside hotel lobby talking to manager – it's him.'

'You recognized him?'

'You are investigating him?'

'No. Just curious. He had no papers on him, name tags ripped from his luggage. No one knows it was him except me. And now you. But you're not the most judgemental man in the world. Why didn't you like him?'

'Is a Nazi. I hate Nazis. I move to Vienna from Berlin to get away from these men and they come to Austria. I come to America, fair and square I come, then I start to see them here also.'

We stood and smoked for a moment.

'Dead, yah?'

'Hm.'

'Shot twice. Well, that is nice to hear, Marlowe,' he smiled. 'It's some days good news, some days bad news.'

'The hole in his shirt was here,' I touched my stomach. 'But the one in his chest was here,' I touched my heart. I raised my hands, 'They think he was holding his hands up when the bullet hit his chest, he was surrendering to someone. Could someone hate him more than you?'

'Many people. He could be killed by an anti-Nazi enemy perhaps?'

'Seems that way.'

'Yah. I am his enemy. He has many but I am one. Might be one with a gun who can't stand it anymore. I was almost that man.'

'I'd be careful who you say that to.'

He nodded his giant German head, 'That's good counsel, Marlowe. I listen to you for that.'

'I hear you're changing your name to Alan.'

He smoked sadly. 'Even my name, they take.'

27.

Sunshine Aziz had nothing to prove to anyone. She was Egyptian, still dressed the way she would have if she was living in Cairo, in long striped colourful robes and sandals, her abundant black hair worn down her back, crazed with grey. She was handsome with wide black-kohled eyes and a fine mouth untouched by lipstick. You could have stood a quarter on either of her cheekbones and come back an hour later and still found them there.

But Sunshine was tough. She had to be. She had four kids enrolled at an expensive private school uptown, kept them in a house with a maid up on Melrose while she lived here and ran the Alhambra with one purpose: to get as much money out of it as possible without putting any money back in. Anywhere else this business philosophy would have put her out of business but not on Skid Row. Here it was ideal.

Nothing ever got fixed in the Alhambra and plenty got broken. I walked into the empty lobby and felt the soles of my shoes stick to the floor. She was behind a desk, telephone held between her shoulder and ear, filling out a form with a chewed-up stub of pencil and a long black pipe nestled in the corner of her mouth.

'What?'

'Hi, Mrs Aziz. I wanted to ask you about what happened at the Brody last night.'

'Don't know anything.'

'Okay.'

I turned to leave, but my escape was impeded by how long it was taking to peel my shoes off the floor.

'You're not a cop.'

I turned back and saw that she had one hand on the cradle. She hung up the receiver.

'No, ma'am, I'm not.'

She looked me up and down. 'What are you?'

'Philip Marlowe. Private investigations.'

I don't know why I told her. Maybe it was that she had authority, head tipped back, looking down her wide hooked nose at me. If anyone had asked me why I'd told her I'd have lied and said it was in case she ever needed a PI. I think a lot of people did what Sunshine asked them to do. We probably all lied about it.

'Who got killed? Was it a somebody?'

I shrugged. 'Seems like it. The cops came.'

She nodded, 'Hmm, they did. I watch. Who?'

'Pavel Viscom. An artist.'

She smiled. 'Fine. You driving an Olds?'

'Yes, have you got spies everywhere?'

'Maybe. You just go to see Adolph?'

'Sure. I think he likes to go by "Alan" now.'

She snorted, 'I know. Too late to change now. Dead somebody is a German man?'

'Maybe Austrian.'

'Same thing.'

'Austrian and German are only the same if you are looking at them from far away.'

'We are far away, Philip Marlowe. America is far away. That's why we come. Get out of my hotel now.'

So I did.

28.

Maude's place looked even more precarious in the thinning light of sunset. Or maybe the ground was opening up to swallow it. The wooden slats around the crawl space were slipping off and leaving a gap a medium-sized dog could amble through without ducking. The house looked abandoned.

I knocked and Maude let me in. Pasco Pete's picture was still standing sentry.

'How are you, Mr Marlowe?'

I said I was just fine, thanks Maude, and asked for Miss Baudelaire. Maude smiled softly and started on the sloping stairs. She was going to lead me up but only made it four steps up before she lost her breath and had to stop. She held onto the banister, waving me away, pressing her hand to her chest.

'I need a cigarette.'

'You'll be glad to get out of here, Maude.'

'I sure as shit will, sonny.'

She stood panting, waving me to go on past her and up the stairs.

Chrissie was in the master bedroom. It was a forgotten room decorated in a high style forty something years ago and maybe not dusted since. The large lumpy bed had a wall of satin pillows banked up against the headboard, the shine all gone from them. At the bottom sat a sun-bleached peach velvet divan. Chrissie was by the window, at a table with a glass-domed oil lamp. She looked low and grey, as if the life was being sucked out of her by the room. She seemed sad and tired, as though she had resigned herself to something.

I sat down across from her and offered her a cigarette. She took it and I lit it for her. She drew a deep breath as she sat back and fixed her eyes on me. Then she exhaled a long, strong stream of white smoke all the way across the table and over my left shoulder.

'I thought you didn't smoke.'

'I'm trying all sorts of new things these days. I can't hide here for the rest of my life like a frightened child. I have to face up to reality. It's how things are. I just have to face that.'

I smoked back at her. 'The person who came into the hotel room and shot that man tricked you into going down there. Do you know why?'

She frowned and shook her head a fraction, as if she was trying to shake the thought away. 'Why?'

'I don't know either but I think they wanted you in the room when it happened. They knew the cops would kick a rug over it if a Montgomery was in there. So that makes me wonder: who knew your real identity and who invited you to the Brody to meet Zimmerman that night?'

'Zimmerman herself.'

'You spoke to her on the phone?'

'Yes.'

'What exactly did she say?'

' "Come to the hotel, I'm checked in under the name West. Come and meet me, and we'll go for dinner and on to Jane Jones' Little Club." I was looking forward to meeting her and said maybe the cabaret would be on but she said no, that was Thursday. She sounded so friendly. Kept calling me "darling" the whole time. It was sweet.'

'She knew when the cabaret was scheduled for?'

'Knew it was tonight, yes.'

'Well, that's swell. Sounds more like a regular than someone who's never been though, don't you think?

Did she call you at Mrs Dudek's?'

'No, at work. Called the gallery. We have a telephone in there.'

'She the one who brought up Jane Jones' club?'

'Yeah.'

'Not exactly internationally famous, wouldn't you say?'

'Are you saying it wasn't her on the telephone? Oh my. I suppose it could have been anyone.'

'Could have been. I met Bruce MacIntosh. He's a fine young man.'

'Bruce is fine. If you like young men.'

'You don't though, do you?'

Chrissie slumped so much that it was as if her joints had been turned off. She tapped her cigarette and looked at the dirty window. Her face was younger, her eyes open properly. 'I never have. I thought it would pass but it hasn't.'

'So you know what sort of club Jane Jones' is?'

She left a pause. 'I do. I've been there many times. I didn't think Miss Zimmerman had been. It took a lot for me to go in there the first time, I had to get loaded.'

'Are you in love with Anneliese Lyle?'

She laughed at that, sincere, off guard. 'Why, are you?'

'Why do you ask?'

'Most people are. She's a rather beguiling person.'

'She's easy on the eye.'

'She certainly is that. But if you look, if you look carefully, she works hard at it. The hair is dyed, the mannerisms are copied from the movies, she never eats.'

'Some people just don't get hungry.'

'She does. She used to be a little tub, you know. She has stretch marks —' Chrissie broke off, her hand resting on her upper back, just under her arm, on an area of Anneliese's skin Chrissie had no business having seen.

'You were romantically involved with her before your father?'

Chrissie looked sad about it, 'I was young. It was me who gave her the job in the first place.'

'What was the job?'

'My assistant. Decorating.' Chrissie looked a little skittish about it. 'She was quite dazzling.'

'She is.'

Chrissie sat back. 'Anneliese is an empty person, a hollow person. She meets you, she measures you up and then she becomes whatever you want. She did it to me. She did it with my father. She's two completely different people with each of us.'

I thought of her in the Dancers, how perfect she'd seemed, a little sad and needing saving, beautiful, loving strange words. It seemed that I had been measured up and served too. It made me feel cheap.

'She knew about me, my girl-crushes. She got me right. I thought I was in love with her until I met someone else. Then Anneliese met her and she fell in love with her too.' She looked deeply unhappy, 'It was the only honest thing I've ever seen her do.'

'Why were you getting married?'

'Anneliese told me to lie about my proclivities, she said I should marry and have girlfriends on the side, lots of women do that.'

'But you couldn't?'

She flinched, 'No. I thought I could, I did it before. That was when I realized I was in love.'

I didn't really think it was for me to dig around there.

'At the Brody, did they want Joan to go there or Chrissie?'

'How could I know?'

'In your new life, who knows who you really are? Mrs Dudek? Evelyn?'

'Neither of them, as far as I know.'

'Mrs Dudek knows you're a widow. Did you leave papers lying around?'

'I told her I was a widow.'

'Someone at the gallery?'

'No.'

'How'd you get the job?'

'Classifieds. I was reading them and I saw the ad.'

'Okay. So maybe Joan Baudelaire was invited to the hotel and they meant it to be Joan who witnessed the murder. Who else do you see?'

She stiffened. 'I keep myself to myself.'

'All the time?'

'Yes. Work and then back home. I eat out, when I eat.'

'Where do you eat?'

'Diners, dinettes —'

'Because if someone in there recognized you . . . What about this girl you're all in love with?'

'My girl?' She squeezed one eye shut, rubbed it, as if the smoke had gone in.

'She know who you are?'

'No. I was planning to tell her, maybe, not yet. It changes things when people know. Evelyn, Miss Maude, they wouldn't be so nice to me if they knew. You can see them thinking about how they're going to get money out of you. Makes it hard to trust . . .'

'The girl, is she someone you met in a club?'

'At the Dancers. She plays piano there. Her name is Hazel.'

'Known her long?'

'Two months.'

'Is she why you left home?'

She nodded. 'She showed me the classified ad for the job because I know a lot about art.'

'You couldn't just give her a job at the mansion or something?'

'Hazel is black.' Her voice was loud. 'You've met my father. He wouldn't even accept her as a servant. You see why I ran.'

I did.

'I never wanted a servant as a lover. I wanted more but I guess that was dumb, really. I thought those relationships couldn't be real. The person in power knows it's a deal and it infuriates them. They always go sour. But maybe all relationships go rotten in the end, maybe some just people die before it gets really bad. I should just accept it.'

'Like your father and Lyle?'

She shook her head as if trying to get the name out of her ear. 'Well, you've seen it.'

We smoked some more and looked out of the window at the

view. Even the tumbledown houses of Vernon looked nice from far away. Chrissie told me how it used to be all fields over there. Her family had a book of etchings of the city back then. They were beautiful. Tiny square fields with popsicle trees in the orchards. A little lake up there and if you looked at it with a magnifying glass you could see a fish popping its head out of the water and looking back at you. She used to do that when she was a little girl.

She was nice to talk to. Calm now that she'd told me the thing she didn't want to say to anyone.

We smoked and lingered by the window and I asked her where Peggy Zimmerman might be now. She'd be out at the beach, she said, at her place in Malibu. A note had been sent to the gallery so that messages could be forwarded on.

'Miss Maude doesn't know who I am, does she?'

'No. She's hiding you as a favour to me. Why? Is she okay with you?'

'We don't see that much of each other. She can't come up here. Leaves my food at the bottom of the stairs. She's got some funny friends.'

'Old Hollywood types?'

'Some. Her crazy neighbour comes over at all hours. She's drunk all the time and draws up in her big old Model T and clatters up the porch.'

'A Model T?'

'Hm, and she's rather vulgar too, if that's not too bad to say. She has a cleft lip, like a little dimple.'

She touched her middle finger gently to her Cupid's bow.

'She does?'

'Yes, and she's kind of a big girl, on the chest, you'd think Maude would take her aside and have a word.'

'You would, huh?'

'I would.'

'Chrissie, I think maybe we should get you out of here. Want to try to get me into a kittens-only cabaret?'

29.

Jane Jones' Little Club was at 8730 Sunset, a low square building of whitewashed concrete and small barred windows with yellow light behind them. No one was outside tonight. The door was shut tight. There must have been a raid or a threat or both. The tattered green awning covering the path to the door looked dirty and old, a length of white trim dangling like a fish hook. A neon sign in red and yellow cut through the black night, declaring the club open to anyone brave enough to come in. A side sign declared that Mammy Eunice was back and ready to serve her famous southern fried chicken dinner to anyone with 90c.

We walked under the shabby awning to the outside door and listened to a boom of laughter from deep inside. A lull, a murmur of song, and then a rumble. It came in waves like the snore of some great dragon dumb enough to choose a bungalow on Sunset as its lair. I couldn't imagine anyone eating their chicken dinner was enjoying it.

A judas window slid back on the door and two eyes looked out, a woman's eyes, red and baggy. Maybe she was too. She looked at Chrissie and recognised her, switched to me and the gaze lingered on my suit. She was searching for some redeeming feature on me. She peered at my face. This didn't make her like me any better. Her mouth came to the slot. It matched her eyes. Even her teeth looked tired.

'Fillies only tonight or it's pervert rates,' she said.

She shut the window and opened the door. A hand came out and grabbed Chrissie's arm, yanked her behind the door and slammed it shut.

I knocked again. The window slid back.

'Twenty dollars. No cheques no credit.'

'Steep.'

'Pervert rates.'

'I'm not a pervert, I'm with her.'

'She ya wife or what?' She had a Tennessee accent. She rolled her words around her mouth as if she was keeping an acorn in there.

The laughter from inside came in splutters now, like the act on stage had stopped being funny and the audience were waiting for them to shut up.

'No. I'm looking for a friend of mine. I'm worried about her.'

'What ya worried about? Ain't nothing but some good ol' gals getting together for a fun littl' sing-song.'

'I don't care if it's gals or gulls. Our friend is in there and I'd like to see she's okay.'

The eyes came back. She looked me over for a moment and then decided against me. The wooden slot shut slowly, like a slider fade in a movie.

'Don't make me,' I told the door.

'Honey bee, I'm not making anyone do anything,' it said back. 'But you should know I've got a bat. And a pistol.'

'I've got two bats and five guns.'

'I've got a tank. And my tank has a gun.'

'Can I borrow your tank? I need to get through a door.'

She opened the slider again and looked out at me, interested now. 'We get husbands in here and they see what's going on and they cause an affray. You're not getting in, buddy, just talk to her when she gets home, okay?'

'I'm no one's husband and I'm friends with Jimmy the One.'

The eyes weren't tired anymore. They were bright and sharp and she looked me up and down. '*Friends* friends or just a friend?'

I almost lied but didn't. 'Just a friend.'

'Jimmy the One,' she was nodding and smiling, 'Jimmy fuck-ing Donoghue. That's my kind.'

I smiled back, 'He's something.'

She still wasn't sure though. 'How'd ya'll meet?'

'Around the place. I'm the bird he called to come and get him out after the Silver Lakes party.'

The eyes hadn't moved but a metal bolt slid back on the door. The slot shut and the door opened. She stepped around it.

She must have been standing on a box to look out at me. She was all of five feet tall in her brogues, dressed like a union fore-man waking up on his couch on a slow Sunday. Her hair looked as if it had been cut blind and for a bet. But the smile on her face was so warm it would have shamed a branding iron.

She held her hand out, 'Sheil.'

I shook it and stepped inside, 'Sheil, I'm Marlowe.'

'Glad to know you.'

We were in a small bright hallway with a curtain nailed up over a doorway at the back, badly hung but weighted at the hem to keep the sound in. Sheil had been having a quiet night by the look of it. She was reading a movie magazine and her ashtray was full.

She alternated between welcoming me with open-armed Tennes-see warmth and wagging a stubby finger at me. I've met Tennesseans before: if they're not shooting at you, they're a-hugging.

'Welcome, friend, to Jane Jones' Little Club. Now, don't you cause me any trouble, ya hear? I'm letting you in, so that's me vouching for you. Remember I've got a bat and a gun and a tank so don't you make me a liar if you wanna leave this fine estab-lishment on the same day an' hour as your nuts.' She shut the front door and stepped over in front of the curtain. 'A straight friend of Jimmy the One, man, I never thought to see it. Surely this is an augur of the Second Coming of the Sweet Lord. Say, that is a mighty fine suit. Finer than a frog's hair split three ways. Where's that from, now? I'm fixin' to get me one.'

'Sheil, if you can live with a six-inch turn-up on the leg, you can have this suit. I'm sick of talking about it.'

'Ain't that neighbourly!' She rubbed the fabric on my sleeve, 'It's sexier than socks on a rooster. Well, come on in, Marlowe, honey.' She put one hand on the curtain, 'And you mind what I said now, no trouble. I've got skin in the game now and I'll be angrier than God at an Egyptian if you mess up my good suit.

'You can sit in the gentlemen's section and look for your friend. They pay to come in and we let them so long as they ain't gonna cause a ruckus. If they's just normal perverts – we'll take their money.' Sheil pulled back the curtain. A steep set of stairs led down to a large, dimly lit room with a bar and a stage. It was bad timing. Half a Ton of Fun was a singing group of three big people in dinner suits, a woman and two men. They weren't leaving the stage as much as running for their lives. The smattering of applause could best be described as angry-sarcastic.

A low fog of cigarette smoke hung in the room. Women were gathered at small round tables, slouched, arms around each other, drinking beers and cocktails. A surprising number of them were eating chicken dinners but the tables were too small for more than a couple of plates and they weren't finding it easy to accommodate elbows.

The light from Sheil's bright hallway broke the mood in the room and caught the eye of the disgruntled audience. Assorted women glanced up at me. I took my hat off. I was not the only person wearing a cheap suit that didn't fit me.

'Ain't a turn!' called Sheil into the room. 'Friend of Jimmy the One. As you were, ladies.'

Disappointed, several turned back around. The chatter started then, rising with exponential speed. Some eyes lingered on me, wondering what kind of a woman I was. I almost felt like bursting into song just to confuse them.

But then a figure stood up from a table, her head rising above the shelf of smoke, into the clear air above. Blonde hair and a badly bruised nose and eyes. Anneliese Lyle was here for cabaret night.

I saw her think about running, twist her shoulder to the back door. I saw her give up and turn back. Then I saw her hope I was a friend, hope against hope that I wasn't here to hurt her or make her do anything she didn't want to.

I couldn't muscle her. I might spill something on Sheil's good suit. Even if she had posed as Peggy Zimmerman to trick Chrissie into going to the Brody Hotel I didn't hate her. I didn't understand her but I couldnt find it in me to hate her. I held my hand up to her and she waved back. That was when I saw Chrissie, sitting next to her, holding her hand. They looked like sisters, those two women, and it was clear they were not in love but stuck together.

I took the steps down and slid through the tight tables to them. People were moving around, getting drinks and going to freshen up, the whole room was molten, moving as a mass. Everyone knew each other here. It must have been intimidating to come into for the first time. It must have been good to come here with a friend.

I arrived at the side of their table, 'I'm not going to do any-thing, I'm just making sure Chrissie's safe.'

Anneliese was on her feet. 'I underestimated you.'

She left a pause for me to speak but I had nothing to add to that.

'I knew Chrissie would come here,' she said, 'when she ran out of road.'

Her beautiful face was a mess. It was hard to look at it. 'What happened to your nose, Anneliese?'

'Having it straightened.' She sat back down and laid her hands on the table in a gesture of peace. 'Won't you have a drink with us?'

'Sure. What are you gals drinking?'

'Old fashioneds.'

'I'll have one.'

Chrissie gestured to a waitress, a small woman in boyish clothes, pointing at our table and gesturing at her to bring three. She was sitting awfully close to Anneliese, I noticed. Something had happened between them. Words had passed.

'Chrissie?'

She looked at me and not warmly either.

'Chrissie, isn't that why you ran?'

Anneliese got up and excused herself. She swept away across the room.

Chrissie waited until she was out of earshot before she spoke, 'Marlowe, you don't know what it's like. I don't want to be married, I don't want my life to be a lie but the money makes it impossible.'

'We're all struggling, Chrissie. It's not really about the money.'

'It is about the money,' she said fervently. 'Don't you see? I can't be near anybody or have anybody real near me. I don't even know my own son. I'm a vehicle for the family riches, he is, we are vessels for the money, for the name, to keep it all going and going and going. My father used my mother to breed a vessel and then he locked her up when she had desires of her own. She died in there. He killed her.'

'I'm sure he didn't mean for her to die —'

'Do you know why people kill?' She looked at me, suddenly intent. 'Hate. Do you know why people get away with murder? No one cares. No one does anything. No one speaks up. That's how he killed my mother: no one said anything.'

I found myself recalling a line from Shakespeare, 'Certain dregs of conscience yet are within me?'

She squinted meanly, 'What?'

'From *Richard III*. The Second Murderer says it. Dregs of conscience are all we have but only some of us act on them. Who is Hazel?'

Chrissie smirked and looked away.

'Is Anneliese Hazel?'

'Good heavens, no. I'm not in love with her.'

Suddenly a hand appeared between us holding a drink. We sat back and the waitress put three Old Fashioneds down, one at a time. Her hair was greased back. She shot me a look that would have made a maiden aunt sob.

'Thanks,' I said.

'Why don't you get —' she walked away mid-sentence and I didn't catch the rest of it but there were a lot of 'f's in it. Stumped for retort and mindful of Sheil's good suit, I picked up my drink and drank it down. It was bitter and strong. I was surprised that it didn't have a nail in it.

I looked around the room.

I've been a lot of places, places people didn't want me to be, but I've never felt less welcome than I did here. Women were watching me carefully and whispering to each other. Some of them had hands resting in purses as if there were pistols in there and they were ready for me. The curtain had fallen over the exit and my buddy Sheil, the only person who could vouch for me, was gone. I felt like a burlesque dancer at a memorial service.

Anneliese came back and moved her seat even closer to Chrissie, their thighs flush together. Anneliese whispered to the side of her face, 'I can be . . .' but then the sound was swallowed up by a singer who'd taken to the stage, a thin woman with a shrill voice and eyes so languorous she might have been sleeping moments ago. She could hardly peel them open.

She sang a bad song badly and then a good one badly. The audience were getting the hang of it and the room was dark when the curtain at the top of the stairs was whipped back, the pure and kindly light of Sheil spilled into the room, tumbling down the stairs to the angry throng, and there stood a vision.

Half the room turned to look at Evelyn Hamilton peacocking at the top of the stairs. She paused there to let them take her in. She wasn't playing the bouncy house guest now, or the cheerful hatcheck girl.

Evelyn's blonde hair was up and curled away from her face, her lips scarlet. She wore a red jacket with large pockets, tightly belted to show off her tiny waist. Her skirt was tight and black and satin and she wore a little hat with a black veil over half her face.

She let them look at her for a moment before she descended to meet her public, half the room sighed with longing as she arrived on the floor. Chrissie blinked away tears. I knew then who Hazel was and I knew Chrissie had been played. But she wasn't the only one. Anneliese met Evelyn's gaze, her face as open and honest as I'd ever seen. She would never look at me like that. I didn't have money but I didn't think Evelyn did either.

Evelyn saw Anneliese and a distinct dislike flickered across her face, passing quickly, a thin shadow on a windy day. It was replaced in an instant by a loving smile. Anneliese had seen it too but blinked that knowledge away and stood to meet her, raising her arms to embrace her, regardless of the fact that Evelyn was lying.

Chrissie suddenly gave a yelp and stood, staggering backwards, covering her mouth. No one heard because of the singer. She was sobbing so hard she staggered. I stood up and grabbed her arm to steady her. She turned away from Anneliese and Evelyn embracing.

'Marlowe, get me out of here. Please.'

I bundled her out of a back door. She was crying.

'You're overreacting, Chrissie.'

'Oh, Marlowe, it's not that. Get me away, please, just away.'

We walked around to the front of the building and climbed into my car. I gunned the engine and pulled out. Chrissie was crying and I let her.

'Evelyn is Hazel? She's a hat-check girl not a pianist?'

She nodded.

I smoked and drove, giving her time. Finally, I said, 'Not every love affair works out, you know?'

She dropped her head against the window, 'It's not that at all.'

'What is it then?'

'At the Brody, when Viscom opened the door.' She raised her arms warmly, mirroring Anneliese. 'He did that. Exactly what Anneliese did. He raised his arms to greet someone, he said "Liebling", and he smiled and they shot him.'

Pavel Viscom didn't open the door and then realize he was being robbed. He opened the door to someone he knew. He raised his arms to embrace someone he loved.

And they shot him through the heart.

30.

It was a crystal blue Pacific morning but I was miserable, ruminating on cleft lips and lies as I drove too fast on the coast road out to Latigo Beach. I'd been set up. Baby Maude had been working me from the get-go. I thought back to Anneliese Lyle calling me a romantic, a rescuer of dames, destined to be angry and disappointed and I thought maybe she was right.

The Malibu Colony sat on the edge of the ocean looking away from the city that spawned it like a sulking child. Steep dirt cliffs rose on the landward side, threatening to spill onto the road. On the left the land fell away into a clear glittering blue ocean. Out here there was no suffocating heatwave, nothing to stick the suit jacket to the back or turn a good hat into a sweat band.

The lapping ocean threw up silver sparks that hurt my eyes as I drove, fastest chump in the west. They glared, bright, white, so sharp it felt angry and hostile, forced me to hold my eyes half shut and my face tight. The air was different out here, thinner, lighter, full of clarity and promise.

A slip road to Latigo Beach dipped down below the highway and flattened out behind what seemed from the road to be small wooden houses, all different but cheek by jowl with one another, looking out to the water intent as Easter Island heads.

I parked on a street with a long garden fence and small doors on the ocean side, found the number I wanted and rang the bell.

The sun beat down on me like a school bully at recess. I was close to giving up and climbing over the fence for a look when the wooden gate was opened by a young woman in pyjamas.

She was twenty or so, not a child but somehow not an adult either. Her hair was pale red and long and tangled, cut into by an unpractised hand, and her face was pudgy, plain, unadorned with make-up. She looked as if she had been dragged backwards through a warehouse full of pillows because everything about her was a mess but she wasn't hurt or drunk or even hungover. She didn't care what she looked like.

Her mouth hung slack as she looked at my face, at my suit, at my shoes. She looked over my shoulder at the road and gave a small spiteful smile without finding out what my name was first. So I followed her.

We passed through a short garden, carefully tended, with a flourishing palm tree and small round topiarized ball hedges scattered around a white gravel yard snaking over to the back door.

The house was deceptive. It looked small but only if you didn't know it went up for two stories and down another to the beach. Inside, a single room covered the whole floor, leading to a row of large windows filled with brutal glaring white ocean. The pyjamaed girl saw me lift my hat to shield my eyes.

'Yah,' she said. 'Hate it.' She clapped her hands twice and a maid appeared from nowhere. 'Blinds.'

The maid pulled the blinds down on all of the windows, working her way along the wall and seeming to evaporate again.

It was a relaxing room. Full of dripping plants and low furniture in mossy colours. On the walls, illuminated with small soft lights, were paintings. These were the very daubs I'd seen in the gallery at the Bradbury. Newspapers and paint smears, variations on the theme of, they were everywhere. The frames were more elaborate here though, gilt and antique. A large radiogram took up one wall. At the end of the row of windows, a small door led out onto a deep balcony.

It opened.

A small, stocky woman in a sagging swimsuit and open robe stood in the doorway, holding a cigarette in one hand and a large cocktail with half a pound of fruit in it in the other. She was about fifty. Her hair was set hard into big curls and she wore gold on her ears, around her neck, on her wrist.

'Who in the hell have you brought in now?' she said.

She was not talking to me.

The pyjamaed girl turned to me with a bitter smirk. 'Probably my new daddy.'

It seemed suddenly dark in the room.

The swimsuit drank. She drank as if she'd never had drink but had read about it and always wanted to try. Assuming she wasn't holding a fruit cocktail, if it was her first, she'd already be quite drunk. It was not her first.

She wobbled over to me. The swimsuit was blue. It had been wet today and sagged here and there, as did she. The whole effect was too much.

She held out her hand and her robe fell off one shoulder. 'Peggy Zimmerman.'

I shook it, 'Philip Marlowe.' I kept my eyes on her face.

She drank again, not quite as much this time, but the fruit got in the way. She held my eye, stuck two fingers into the juice and lifted out a slice of pineapple. She sucked the red juice from it and dropped it on the floor. Something had happened to her nose. It wasn't a plastic job because there was no nose that this was an improvement on. It was narrow with a scar across the bridge, too neat and thin to be from an accident. It came to an asymmetric bulbous end and wide nostrils.

'You're looking at my nose.'

'It's unusual.'

'Isn't it? I paid a lot of money for this masterpiece. You think I should get it fixed? I tried. Wouldn't let them put me under though, I have a problem with that. Got the best doctors in the whole of Europe to work on it. San Tropez. Miracle workers.

They laid me out and opened me up but when I saw the tools they were planning to use, a little silver hammer and chisel, I made them sew me back up and let me go.'

'Well,' said the pyjamaed girl spitefully, 'it looks gorgeous.'

'Get lost, Pegsy,' ordered the older woman.

I was confused. 'I thought you were Peggy Zimmerman?'

The pyjamaed girl glared at her mother. 'I'm Pegsy Bradshaw. *She's* Peggy Zimmerman. Couldn't even give me a first name of my own. Mother, are you drinking alcohol?'

'It's a fruit drink. The doctor in Zurich said I had to eat fruit with the vitamin injections or I'd get sick again.'

The mother and daughter looked at each other with all the warmth of fast-draws waiting for the noon bell.

A maid scurried between them, in a crouch, as if she might be hit if she stood tall, picked up the dropped fruit and wiped the sticky wet splatter off the floor. Neither of the women acknowledged her.

She left.

Outside, the ocean hushed softly. A man called after a dog out on the beach, an angry command to return to his master.

Peggy Zimmerman was looking me up and down as if she was about to guess my weight. Then she paused to let me get a good look at her. There was a lot to look at. She was small, dumpy and had a broken nose. Very tanned. She exuded a sexual confidence that only made sense if you knew about her bank book.

Her hair was teased up to make it look thicker and her thin lips twitched in frowns as she walked down the long room with her hand out.

'What do you want here, Philip Marlowe?'

'I thought you might know something about Pavel Viscom being murdered two nights ago.'

The girl let out a small cry like a mouse that had been stepped on. Zimmerman was so shocked that, for just the briefest moment, she looked sober.

31.

Peggy Zimmerman had done her robe up, which was a mercy, and took me downstairs, into a lounge room that led onto the beach. The sand was white. The water was blue. The sky was brilliant and clear.

'I feel sick,' said Peggy, holding her stomach, 'and I don't know why you'd make up such a cruel lie. If you weren't so tall and handsome I'd have had you thrown out already.'

'I'm not making anything up.'

She clicked her fingers and I saw some movement behind us. The servants were small people who managed somehow to always remain in the blind spot. A maid held open a box of Turkish cigarettes. The paper was yellow, the tobacco a deep, moist brown. She offered a flame to her boss and Zimmerman took a deep inhale and exhaled a thick brown stream. It smelled as thick and rich and warm as pipe smoke. She tipped her head and the box came to me. I took one.

The cigarette paper had Arabic writing along the side. It was smooth and delicious and instantly nauseating, like drinking a pint of melted butter.

She offered me a drink. I said a whiskey and soda would work. Zimmerman didn't really want to offer me a drink. She wanted to let me know that we were not alone. I couldn't harm her or say anything private.

I took my drink from a silver tray held by a different maid

who didn't look up. They kept their heads down as though admitting they existed would be a breach of contract. She slipped back into the shadows.

I sipped. It was very nice whiskey.

Peggy took herself and her cigarette outside to a beige lounger on the deck and invited me to lie down next to her on its twin. I sat down on the side of it as she slipped on a pair of large sunglasses and pulled her robe together at her neck.

'Why did you say that awful thing?'

'About Viscom? Because it's true.'

She smoked and tapped her ash on the floor, cleared her throat, and squinted at the sea.

'Mr Marlowe, Pavel Viscom was my lover. He died in Paris four months ago.'

'How do you know that? Did you see his body?'

She looked at me from the side of her sunglasses. Her tongue felt for something on her front teeth. She sucked a hiss.

'A body, yes. His face was gone but it was him. His gold cigarette case was in the pocket. Had his initials engraved on it. A gift from me. His body was dumped in the driveway of my villa.' She swallowed and looked away.

'Is there any possibility that it wasn't him?'

'Did Pavel dress someone in his clothes and murder them for some scheme of his?' Her chin trembled. 'Possibly. He's an interesting man. Was.' She laughed as if she'd been holding it in, a breathy, devil-may-care, half-scream, 'He didn't have to die to get away from me but it didn't hurt that I thought that!'

'If he did fake his death and turn up here, what's in it for him?'

She shrugged.

'Is that when you bought up all his paintings?'

'No, I'd already bought the contents of his studio.'

'And then you became lovers?'

'No, Mr Marlowe, that's not how it works.' She gave her drink a sad smile. 'I buy some of their work and then they sleep with me. Then I buy more of their work.' The eyes slid to the side again, 'That's how it works.'

'Maybe they'd sleep with you anyway?'

Without looking at me, she let her robe fall off her legs. Her calves were mottled and grey, marked by thread veins. She smirked, knew she'd won the point.

'You know the value of art is all about the stories behind it.'

'Someone else said that . . .'

'Who?'

'Joan Baudelaire who works in your gallery?'

'Well. I don't know staff.' She threw the burning cigarette away into the hot sand. No one came to pick it up. Maybe they'd get it later.

The imperious hand came up and she flicked a finger at the water. A fruit-filled cocktail arrived. She looked at it, disgusted, and murmured to herself, 'I hate fruit.'

It felt like the first thing she'd said that wasn't cribbed from a bad movie script.

'Can't you ask them not to give it to you?'

Her head slumped on her neck. 'They'd do it. But I need to eat fruit so I make them bring it. Then I don't eat it.'

Out on the water a sail boat coasted by perfectly on the razor-edge horizon. A dog further down the sand caught a ball in its mouth and brought it back to its owner.

'Kind of perfect out here, isn't it?'

'Yes,' she said sadly. 'I hate it. Pegsy makes me come here because she knows I hate it. It's so tasteful . . . What makes you believe it was Viscom who was killed?'

'A man calling himself "West" was shot and murdered two nights ago in the Brody Hotel.'

'West?' She looked at the water sadly.

'All the murderer took was his papers.'

'No ID on him?'

'None.'

'It wasn't him in Paris, huh? Well . . .'

I hadn't really made a case for the body at the Brody being Viscom yet. I didn't understand why she was so willing to believe me.

'The man had just arrived in California, only spoke German. And he had shoes from Vienna. And he had teeth up here,' I showed her the distinctive place his canines were. 'Tucked right up under his top lip. You only saw it when he smiled.'

'Family trait. His mother had the same teeth. Pavel called himself "West". It was his pseudonym. If he was travelling under any other name, it would be West.'

She knocked the fruit garnish to the floor and drank, raising a hand at her side to tell the servants to leave the pineapple and cherries on the wooden decking. The pink from the cherries soaked into the salt-dried wood, staining it. She saw me looking.

'I own this house. I come here for one or two weeks a year. The rest of the time the staff live here, rent free. Paid to live here, in fact. They cower when I come. They want me to love it. They want me to keep this house so that they can live here. Without me, they have nice lives and live by the beach. Now I can't get rid of it without ruining lives. I wish I'd never bought this damn place.'

I looked back into the darkness of the room. A pair of anxious eyes flashed at me, blinked and then slid further back into the dark.

'Where do you live the rest of the time?'

She sighed. 'I have houses . . .' She looked at her wrinkled knees, smirked as if remembering someone she liked. 'I've houses comin' out the wazoo.' She looked at me through her dark glasses. 'You don't come from money.'

'No.'

'Yes.' She settled back in her chair. 'Our fortune is almost infinite. I can have anything I want, at any time, go anywhere, do anything. I buy lovers, I buy houses, I buy friends to laugh at my vulgar jokes, men to tell me I'm not old and my nose is characterful. I buy cars and yachts, I buy things. Poor little me.'

'You buy art.'

'I do. Do you like art, Mr Marlowe?'

'No.'

She laughed at that and it sounded sincere. 'You don't mess about, do you?'

'I saw the paintings in your gallery, the Viscom ones at the Art of Now. I thought they were garbage.'

She laughed but it wasn't sincere. She was a little annoyed. 'Well, you ignoramus, you're wrong. He has revolutionized looking. He has made art relevant again in the age of photography. His genius is seeing beyond the canvas.'

'None of that means anything to me.'

She nodded, 'Then don't invest in art.'

'Why d'you bother investing in art if your money is infinite?'

'Why bother having a gallery and running around Europe buying paintings from men who'd fake their own murder to be free of me?'

'If that is what happened, yes.'

She hummed. She drank. She settled back on her lounger. 'My uncle, Solomon Zimmerman, built a museum in New York for his collection. Old Masters of the French Academy mostly. Impressionists. Pointillists. The good ol' boys. His cut-off point is around the turn of the century, as if art stopped then. My gallery challenges that conception of art as stagnant and finite.'

'You're doing it to contradict your uncle?'

'Solomon doesn't approve of me.' She tapped her cigarette fast. Anxious. 'He doesn't like women smoking or drinking or being divorced. Three times. Or travelling alone. He's wrong.'

A tray of fruit was suddenly on the table between us together with a fresh whiskey soda for me. The ashtray had been replaced with a clean one. The serving staff were so unobtrusive it was eery. When they were out of sight I asked, 'Who killed the Pavel Viscom in Paris?'

'I was told it was the anti-Nazis. They hated him because he was a Nazi. Everyone is a Nazi over there, Mr Marlowe. Except the anti-Nazis which consists of two men, a boy with one eye and a three-legged dog.'

'Aren't you Jewish?'

'Yes but I'm also rich and, more importantly, American. They don't want to antagonize the American government. Don't want us getting involved in the war.'

'There was a girl working in your gallery here, Joan Baudelaire. Do you know her?'

She rolled her eyes up and thought about it, rollerdexing through girls she knew. 'No,' she said finally.

'Never met her?'

'Can't say I recall.'

'How about Pegsy? Would she have met her? They're closer in age.'

'Pegsy never goes anywhere or does anything. She never leaves my side, wanna know why?'

'Why?'

'She hates me.'

She held my eye angrily, a trace of disgust on the edge of her gaze, wanting me to ask what she meant, how much did her daughter hate her, why was she wrong. I'd rather have eaten a rat. Live. Without salt.

'Joan thought she was taking you to Jane Jones' Little Club.'

Peggy sat up, excited, 'The butches' bar? Oh really? Who is she?'

'She worked at your gallery. She thought she was taking you there the night Viscom was killed.'

'I'd like to go there. Tell her that. I'd like to go.'

I stood up. Zimmerman knew Jane Jones' Little Club. She knew what it was and the sort of women who went there. She was starved of excitement. All the normal thrills of life, finding a parking space, cashing a cheque, making rent or buying a steak, she was dead to all these pleasures, finding fresh meat in the form of young bodies, she could connect with that. But she didn't know who Joan Baudelaire was or who she had been.

I said I had to go, I had an appointment. She didn't want me to leave and the drink had hit her hard. She was slurring as we walked back up the wooden slats that served as stairs to the room I'd come in through.

'Tell her, will ya? This Joan girl. Tell her I said it's yes to that night out?'

'Sure.'

Pegsy was sitting on a chair, watching us emerge from the stairs. She had dressed in a smock dress, white with blue flowers, but her hair was still tangled and ragged and dirty. She looked angry. Her chin was smeared with butter.

Peggy stood in the room, her robe open, stocky legs uncertain, tramping the floor as if it was moving. She blinked at Pegsy. She blinked at me. She blinked at Pegsy again.

'How'bout,' she drawled at me, 'how'bout you take your jacket off?'

A slow grimace of self-disgust made her bare her teeth and roll her eyes back in her head. Pegsy stood up and screamed at her mother, 'DRUNK!'

'I'm eating fruit!'

Shadows shifted in the corner of the room, ready to catch or serve or separate, whatever it would take to make these two unhappy women love it here.

I didn't take my leave. I just left.

Peggy Zimmerman had said a lot but the one thing she hadn't said once was 'darling'.

32.

Driving back to the city, looking forward to the wholesome company of corrupt cops and drunken bums, I came to the edge of the Palisades Beach and found myself swinging right off the road, doubling back onto a dirt track that led down to a row of low shack houses, cheek by jowl looking out at the water.

There was the little green Plymouth parked right behind them. I drew up next to it and got out.

Half a mile away, down at the waterside, the beach was full of families enjoying a Saturday at the ocean after a week of hot offices and bus journeys and trolley rides. They gathered around blankets or sunshades, in little groups, pops reading newspapers in folding chairs, moms drying kiddies fresh back from the water. Out in the slow waves people were playing ball, getting on and not attacking each other or opening museums to spite their uncles. It was nice to see. Hopeful.

I walked past a truck selling donuts and ice cream, the queue was fifty yards long, all watching, all excited. Beyond it a gang of Latino kids was gathered around a red convertible with yellow leather interior. Their hair was too slick to go swimming, their shirts too starched for sitting on the sand. They smoked and paraded around in front of each other, talking Spanish loudly to catch the eye of a group of girls standing nearby, pretending not to have noticed them, the only other people in the car park. I thought of poor Manny Perez.

I walked around the front. My feet sank and sand worked its way into my shoes. Seagulls called overhead, riding the high winds, and the waves broke on the beach.

Calling it a beach house was overstating it. It was a pink walled shed, sitting on a concrete platform with three others. Each had a faded green corrugated iron roof, a door with a window on either side. They looked functional and unadorned. The army could have been using them to spy on the sea.

Sitting outside, reading a paperback under a red and blue sunshade, sat Anne Riordan. She wore a green bathing suit and dark glasses with just the faintest smear of pink lipstick. She looked up and saw me and her face brightened with delight.

'Marlowe!' But then she caught herself and beat back her surprise. 'What are you doing all the way out here?'

'Came to see you.'

'You did, huh?' She folded over the edge of her page and shut the book. Poetry. John Donne.

I sat down on the concrete platform next to her chair and looked out at the scene. Anne's hand fell to her side. I was acutely aware of how close it was to my face.

'Nice out here.'

'Sure is,' she said.

And we sat and we looked and it was nice.

'Chrissie okay?'

'I think so. For now. Had to move to her last night but she's stashed away nice and tight.'

'Want to tell me where you stashed her?'

'For the bonus? You can't take her back there, Anne. He's beating Anneliese Lyle. He'll hit Chrissie.'

'He already does. Anneliese told me he gets her to beat Chrissie on his behalf. Test of her absolute loyalty.'

She could see I was surprised.

'Oh Marlowe,' she patted my shoulder. 'Women tell each other things we would never tell a man. You don't know how it is. There's just so much backstory to being a woman. Chadwick used to be a lot worse. He committed her mother to a sanatorium and they drugged her so heavily she drowned in a bath. It's not as dramatic as it looks. Anneliese bruises easy and every time he beats her up she figures he's bringing himself closer to death. Chrissie may still be safer there than out here.'

'I don't know everything you know, but you don't know everything I know either.'

I sounded petty and low but when I looked at her, looking up for once, she smiled kindly at me. Her nose was small and round at the end. She had a little chin that would fit perfectly between a thumb and the crook of a forefinger. I looked away.

After a little while she said, 'I was about to get a sandwich. Would you like to come inside?'

She took her book and I carried the chair to the little pink door of the little pink house. She opened it into a room that suited beach living. Bare, bleached wood chairs. A table. A lamp.

An ice box was tucked into the corner. At the back of the room a single cooking ring sat on the worktop with a gas canister on the floor beneath it. Through an open door I saw a bed with a green cover on it. She was nothing if not consistent.

She took down bread from a cupboard and cut some slices, took a plate of meat cuts, some butter and a small block of cheese from the ice box, and put them on the table. From a cupboard she brought out two small plates, some knives and a couple of napkins, made up two places, got us both a glass and filled a jug of water.

I watched her glide around the small bare room, watching her hands more than anything. They made no moves other than those that were absolutely essential, sliding the plate to the table, laying a napkin down, lifting a glass from a cupboard. But they moved gracefully. There was no nervousness in the hands, no hidden thoughts finding expression in the fingers. Here are the plates we will eat from, said these small delicate hands. Here are the glasses we will drink from. Here is your place, Philip. Here is mine.

We sat across from each other and ate. She offered me the bread and then the meat and cheese. I poured her some water.

'A suit's a bold choice for the beach,' she said.

'Fashion is boldness. I didn't plan on coming by.'

'I'm glad you did.'

'I'm glad too.'

The front door lay open and we could hear the families and the ocean, hear the Latino kids flirting and shouting around the back, feel the heat of the day wafting in and out of the door.

We sat across from each other and ate quietly. I could have lived there.

'Why did you come here, Marlowe, to check out the spoils of a well-run business?'

'I was passing by.' I took out my cigarettes, lit two, and handed her one.

She was looking at my matches. 'You don't go to Coomes.'

Had to wonder how she knew that. 'Moochie Ruud does.'

She smiled, 'Does he?'

'Moochie Ruud couldn't work out where rain comes from. He's a fool.'

She smiled. 'Those cigarette girls you disapprove of sure do see some sights.'

'Coomes is one of Tiny's places, is it?'

'Why yes, it is.' She smiled again, pressing her pretty little lips together. There was something behind those lips.

I was smiling too. 'Ruud doesn't drink alone, does he?'

'No, he does not. And he doesn't drink with his wife either. Or his father-in-law.' She smiled out of the door. I'd bet she knew a lot more than that about a whole lot of people.

'Hear any more about Manny Perez?'

'I went up to Pico at the time of day when you let him out. Only women and children in the street at that time. All white women. And no one saw anything. Whoever did it just slipped in and out without being noticed so I'm tracing Chrissie's friends, anyone who fits that description.'

'Cops don't have anything?'

'Cops don't care about Manny Perez. No one seems to care.'

'The only thing anyone noticed out of the ordinary was a Ford Coupe missing a white wall on one of the tyres. It's that sort of area.'

'Who you got so far, apart from Evelyn Hamilton and Mrs Dudek?'

'And Anneliese Lyle. What do you know about her background?'

I knew nothing. I'd met her a few times and been drinking with her but hadn't looked further than her dazzling face. 'Not much.'

'I can't find out a thing about her,' said Anne. Where did she come from? Did you ask her?'

'Sure. She was kind of squirrelly about it but said nothing much. Say I needed Ruud to look into a case he already solved. Can you help me?'

'Why do you need him to reopen it?'

'Ruud has a slam-dunk on a cowboy called Black Jack Beau. I helped him. Now Beau'll fry if I don't do something quick but I can't see Ruud giving up the win.'

She listened as if she was interested, as if Black Jack Beau's wellbeing was all she'd been thinking about, and then blindsided me: 'What were you doing on Skid Row the other night with a dame who sounds an awful lot like Chrissie Montgomery?'

'What was I doing?'

'Ruud has a case. A stiff who booked into the Brody under the name West. And by coincidence he finds you there. Has he followed up with you about that?'

'No.'

'Well, isn't that odd,' she said. 'Ruud backed off faster than a dancing chicken at a State fair. Almost as if someone told him he shouldn't be interested.'

'Hm.'

The white light reflected off the sea lit her skin silver. Her eyes flashed and her auburn hair fell over one eye. Movie stars would kill to be lit like that.

'You're smart, Anne. You'll do so well in this business.'

She was surprised by that, 'Thank you. Thank you, Phil, I appreciate that.'

She'd never called me Phil before. No one called me Phil. She'd been thinking about me when I wasn't there. She'd been talking to me in her mind. Using an informal form of address. I don't know if I've ever felt better.

'Where have you stashed Chrissie?'

'Someplace safe.'

'We have to take her back, you know that, don't you? Before she gets in more trouble than covering up a murder.'

'Anne, it could be worse. It could be two murders.'

Half joking, she threw her butter knife down on the table. It bounced and landed on the floor facing the door.

I thumbed over at the knife, 'Nice.'

'Thinking of starting a knife-throwing act.'

'Want me to get it?'

'No,' she sighed and sat back down. 'Let's leave it there to deter burglars. Tell me where Chrissie is and I might talk to Ruud about your cowboy.'

I saw her in that perfect light, haloed in the glare from the sea. I saw her old and me old, and us still sitting here, eating endless lunches and bickering.

'We need to take her back, Marlowe, she'll get used and used until she's all used up.'

'One way or another we all get used, Anne. Chrissie's holed up in room 118 at the Biltmore. Just give me one day?'

'She's not safe.'

'I don't know who she's in most danger from just yet. Can you give me a day to figure that out?'

'One day, but –' Anne's back stiffened. She looked past me and her eyes widened as if she'd been shot.

'Hello, Marlowe.'

A figure blocked the light of the door, ending the little play we'd put on for ourselves as suddenly as a dropped curtain.

Errol Cooper was no longer the restrained butler from the Montgomery place. He'd dressed for the beach in pressed cotton slacks and a white shirt, canvas shoes worn without socks. In one hand he held a small cake box on a string and in the crook of his elbow he carried a small bunch of jacaranda flowers wrapped in newspaper.

His eye was still bruised. He looked from me to her, his face asking a question so angry that I hoped he wasn't carrying a gun. He put the cake box down carefully on the table, bobbed down and picked up the butter knife. He held it out to Anne by the blade.

'Cooper,' I said. 'I was passing by and I dropped by to ask Anne something.'

'Passing?' He spoke to me but he was watching her.

Anne stood up. She was annoyed at being asked the unspoken question. This was her place and she could have whoever she wanted in here.

'Hello dear,' she said, making him not sound dear to her at all. 'Marlowe came by.'

'I can see that.' He jabbed the flowers at her. His accent was soft but at least from the right continent. Out of uniform he seemed younger, uncertain and a little frightened.

She hesitated before she took the flowers from his hand. She smelled them. 'They're quite lovely. Thank you.'

'Yes,' he nodded sternly. 'They're lovely.'

Anne went to the cupboard and took out a glass vase. She filled it with water from the tap and set them on the table, arranging the long stems counter to one another. They were too long for the makeshift vase. A lilac finger pointed me to the door.

Cooper looked at me. 'I got a few hours off,' he told me. 'I thought I would surprise Anne. And I think I did.'

Anne looked at him. He looked back at her. I stood up and picked up my hat. 'I was just leaving.'

'Don't leave on my account,' he said, as I brushed past him.

I was leaving on his account. If he hadn't turned up I might have stayed there forever and gotten old and been halfway happy for some of it.

33.

It was a snapshot kind of night. Moments dredged from the darkness. Flashes of conversation and disjointed images that make no sense.

I recall driving to the city. I recall going to Frenchie's beer hall, though I don't know why. Adolph wasn't there so I went away to a different bar and drank whiskey.

The shutters came down.

Fifth Avenue as full as a New Year's party but no one was celebrating. Lights ached through the dark as I stumbled into a bar that could have doubled as an emergency ward. Men slumped on tables, over the sticky bar top, one sleeping on a stool, a smoking cigarette stuck on his dry lip, acrid stench of burning hair from his beard. I was drinking gin in there. I don't know why. Gimlet memories or maybe they only sold gin. I can taste it yet, the warm sticky feel of it in my mouth and the acid flare when it hit the back of my tongue. A man was fighting two other men in there. It was a real fight, punches were swung, but moments were lost and then there was blood and then the men were gone. A smear of blood on a bar and a broken tooth sitting in it. A smoke-racked voice that seemed to be me told the barman he should clean it up but he said someone might come back for the tooth and he didn't want to touch it.

Shutters.

Steadying myself against a store window in the warm street.

Neon blue and yellow lights made a show of passing faces. Crooked, worn, sun dried and broken. Woman in flaking make-up, powder on shoulders and the cover-all-sins smell of lavender, a pungent stiletto of a perfume. Faces turning to me as I struggled to stand and breathe at the same time. Looking at me or the window behind me, I don't know. Far across the road I saw a body on the sidewalk. Shapeless clothes, rags, curled on his side. People stepped over him and shambled on, looking back sometimes, ignoring other times. I felt he was dead. I felt he was me and I should go over and look after him or kick him to death or wake him up and buy him a coffee. It changed every minute.

I heard a child's shout from the open window in an apartment over a bar. A wordless call, shapeless, a caw of a voice. Anne at her beach house and the children playing on the beach. Silence at the table and cold cuts from the ice box. Cooper. I had sent her away when she asked to be close to me, this wonder girl, this cream-skinned wonder. The air, it hurt, and my heart and my hat, just as Lorca said. Every time I met her we fought and I liked it. I liked everything she did. The way she drove and threw a butter knife at a door. I looked down at my forearm that no one was touching and it was on a bar and the bar was wet.

Shutters.

I was the one fighting this time, wrestling a small man on the sawdust-covered floor of a bar. Around us legs moved out of the way but no one paid attention. We got stuck under a table. Someone shouted across the room, and a woman sang an old Irish song about hills.

Shutters.

This was the worst part. The shutters came up for just a moment at a long table in a dark bar. Everyone in the room was looking at me. These were the lowest of the low, tramps with the dust of a thousand miles of box-car riding ingrained in their wrinkles, one-eyed men with scars from brawls. Men with wild hair or no hair or hair pulled out at the sides. Everyone was ageless and everyone was worn out and everyone was sad. But they were all looking at me, shocked at something I had said or done. That time I reached forward in my mind and pulled the shutters down myself.

Shutters.

A dust-floor car park next to the flower market. Smells of sour vegetation. Men around a fire brazier, singing a song in a language I couldn't understand. Silence. Footsteps through the dust. A woman's voice. My collar being yanked.

Shutters.

A man lay on my feet. He was a big man or my feet thought he was big anyway. They were having a shutters moment of their own. Completely numb, feeling nothing. I envied them. I tried to wriggle them back from under the weight of him but he shifted and I got more stuck. My heels hit something solid. I couldn't pull the lumps of meat out or get away from him.

I opened my eyes.

The sun rose in the lobby of the Alhambra Hotel, lighting up a sea of men with no place else to go. The windows caught the morning light, slicing down through the low streets and waste ground all around us. I was one of the lucky ones. I had a chair. The floor around me was carpeted with sleeping men, grunting and turning away from the bothersome morning rays burning in through the window.

I looked up at the desk. Sunshine was sitting there, reading a detective novel with a lurid cover. A gun, a dame in a ripped blouse, bright and red with yellowed pages. She licked her lips and looked over the top of the pages and caught my eye. She gave me a kindly nod and mouthed my name.

I shook my head and burst a firework behind my eyes. I held myself still until it stopped. When I opened them again she was standing next to me, holding out a glass of watery blood.

'A red eye.'

I took the drink. It smelled of petrol and tomatoes.

'Drink it. Is good.'

I took it. I drank. It had beer in it and the tongue-cling of a raw egg. Tomato and something else, something strong. But I drank it. For a moment it seemed like it wasn't going down. But it did. Then it seemed like it wasn't going to stay down. But then it did. A slow warmth seeped into all of my limbs, up the back of my head, it rubbed my back and stroked my elbows and covered my eyes and I thanked it.

'Good,' said Sunshine. She flicked two fingers at me, telling me to follow her and to not dare wake up the men lying all around us. I did as she ordered and followed her to the desk and a small door behind it. We stepped into a room with bare wood shelves of grey, threadbare linen.

My head suddenly felt that it might split open. I slumped against the wall. 'How did I get here?'

'I found you on my way in here last night, lying in the street. Adolph says you're good man. What you doing down here? You don't belong.'

'Trying out the lifestyle for size.'

'Try something on too much it might start to fit.' She crossed her arms at me. She made a sound like a cross between a hiss and a sigh. 'I see you here again I pay my men to rip your arms off.'

I tried to laugh but my stomach hated me for it.

Sunshine didn't like it either. 'No joke. Men die down here all the time. You got shoes and a job. You got a car. Get out of here. Be American man. Fix yourself.'

I looked out at the sleeping men. 'They're American men too.'

'They're broken. You're sad. Different thing.'

She was right. It was different. And the lifestyle would start to fit if I came here too often, I knew that.

'The Brody. Can you get me in?'

'To live there? No.'

'To look. I want to see the room the Austrian died in.'

She looked at the empty glass in her hand and she looked out at the men in the lobby. She'd already done me a favour, several in fact, but she must have remembered something, another night, a chance she missed to save someone else.

'You go. I call across to Flaky Hondrat. He the desk man. Now, you get out of my hotel and don't come back here.'

So I did.

34.

The Brody was different in the daylight. It was dirtier and more intimidating. Two men were sleeping on the bench outside and a busted old jalopy was parked drunkenly, its front tyre pressed tight to the kerb. Inside the floor was tiled white and filthy, the windows onto the street netted with dust and dirt, keeping the morning soft and out of there.

The night porter was gone and in his place was Flaky Hondrat, a small man in a short-sleeved lounge shirt. He had a skin complaint that made him look flayed, white peeling flakes on top of raw pink, as if his skin was trying to get off of him and it looked painful. Here and there the skin had split in paper cuts, at junctions where the skin stretched, on his knuckles and at the crease of his elbows and his neck. He was smoking a cheap cigar, chewing the end of it so it turned in his mouth incessantly.

He gave me a look as I walked in and his right hand fell to the shelf below the counter top. I raised both hands and stalled.

'Who sent you here?' he growled.

'Sunshine Aziz.'

'Watch me,' he slowly raised his right hand. It didn't have a gun in it. That was the whole trick. I showed him that I didn't have one in my hands either and he said, 'All right. Come in.'

I walked over to the desk. He chewed the ragged end of his cigar and then puffed on it. 'What you want to know?'

'In the register. How many people by the name of West were booked in that night?'

He pulled the tome over and flicked through to the day. 'Just the one. The German that got rubbed. Sunny says you wanna see the room?'

I nodded, 'Can I see both rooms?'

'Each to his own.' He snarled. 'Not my idea of a good time. We get all sorts in here.'

I was too sore to explain.

'Get many like him?'

'Nah. He was in the wrong place. I tells him he is. They don't listen to me on account of I'm short.'

'What did you say?'

'I says: friend-o, this place ain't for you. You got nice luggage, pricy clothes. Go up town, get a nicer room in a better place. Says he thought so too but it was all paid up. Seemed like he was meeting someone here. Waited in every night. Every morning he asked if a frail had come by for him.'

'A woman?'

'Yes but not the fun kind, didn't get any liquor in or anything. He described her in broken English. "Young", "Aryan", "beautiful".'

'That could be anyone down here.'

Flaky almost laughed. It felt like a breakthrough. He reached behind him and took down two room keys from their hooks. Both had big wooden balls attached to them to stop guests slipping them into their pocket and taking them away.

'Who was staying in the other room?'

'No one. Just the boxes he brought with him.'

'They still there?'

'Oh no.' He gave me a serious look. I took the prompt and gave him some serious money. He leaned over to me and whispered, 'Day after the day after? Removal men came and took 'em away.'

'How many boxes?'

'Four or five of 'em,' and he showed me the shape of them: each three feet squared.

'Didn't happen to mention where they were taking them, did they?'

'I asked and they delivered.' He wrote the address down. It was one I knew well.

'This dame who booked the two rooms, what did she look like?'

'Kind of skinny. I suppose young, Aryan and beautiful might cover all bases but she wasn't my type.'

'What is your type?'

'Breathing in and out.' He handed me the keys and the big wooden balls. They had to weigh ten pounds each.

'She wasn't breathing?'

'Yeah, but all tippy toes and fresh. Didn't want to touch the key balls. Held them with her sleeve. It's not contagious, what I got. Lucky I didn't punch her in the mouth 'cause she might have liked it. Don't wanna get me on the wrong day, know what I mean?'

He wanted me to think he was tough. Tough enough to punch a young woman in the teeth for looking at him wrong.

The truth was Flaky was hard to look at. Even his eyelids were raw. It must have been painful and would have made a lesser man a whole lot meaner than he was.

'Say, I'm letting you in for Sunny. Don't tell no one you were in there. The cops told me not to let anyone in there until they were done.'

'They know about the second room?'

'Nah, never asked me. Seemed like it might be worth something to someone one so I kept schtoom.'

The mirrored entrance concentrated the morning light to the brink of painful. I had to get out of there. Flaky saw me narrow my eyes and cringe.

'I'm on for ten hours. I have to look at my own face for all of that. How do ya think I feel?'

'Tough shift.'

'Sure is, bub.' He pointed up the mirrored stairwell. 'One floor up. Turn left.'

'I owe you, Hondrat, thank you.'

He was surprised by that. Maybe thank yous were thin on the ground at the Brody. I gave him ten more of Chadwick's dollars just to be fancy and thought he might cry. I'd have bet large on him being a sentimental drunk. Tough nuts usually are.

At the top of the stairs the mirrors ran out, the light deadened and I caught my breath.

It was quiet up here. Warm. The floor was stone and my footsteps smacked off the walls as I walked down to the room. Whoever booked the rooms had come up here to see the layout so she could have hidden a gun behind her back, smiled at the spyhole and pulled it when the door opened. She'd have scoped it to work out how she was going to get away afterwards. It was all planned. He waited for her every night, this dead man, and when she finally came, she killed him.

I used the key and let myself in. They had taken the bloody rug away. It was replaced with another one, same pattern. I lifted the corner. The bloodstain was still there. I stood up and saw the scene. Chrissie was standing over by the window, next to the bed. I was Viscom. I stood looking at my imaginary Chrissie then turned to the door. There was a spyhole bored into it. I stepped over and looked through. A fish-eye view of the hall. He had seen whoever was out there, he chose to let them in.

Chrissie said he was smiling as he raised his hands. Did the person pull the gun then? It had to be someone he trusted.

I opened the door to the corridor as he had. He'd opened it willingly and opened his arms so the hole in his shirt was two inches below the hole in his chest. I did the same, looking down as my shirt rode up. Two inches wasn't that much of a difference though. I lowered my arms watching my shirt. He didn't throw his hands over his head or anything, he wasn't surprised, just raised them a little and then backed into the room, crossing the rug, back and back until he trapped Chrissie there. It was the woman he had been waiting for and he let Chrissie in, thinking she might be her. Shots. One into the chest, one more into the jaw.

Then, here comes Marlowe, running up the stairs, two at a time. Along the landing. Finds the door open. Gets Chrissie across the bed. Gets her purse. Hears the siren. Meanwhile the killer is sliding down the fire escape and she's alone: the fire escape nearly came away from the wall when there were two of us on it. She was slight.

I left the room and locked it, went to the second room and opened that door. It was a mirror of next door without the corner window. A big bed, a chair, a rug all the same. Jagged sunshine lit the thin layer of dust on the floor and an absence of dust around three feet square. It was very clean so whatever was there was heavy enough to keep the dust out from under it but not enough to leave a mark on the floor. Viscom had brought a bunch of paintings with him and someone had taken them.

Walking down the mirrored stairway I heard Moochie Ruud before I saw him. I tipped the hat over my face and changed my walk to a limp as I came downstairs. In the mirrored wall I saw Moochie, hands splayed over the mirrored surface, using up air. He had some uniforms with him and they were slouched around the desk as Ruud pressed Flaky.

'Give us the room key, Flaky, otherwise this is nothing but a trip for biscuits.'

Flaky was filling in like a champ, 'Come on, I already told you I don't have the key, Lieutenant Ruud, sir, your guys took the key.'

'Specifically, who?'

'Hmm, maybe him?' Flaky pointed vaguely between the uniforms. 'This one.'

Ruud backhanded a slap into a uniform's chest, 'Well, where is it?'

The young man looked surprised.

'Not him, *him*,' Hondrat pointed at another one of the uniforms. 'He's took it.'

Ruud spun to look at him and a black band of vibrating hats
circled the room. 'Did you?'

The second uniform shook his head.

'Oh,' said Flaky, 'I can't tell youse guys apart. Someone, one of
youse guys, took it to the car youse was driving yesterday.'

Ruud and his uniforms turned to bustle out to the car in the
street. I palmed Flaky one wooden ball and then looked up.

Moochie Ruud caught my eye in a thousand mirrors.

If he had glanced down he would have seen Flaky's hand
under the counter, now holding a greasy wooden ball, and he'd
have known that it must have come from me. But Ruud didn't
glance down because he was too happy to see me on a losing
streak to notice anything very much.

'Well, well, well, Philip Marlowe. You're staying here?'

He looked around at the dirty mirrors, at Flaky, at my crumpled suit and matching face. He bobbed on his heels. I swear he
was actually sweating with glee.

I handed Hondrat the key for the second room.

'That you leaving?' asked Flaky.

I said yes and made to slip past to the door.

'So much for the lead, Marlowe,' said Ruud, 'Perez never borrowed no money.'

'Didn't pan out, huh? Couldn't find brothers called Chavez in
Boyle Heights?'

'Marlowe, look at the mess of you, you two-time loser, be careful who you're squirrelling around. I can get your PI ticket taken
away like that –' He tried to click his fingers but it didn't
happen.

One of the uniforms accidentally snorted a laugh. It was a
mistake.

'Don't you dare take me on, officer. Don't you even dare. Do
you know who my father-in-law is?'

It wasn't just my mood or even my hangover: Moochie Ruud

spoke in banalities strung together with clichés. Seeing him draw a breath to start a sentence was despair-inducing.

'Why, I oughta write you up right now —'

Flaky couldn't stand it either and interrupted him, 'I thought you guys were done up there.'

'We are done. We're going through the motions. We'll put this case to bed in an hour.'

I lit a cigarette and gave one to Moochie more out of reflex than courtesy. 'What case?'

'Straightforward suicide. An Austrian killed himself in one of the rooms up there. That's where I was going when I met you the other night.'

'I heard there were two shots.'

'No,' said Ruud, blinking slow.

'And I can rent out the room again, then?' asked Flaky.

'Yes. Just need to go up and check again, make sure there's no bullets laying around and then the case is getting filed.'

Flaky liked that idea, 'Oh, say, here it is. I just this minute found the key down in here.' He held it out to Ruud, as innocent as Eve offering Adam a mid-morning snack.

'You had it all along, Flaky? What are you playing at, you disgusting —'

I said, 'Wrapped that investigation up kind of fast, didn't you?'

He looked at me, 'He was alone in the room. Had no money. Just arrived. Get them a lot down here.'

'Ah yes, the old two-shot suicide. Happens all the time. That what your father-in-law told you to find?'

'It was one shot. People in the street heard the echo of the shot, okay? They thought they heard two shots but it was the same sound they heard twice.'

He didn't know I'd seen the body and knew it was a lie. But this he did know: the shooting was deemed a suicide. Someone high up had decided that it was to be called a suicide because a Montgomery was involved. Whatever else went on in this town, no member of the Montgomery family would ever be reported as present at a murder, or even a suicide, in a hotel like the Brody. The up-highs would rather blow up a full block of the down-town area than cross that family.

Flaky was trying to catch my eye but I didn't dare look straight at him while Ruud felt he was winning. Anyway, he said, the stiff definitely wasn't Pavel Viscom. They had confirmation of that.

'How do you know?'

'Thinking you're a cop now, Marlowe? I knew you were on the ropes when I saw you down here the other night. You living down here?'

I saw Flaky's raw and panicked eyes reflected back at me a million times.

'Only when I can't make it home,' I said, and pushed past him to the door.

'He used to be somebody,' I heard Ruud murmur as the door shut behind me. 'That's a pitiful shame.'

I could have ripped his lips off but I had to get Chrissie Montgomery before Anne took her home.

I was twenty feet down the street when a hand grabbed me by the neck. 'Hey smart guy, we seen you hand the key back to Flaky. You're coming downtown with us.'

Then I was off my feet, being bundled into a cop car, contemplating the balletic artistry of Moochie Ruud's conversational style.

35.

They were going to lock me in the drunk tank. This was bad. They could hold you in there for three days and let you go with no charge. They did it all the time to get people off the street, the tank was wild. DTs will make a good man do bad things and the cops didn't watch them much. I sat forward in my seat, bulky uniforms on either side.

'But I'm not drunk, Ruud.'

He smiled to himself. 'You seem drunk to me.' He turned his face to mine, 'A bang on the head looks awful like drunk to most fellas.'

I sat back. Anne would take Chrissie home by the time I got out of this.

We all got out of the car outside the Central Police Station on First. I tried to walk as soberly as I could, being part of the party, as though we all worked together.

I walked into the foyer like a visiting dignitary, taking off my hat, smiling and nodding to the desk sergeant, an Irishman called Bullet Borman on account of the shape of his bald head. Borman was known for his abrupt mood swings.

'Public intoxication,' said Ruud, shoving me towards the desk.

Borman looked at me. 'Two blues and a Lieutenant bringing you in? That's shameful drunk.'

I looked at him steady.

'Are ye drunk?'

'No.'

'Didn't think so.' He looked at Ruud. 'What are you pulling?'

'Book him in, Sergeant.'

Borman threw down his pen. 'This man is sober as a judge. He'll be down there causing ructions and this is why, as well you know, we only take them if they're moroculous. If you're hell-bent on holding him here I'll book him for something else but I'm not dropping him into the tank to save you the trouble of thinking up a charge.' He lifted his pen, 'So, go on, Ruud. Name a charge or let the man go but make it quick, I'm about to clock off and it's been a long ol' night.'

If I got charged with anything I could lose my PI licence. Ruud considered his options but he was determined to keep me here as a punishment, as a put down, for wasting his time and hiding the keys. He might try for the murder of Manny Perez if he got desperate enough. I slumped over the desk, opened my mouth and started to sing 'Back in the Saddle Again' with both gusto and a drunk's disregard for rhythm.

I was explaining, through the medium of song, that I slept out every night and the only law was right when Borman slammed his hand on the desk.

'Mr Philip Marlowe, SIR.'

I stopped. I slumped.

'Will you at least allow me to join you in the chorus, sir?' He sang in a rich baritone, 'Whoopie-ti-yi-yo.'

And I joined him, on descant: 'Rocking to and fro!'

Some officer behind the desk joined us for a finale and a couple of joe publics, 'Back in the saddle again!'

'NOT YOU!' screamed Borman at a very small sorry man waiting on a chair against the wall. The man stopped singing and looked down, pressing his hands between his knees. 'You DO NOT get to desecrate the medium of song,' Borman glared at him. 'You'll be ridin' the range for real if I hear another peep out of you, sir.'

The small man had done something very bad. Suddenly calm, Borman turned back to me and huffed an end-of-shift sigh.

'So, acting drunk, is it?' said Borman. 'Fine. Well, you'll need to keep that up if the tank's what you're after. Think ye can do that?'

'For you, Sergeant Borman, I can do anything.'

'He *is* actually drunk,' said Ruud. 'We picked him up on Skid Row.'

'Is that right, son? Mr Marlowe, were you down there indulging all night?'

'All night,' I drawled theatrically. 'I had a fine time!'

'Well, that sounds grand. I'm a slave to the drink myself. Would you have the telephone number of your mother so I can tell the good lady who has the great good fortune to share her life with ye that her favourite son isn't dead in a ditch?'

'I'm not her favourite. She prefers my brother. He's taller.'

'Sweet Mary, Mother of Mercy, isn't that always the way. Sure, my own brother has half an inch on me and he's a bishop up in Boston and here am I, singing along with a man who can barely hold a tune or passably act drunk. Give me some kind of a telephone number if you like, otherwise go on with yourself and be sure to get singing lessons before I stumble across your sorry carcass again.'

I gave him Anne Riordan's number.

'A proper disgrace ye've made of your God-given self. Get this drunken fool off to the tank, so.'

Two officers bundled me down to the basement. One opened the cage door, the other threw me in, then they locked the gate and walked away, back upstairs where they kept the fresh air.

The Central Police Station drunk tank is no place to have a hangover. It's an old building with an old building smell and sanitation. It was hot. The water fountain was broken. The bars were painted and chipped. The windows high and painted shut. The floor was concrete and damp with sweat and urine and, possibly, tears. I pulled up a bit of dry floor and sat down.

I lived a lifetime over the course of a day and a night inside that tank.

I ate and slept and avoided arguments and got in fights. I made friends and saw friendships form and dissolve and deepen.

The other denizens came and went, they slept and pissed and talked. I watched.

Here were the seven ages of man: first the vacant-eyed mewling and puking baby, begging for succour and crashing to sleep. Then the schoolboy whiner, pimpled and sorry, moaning and groaning at any request. The most annoying was the lover. He was incarnated as a fat Belgian, moustachioed and full of passion, sighing like a furnace, demanding cigarettes from everyone as the self-pity roared from his eyes. In the middle of the night we were joined by the furious soldier. He paced the length of the bars, watching the stairs down and muttering strange oaths, building and building his ire until he burst into shouts for the cops to come and fight him. A few of us got him to be quiet and it didn't take much. He didn't seem as interested in a fight inside the cage. By the end of the discussion his nose was burst, his knuckles covered in dried blood.

All through this, observing from the bench sat the jury. They may have been there since the jail was built: three old men. These were Justice and Mr Pants and Second Childishness. Justice cracked wise, narrating the whole scene for the other two. Mr Pants had lost his suspenders and held his too-wide pants up with one hand. He followed his companion's rant, chortling companionably at his jokes. Propped up between them was an ageless man, so pickled he might die at any moment, steeped in his second childishness and mere oblivion.

I lived there for so long that I got used to the smell and I knew that at any moment Anne Riordan could be arriving at the Biltmore lobby, taking the stairs and walking down the corridor to room 118, knocking and reminding her they'd met in my apartment. I didn't know what she would say to get Chrissie to leave with her, the truth probably. She might even give her a business card. Then she'd get Chrissie into her car with a scare story and she'd take her home. They didn't want her there. They didn't like her there. No one really wanted her back but Anne thought this was safer than anywhere else. It might be for the best. It might be safe but I didn't know anymore. I'd never seen Anneliese Lyle give a full smile. I'd like to see her teeth.

Dawn was breaking over the drunk tank and we were all asleep when a voice spoiled the peace.

'Philip Marlowe! Hey, is there a Philip Marlowe in here?'

I looked up. It was Borman coming back on shift, his face sleep-puffed and clean. 'We've your sister here.'

He had them open the cage door to let me out. I stood up but hesitated to take the way out. I don't know why. I'd gotten used to it maybe.

Borman tutted and walked away. 'Get him out,' he said as if he'd seen this happen before.

A uniform reached in, grabbed me by the hair and pulled me out. The door clanged shut behind me.

'So long, buddy,' said Justice.

'Take care on the road,' called the Whining Schoolboy.

I wanted to turn around and wish them all good luck in their endeavours but the time was never right: the cop who'd pulled my hair wrapped a fat hand around my upper arm and lifted me up so I was running on tiptoes up the stairs to the foyer.

The light and fresh air swamped me. I felt as if I'd never stop breathing in.

'Oh my gosh, Marlowe.'

I blinked and a face resolved in my eyes.

'Oh good gosh.'

It was a fine face with a small nose and a long lip. It was a face you could look at for the rest of your life and not get bored.

'Oh sweet mercy, what a god-awful smell.'

36.

She wouldn't let me get in her car until she'd bought a newspaper and laid it down on the seat. Then she lit us both cigarettes and rolled down as many windows as she could. If they wanted Hitler to back off, she said, they could shoot me at him. She drove me to my car down in Skid Row.

'Phil,' she said, when we were parked in the street outside of Frenchie's, looking at my car, 'I'm sorry.'

I'd been thinking about Cooper and the beach house, that elusive life of sun and kindness and Anne. I'd been thinking about it all night. I'd made a decision.

'It's your choice, Anne. You're entitled. It's completely your choice.'

She looked at me, confused, 'What?'

It was killing me but I said again, 'It's up to you.'

'I know that, Marlowe. I've always known that.' And she reached into her purse and brought out an envelope. 'This is yours.'

I opened it. It was a lot of cash. 'What's this?'

'It's your half of the bonus. I took Chrissie back. Why, what were you talking about?'

I shut the envelope. 'How'd you get her to leave the Biltmore?'

'I told her you'd sent me. She trusts you.'

The low risen sun was shooting long shadows across the street. Passing laundry trucks swung past, sweeping screen-swipes of shade over the street. They stopped further on to get loaded up with clean towels and linen to take to the nice places in town. This was not that.

The street was filling up with men as Sunshine's bums got thrown out of the Alhambra lobby. An army of grey, exhausted men wandered down the street, scanning the floor for cigarette butts. One had gotten out early and struck gold, smoking tobacco rolled up in newspaper, tipping his head back to stop the tobacco falling out. Another man watched him enviously. None of them wanted their day to start, none of them wanted back on the treadmill of finding drink and drinking drink and wishing they had more to drink even while they were drinking it. Those small triumphs that made a day, the discovery of a ten-cent-shot shop or a half-smoked cigarette didn't make up for every waking moment being made up of yearning.

'Is this what you want for yourself, Marlowe?'

'Do you know what I really want, Anne?'

'What's that?'

So we sat there and I told her. It took a while. At the end of it she turned to me and said she thought she could fix it so I got exactly what I wanted.

She drove me up to Mrs Dudek's. Evelyn was out but Mrs Dudek opened the door to her room with her spare key and let me look inside. If I'd asked Mrs Dudek to let me burn the house to the ground with her inside she might have agreed at this point.

It was clean and spare. At the back of the room were paintings, all stacked up, all still in the crates. One of the lids was off and we looked inside.

'These're absolute garbage,' said Mrs Dudek.

I agreed but Anne wasn't sure. We left everything as we found it, told her to lock the room and not mention we were there.

Then Anne took me home so I could wash and change and we went for breakfast in a small dinette. She had coffee and eggs. I had grilled cheese. The food was bland. The coffee was burnt. The waitress was surly. We sat at the counter and Anne Riordan nudged me softly, drawing my attention to the coffee bubbling down to a tar on the hot plate.

'It's where it gets its flavour,' she grinned. I believe she meant it as a compliment.

She paid the cheque and we stood up. I felt almost human again. On the way out I held the door open for her.

'Ready, Marlowe?' she said.

'I am now, Riordan.'

'Let's go see Ruud.'

37.

The Ruud household seemed to be doing very nicely, thank you. They had a lawn. They had a door with columns. They had a dog and four blond sons playing out on the perfect lawn with said dog before setting off for school. Two of them were teasing the dog with a stick while the smaller two wrangled over a bike. They all wore the uniform of the Balliol School, maroon ties and grey blazers. It was the most expensive school in the city. You had to be related to God to get in.

As we walked up the path to the house the boys stopped playing and watched, trailing our route like guard dogs waiting to see if there was anything worth eating here. The oldest was twelve, youngest around nine. They all had the same face and it wasn't a nice one. The nose was upturned at the end so you couldn't help but see right into it and it dragged the top lip up with it, making them look rat-like and toothy. None of them looked like Moochie Ruud. I had to assume it was his wife's face.

'Good morning, gentlemen,' said Riordan.

The oldest boy conceded the stick to the dog and stepped through a carefully tended flowerbed to get into her way.

'What do you want here?' he said. 'Father has been told not to bring his underlings to the door.'

She looked at him, 'We don't work for your father.'

He looked around at his rat-fink brothers. 'Are you from the school?' He wasn't going to let us pass him, not without answers.

'Son, we're here to see your daddy,' I explained carefully. 'So git. Because if you don't git I'll get angry and you'll be picking little tiny bits of your pug-ugly face out of that flowerbed over there.'

The boy did git which was judicious of him. He was used to talking down to people who worked for his father but I like to think I extended his repertoire of engagement with underlings that day, perhaps in a way that was useful. We walked up to the door.

'Father of the year over here,' said Riordan. 'Is it snotty kids you hate or all kids?'

'I don't hate kids. I hate people.'

Anne rang the doorbell. A maid answered and kept us on the doorstep. She asked who we were there to see.

Ruud arrived at the door, freshly shaved and doing up his tie. He was not happy to see us but Anne managed to turn that frown around with one word and that word was 'Samantha'.

We were taken into a small book-lined study that looked as if no one ever read or went in there. The rug was blue, the walls were white and the desk was tidy and paper-free. We sat in armchairs and left the door open, making small talk. Yes, it was hot. Anne was getting on just fine in her new offices. That tank thing Moochie asked me to attend, that was all finished, don't give it a second thought, Moochie, we're not here about that.

We had to wait for the kids to get chauffeured off to school. Then we had to wait for Mrs Ruud to come in and, through the medium of facial expressions and pursed lips, express her disappointment and annoyance that Moochie's insalubrious acquaintances had darkened their door. I knew he'd catch hell for us being here. The children did have her face. It looked even more rat-like on an adult. Then she went off with another driver to a charity meeting of some kind, perhaps an outreach programme to teach over-privileged children basic manners.

A different maid came in and brought us coffee in tiny cups

with tiny handles and matching saucers and tiny teaspoons. The cups may have had their own tiny car and driver. I didn't think to ask.

We were finally alone. Moochie Ruud was sweating so much he would have to change his shirt before he went out.

'I don't have access to money to pay you off.'

'We don't want money,' said Anne. 'We want you to do your job. Reopen the Baby Maude case *and* name the dead man at the Brody as Pavel Viscom. We're not asking for you to admit it was a murder but just name him.'

'I can't do that. You know I can't.'

'We think you can. And really, when you think about it, it's not such a stretch. Both cases were decided on the basis of what was good for your career. Telling everyone about double-jointed Samantha at Coomes' Nite Spot would be bad for your career. It's the same aim, just a different slant on it, isn't it?'

He was shaking. 'But I'm already in the newspapers arresting Black Jack Beau for the murder. It's in print. I've said Baby Maude is in the clear.'

I smoked at him, 'You didn't really investigate it though, Moochie. I took you to a body and I told you who it was, didn't I?'

'This is blackmail.'

Anne agreed, 'We're blackmailing you to do the job you're supposed to be doing anyway.'

Miserable, Moochie sipped from his doll's-house cup while his eyes raced around the rug. He was trapped. 'How did you know about Samantha?' He asked me, 'I know you saw the matchbook but I never saw you at Coomes. Someone told you. Who told you?'

I wouldn't tell him about Tiny's cigarette girls. After all, Moochie and his father-in-law were on the other side in that particular war. I wouldn't have anyway. Anne didn't need the Baby Maude case reopened. She hadn't been fooled by an old actress with a good line. She didn't even need the body identified as Pavel Viscom instead of a nameless German traveller. She'd found Chrissie Montgomery and returned her to her powerful family as requested. She had won. Everyone powerful in this town who was looking for a private detective would hear about Riordan Associates. She was only doing this for me. Knowing Moochie Ruud had a side piece was a big chip and she was using it for my benefit, so that I could sleep nights.

'You should be worried about who we're going to tell, Moochie, not who told us.'

That shut him up. I could see him coming around to the idea.

'Okay,' he said. 'The Baby Maude case, I can do. I can say a new line of investigation has been opened up in light of new information. I can do it quietly. The cleft-lipped girl is coming to her house, you say?'

'They know each other. A neighbour might be a daughter or a niece or a pal, but they shouldn't know each other. Pasco Pete was set up so Baby Maude could get the insurance payout. You can spin that to a better story than jealousy over bit parts. It makes you look less gullible.'

He nodded at his tiny cup, 'But the body at the Brody, I can't do much about that one. We've investigated that line already. Pavel Viscom's daughter came forward and saw the stiff in the morgue. She said it wasn't him, that he'd already died in Paris two months ago.'

'His daughter lives here?'

'Her mother moved here when she was a baby. They never met but her father kept in touch, letters and birthday cards. She knows him well from photographs.'

Anne shook her head, 'No, no, Moochie listen to yourself: you're saying that a man beaten to death in Paris has papers in his pocket claiming he is Pavel Viscom. Two months later, by pure coincidence, a completely different man who bears a striking resemblance to Viscom appears in a city halfway around the world, a city where his only known living relative also lives and *that* man is also murdered but the only thing stolen from his luggage is his ID papers? It's just happenstance, is what you're saying.'

He could see it didn't sound believable.

'What would the newspapers say about that conclusion? Would they say you're smart?'

'But it's not me,' he was shaking as he told Anne. 'You don't understand. Powerful, powerful people decide the outcome of these cases, not me. They don't need me. I need them. I'm a powerless man. My wife, my sons, they don't respect me. She doesn't even like me. If she wasn't so presbyterian she would have divorced me years ago. All the power is in her family.'

She nodded kindly, 'We're not here to make you look foolish, Moochie. How about if we make it that you're the hero of the piece?'

'How?'

'Well, how about if we tip you the wink that Viscom faked his own death in Europe as a scam? His prices shoot up because he's so interesting, a martyr to the Nazi cause and there's plenty of them over here —'

'Plenty,' agreed Moochie a little too quickly.

'They buy all his garbage paintings for high prices, then he turns up here, alive and ta-da! Not dead but rich. Only someone doesn't want that to be the case. That someone lures him across here and kills him in cold blood. No one else in the room. It's complex. It's international. It takes a mastermind to solve. And that mastermind is —'

'Me.'

He loved it.

'We get you back into the newspapers as the wonder detective leading the most effective and fearless department on the force.'

'Yes. Me.'

'Could you reopen the cases then?'

'And no one mentions Samantha?'

'I've forgotten the name already.'

38.

'Philip Marlowe.'

'Jimmy Donoghue,' I blew the smoke out of the side window. 'Say Jimmy, how d'you like to get the sack from this job?'

Jimmy smiled but he didn't answer right away. He swung the ring with the keys on it around on his finger and looked at the gates. 'You know, I think I kind of would like that.'

I looked at the oily air rising up from the ground. 'You know, I can get you the sack from here, there, anywhere twice. The sky's the limit when you've got friends in low places.'

Jimmy smiled and swiped the monkey hat off and scratched his head, making all his hair stand up on end. 'I'm gonna get some things.'

He moseyed into the gatehouse and moments later came back with his own suit on, tie undone. He threw his bag into the back of the car and went over to unlock the gates. When I was half-way through I stopped and he got into the passenger seat.

'Nice suit. You'll get a better job wearing that.'

It was black, a double-breasted jacquard pinstripe, with loose pants. 'This wasn't on discount,' he said, giving me a derisory glance.

As we drove under the arbour of gnarled jacarandas he asked me if we might go to prison for what we were going to do. I said I doubted it but couldn't be certain, not with people like this.

'You didn't bring a gun, did you?' he asked. 'If we go in with a gun they can shoot us.'

He had a point.

'I'll leave it in the car.'

I could feel his commitment fading though. Did he want out? Jimmy the One stuck his face out of the window to catch the breeze and said vaguely, he didn't mind jail, it wasn't the worst.

Errol Cooper answered the door and let us into the hall. He'd tried make-up on his black eye, to detract from how painful it looked. He'd done it badly though and now it looked like a black eye with make-up on it. It was all you could look at.

Jimmy whispered at him, 'What's going on with to your eye, Mr Cooper?'

'Shut up and follow me.'

He led us up the stairs to the balcony where I'd seen the boy, led us through the doors. We were in a narrow corridor with a red runner rug on the floor. Doors led off, to the left, to the right. It was the living quarters for the family.

'Through the door at the end,' said Cooper. 'A set of stairs. Go up to the top and use this key.' He held it up. 'She's in there. I'll make sure you get out. Trust me.'

I did trust him. I could see why Anne liked the guy suddenly. I thanked him but he'd already left.

Jimmy and I went carefully along the silent corridor to the door and opened it to a spiral set of wooden stairs. Up and up we went.

It was a wide attic room with dormer windows, bright and cosy with two single beds and a chest of drawers and a scattering of toys in a corner on the floor. An old woman, small, grey, in a long blue dress, was sitting on a chair and stood up as we walked in, 'Who are you?'

A figure stood up from the bed. I hardly recognized her. Chrissie Montgomery's face was grotesquely swollen, black and yellow across her temple and down to her jaw. The tops of her hands were black and swollen from shielding herself against blows.

Jimmy D. ran forward to grab her hand but she pulled it away. She held herself stiffly, pain racking her frail body. The bruises on her face were the least of the beating.

'Did your father do this to you?' I asked.

'Anneliese. Anneliese beat me. He told her what to do and she did it,' she began to sob. 'Please get me out of here. They're going to send me to a sanatorium.'

The old woman stood up, 'Now, now Christine –'

'No, Nanny, no! You let them beat me. You let them! You let them.'

The old woman fell back against the wall but shouting had hurt Chrissie and she held her side and had trouble breathing.

'He beat me for running away. She beat me for escaping. She's showing how loyal she can be.'

We sat her down and Jimmy asked where it hurt. Her side, she said, shooting pains. Jimmy said it sounded like broken ribs and he felt them and said they were okay, nothing out of place, there wasn't much they could do for that.

None of us noticed that the old woman had already left. We should have.

Jimmy and I helped Chrissie down the steep set of stairs to the corridor. We made a strange group, Chrissie hobbling along, holding her side as she hurried. Jimmy was carrying her bag and led the way down the stairs.

We got to the door out to the hall and I made them stop so we could listen for people coming. Nothing. A strange kind of nothing. Air sifting silently through hallowed halls. Ghosts of miseries past. Water hissing in the open courtyard but another sound too. Another fountain. The one out front. I stepped forward and glanced down, standing where Chadwick the fourth had stood when I first came up here. The front door was open, just slightly.

Chrissie was struggling to walk, holding her side and breathing heavily.

'Is there another way out?'

Chrissie puffed, 'Miles back. Along there and up to the kitchen and then back up.'

I couldn't chance it. We made it down the stairs to the front door. As I pulled it open Chrissie Montgomery screamed.

Anneliese Lyle was standing in front of my car and she was

holding a pistol. 'Chrissie, darling, please go back in,' she said quietly. 'Daddy wants you to stay.'

Chrissie cowered behind us.

'Please, stop it, Anneliese,' Chrissie pleaded. 'Please, please let me go.'

Anneliese Lyle pointed the pistol at me. 'Marlowe, get in the car and leave us alone. If you leave now we'll give you a two-hour head start.'

'Anneliese,' Chrissie stepped in front of me, 'please . . . ?'

Anneliese lowered the gun, 'Oh Chrissie, Chrissie, it doesn't have to be this complicated. It won't be long. He won't be long and then we can be together.'

'Now that Evelyn has no more use for you, you'll take me as a consolation prize? I want more, Anneliese. I want a real life.'

'We can have that, I'll make that happen for you, but this isn't the way. You know me. There are no surprises here. I can't hurt you because you know who I am. We just have to wait for your father . . .'

They were waiting, these women, waiting for him to die and for their lives to begin. Anneliese was going along with him, doing whatever he told her to do, waiting for him to die. She didn't need to get her claws into Chrissie. They were already there.

'You beat me because he told you to,' sobbed Chrissie.

'He made me,' purred Anneliese sadly.

'He asked you, that's all.'

'And then you'll be in charge. If you ask me for anything I'll make it just how you want it.'

Chrissie looked at her and Anneliese smiled. I'd never seen her smile properly before, never seen her bare her teeth. It had bothered me. But I saw her smile now, a wide warm smile with just enough flaws in it to make a slave of anyone. Lyle's eyes narrowed into half moons, her cheekbones rose to roundels and her straight white teeth were perfect.

Chrissie sighed, 'Anneliese . . .'

'Put the gun down,' said an unfamiliar voice in a thick Bronx accent.

Errol Cooper stepped out of the front door.

Anneliese squinted, 'Who said that?'

'Me,' said Cooper. 'I says it. I'm saying let them all get in the Olds and get outta here.'

Chrissie looked at him, confused, 'Coop, are you doing a voice?'

Anneliese shook her head, 'I don't know what's going on. Get away from those people, Cooper, they're trying to kidnap Christine. Get away from them right now.'

But Errol Cooper raised an arm high by his side. It took a moment for Lyle and Chrissie to follow the line of his arm to his hand. He was holding the Midas vase.

Anneliese gasped, 'Cooper – oh my God, don't!'

'Get away from their car, lady, and drop the pistol.'

She did. Cooper picked the pistol up as Jimmy and Chrissie climbed in. I pulled away and I heard Anneliese say something to Chrissie through the window.

We slid down the hill.

'There is no Hazel?'

'No.'

'What'd Anneliese say to you just then?'

'She'll make it safe,' said Chrissie, 'she says she'll make it safe for me to come back.' It sounded like good news but she was crying.

We drove downhill and out of the open gates, took the winding road as fast as we dared, heading for the open stretch of Sunset.

It was only because of the light, and because we were coming at it from the side, but as we arrived at the turn for the Boulevard we were facing behind the Dancers, looking straight at the car park. And there it was. A Ford Coupe with one white wall tyre missing.

Without warning I swerved sharply on the corner, tipping the car on its side as I pulled in.

Chrissie and Jimmy shouted, clung to the sides of their seats. I didn't care.

I didn't care when the valet parking attendant, not even in his jacket yet, saw me and came over to say they weren't open yet, come back later. I walked straight past him and up the steps. I threw the door open and I saw her.

Evelyn Hamilton was in the open bar. The chairs were all on the tables, the place smelled of last night's smoke and gin, but she was smiling at the barman. And there, nestled up just above her gum line, were two little nubs of teeth, undescended canines, the family trait of the Viscoms.

39.

Chrissie didn't speak as we drove down to the ocean. She smoked cigarettes and watched the city passing the window, her hair falling over her face, jaw slack with misery. I thought back to her stepping off Mrs Dudek's porch the first time I saw her, the lightness of step and her face full of hopeful anticipation. They hadn't been careful enough. That beating would scar her face. I could see her bruised eye in the corner of my rear view mirror. The skin was blackened, trimmed with green, like a piece of badly spoiled fruit.

We had been at the Dancers for hours, answering Ruud's questions while they searched Mrs Dudek's house. We were all sick and tired of each other's company.

Jimmy asked us to drop him at the beach so we did and then Chrissie and I drove on. Her hands were folded in her lap, unmoving. 'Pavel Viscom was her father.'

I wasn't certain she was talking to me but who else would she be talking to.

'Ruud said she looked at his body and said it wasn't him and she had a bunch of his letters. I just found six crates of his paintings stacked up in her bedroom at Mrs Dudek's.'

'Ah!' She nodded too long, and said Ah again but it sounded like a sigh. 'He brought them from Europe?'

'Seems so. He thought they were in it together but she had other plans. He put his papers in the pocket of a murdered man

231

to give Peggy a good story, she came over here and sold his work and they were going to cash in.'

'How did he get out of the country if his papers were on a dead body?'

'I don't suppose a dead man's papers are looked at very carefully. He gives Peggy what she needs, a good story, she makes him a star and then, together, they flood the market with a whole lot of paintings and cash in on all the work the gallery has done. But Evelyn doesn't want to share, or mess up the nice clean story about the dead Nazi genius so she shoots him.'

Chrissie nodded, 'and she's smart enough to know that if a Montgomery is in the room when she kills him then the cops will make out that there was no murder. They find out who I am and suddenly there was no murder.'

'Odds on she told them who you were and that you were there.'

'Then she doesn't need me anymore.'

'Ruud says, according to the letters, Viscom had been writing to her since she was little and her mother brought her here to get away from him.'

'Where are you taking me?'

'Out to Malibu. You'll be safe with the Zimmermans. Safe for a while.'

She tried to sigh but winced and held her side. Bruised ribs. They'd heal but there was nothing much you could do to help them along.

We came to the broad Coast Highway and the land dropped away. She lit two cigarettes and gave me one. We drove and smoked for a spell.

'It seems like you're always finding places for me to go, Mr Marlowe.'

'It's just for a little while, Chrissie, just until you heal.'

'There is nowhere for me, don't you see? There's nowhere I can hide but the place I came from. They fixed it that way. All I can do is wait for him to die.'

I could have said a number of things but they would all have been lies.

I pulled off the road to the beach and slowed on the quiet little road. We got out and walked over to the unassuming little garden door.

Pegsy met us at the gate. She was unenthusiastic when she saw it was me but then she saw Chrissie.

Her gaze trailed her up and down, from the shoes to the skirt to the blouse. She read the signs and signals, where the shoes were made, what the skirt length meant. She didn't seem to notice the bruises but saw straight through them to the bones. They knew each other, these two lonely girls. Like solitary animals alone in the Arctic for ten years who lift their heads and find a trace scent on the wind, a smell so like their own that for a moment they're stunned still, unsure if they're really just smelling themselves.

'Which are you?' asked Pegsy.

'Montgomery. You?'

'Zimmerman.'

'Oh, you're the younger Zimmerman?' She glanced at me, her driver, as if she hadn't known she was coming here. Maybe that she had stopped believing Pegsy existed.

Pegsy opened the garden gate and let us in. 'Mother is still asleep. Drink and jetlag.'

Chrissie nodded. 'Well, I don't really know how long we'll stay here . . .'

They both looked at me. 'I thought you could hide out here for a while, Chrissie. If that's all right with the Zimmermans.'

'Sure.' Pegsy led us into the house. 'Was it Pavel Viscom after all?'

I said it was.

'Good,' said Pegsy, 'I'm glad. Can't think of a better place for him to die than on the floor of a dirty hotel room.'

'It wasn't so very dirty,' said Chrissie vacantly.

'You were there?'

She nodded. 'I thought I was meeting your mother.' It had exhausted her. She shook her head.

Pegsy waited for more but she had nothing left to give. 'Let's go inside. Maybe you could eat something. Do you like fruit?'

Inside the blinds were up on the windows overlooking the water and it was flooded with a blue-white light so intense it was like a visual representation of having a stroke. We all reeled away.

Pegsy explained that it was the combination of this dark room and the glare from the water and we should go outside, it would feel better. She led us out onto the balcony and sat us down in big wicker chairs with cushions on them. She folded her leg under herself and waved a hand. A jug of pink fruit juice that no one wanted appeared on the table, crammed with fresh pineapple and cherries and sliced orange. It wasn't appetizing but it did look as if a lot of work had gone into it.

She poured us each a glass. There was an inevitability about the Zimmermans' way of doing things. If they dropped fruit on the floor it meant that fruit should be dropped on the floor. If they walked around in pyjamas all day then that was how it should be. Out here in Malibu it seemed like none of the rules were immutable. Men wore straw hats. Women didn't brush their hair. There were no lawns or children or butlers. Everyone did whatever.

Pegsy handed Chrissie a glass of pink, 'Tell me what happened to Viscom.'

Chrissie slumped in her chair. She put her drink back on the table and gripped the arms of her chair. 'A trick. I got tricked into being there when he was killed so that the police wouldn't investigate it as a murder.'

'Oh, tipped off a Montgomery was in the room and suddenly – what?'

Chrissie hung her head, 'They called it a suicide and it's case closed.'

'Oh, I see. How did she trick you into being in the room?' Pegsy wasn't being sympathetic, she was asking so she didn't make the same mistakes and that made it okay for Chrissie to tell her. She hadn't done a silly thing or been fooled. They both knew and both acknowledged that this was an inevitable fact of their lives as very rich heiresses, like the rest of the world has accepted that flies are attracted to food.

'A long build-up. You can be free, she said, those things we like to hear that aren't true. You can be free. I thought I was in love.'

'With her?'

'Yes.'

'A servant?'

'A hatcheck girl. So was our housekeeper. We were both in love with her.'

'That's a mess.'

None of this was said in a judgemental way, they were just sharing information, these two richest of the rich girls, preparing themselves for heartbreak and confidence tricksters, hardening their hearts against a world that wanted to get their money off them.

'She told me to leave home and gave me the classified ad for the job in your mother's gallery.'

'A classified ad? In a newspaper?'

'I applied for it in another name. Said I knew all about art. I got it fair and square.'

'We don't advertize. We asked the Galbraiths to find someone.'

'The Monterey Galbraiths?'

'Yes. We asked them to get someone. They must have asked her if she knew someone.'

'And she placed the classified herself.' Chrissie smiled ruefully. 'I thought I got myself a job.'

'Yes, confidence tricks always start with flattery. But no, you didn't get yourself a job.'

'So I see. She so wants to be rich. One way or another she was going to get it.'

The ocean twinkled like it was ocean Christmas. A man walked by on the beach below. He saw us watching him and smiled up, called 'Hi there!'

Pegsy ignored him.

'How are you two pretty ladies doing today?'

'Men come here,' she explained to me, 'to meet rich lonely women . . .'

The man on the beach below put his hands on his hips and grinned, 'Not talking to me, ladies?' He refreshed his smile.

Chrissie and Pegsy stared at him. He was in shorts and a loose shirt with short sleeves. He was tall and dark and had all his own teeth. His legs were muscular and he was walking barefoot in the white sand, his steps sinking deep. He was better looking than either of them, half Cary Grant, half Jimmy Stewart.

They looked down at him, impassively observing, the way Piggy Poltroon stared at me in the hallway of the Montgomery Mansion. They were trying to work out the man's motive.

'Would either of you care to come for a swim? There are fish out there today.'

They didn't answer. Pegsy's eyes remained blank. Chrissie though, Chrissie was something to see. She looked him up and down, saw the good and the flaws. Then she looked out to the horizon, her mouth open. She looked old and frightened, as though she'd seen that she was cursed, knew that no happiness would ever come to her. She looked back at the man. He waved goofily.

'Go away,' she said spitefully. And he did.

The door opened behind us. Peggy stood there in a north-African robe and turban and big round dark glasses. She'd just woken up but seemed quite drunk already. She asked Chrissie who the hell she was and nodded when she told her.

'What are you doing here?'

'Hiding. I worked at your gallery.'

'You *worked*?'

'Under a pseudonym.'

'Well, that sounds perfectly ghastly.'

Peggy tried to make her way over to sit down but staggered as if she was on the deck of a ship in a hurricane. She clung to the back of my chair.

Pegsy glared at her mother, 'Have you taken those pills again?'

'I needed to sleep.'

'That doctor is a liar.'

'He's helping me.'

'He's keeping you stoned. If he comes here again I'll throw his bag out of the window. He'll kill you.'

Peggy waved away her concerns again with a flail of her hand and spoke to Chrissie, 'Why are you hiding here?'

Pegsy answered for her, 'She's a Montgomery. They beat her because she fell for a con.' She reached forward and pressed Chrissie's hand. 'Didn't they?'

Peggy trod carefully over to her seat and fell into it sideways. She turned herself around to face the women. 'Well, that's not fair. We all get taken in sometimes. It's a matter of degree. How much did you lose?'

They watched her as she struggled to explain that she hadn't really lost any money, not really. She'd lost something else. Something more than that.

Peggy shook her head, 'But how much?'

They stared at her. She didn't know what she'd lost. She looked as though she didn't know if she'd been entitled to it in the first place.

'So what do you care?' said Peggy. 'They can't hurt you. She's like you Pegsy, she's an only.'

Pegsy stared hard at her mother. 'She has a child.'

This changed things for Peggy. 'Oh.'

'They don't need her anymore. She bred already. They can throw her in the sea or put her in a sanatorium for the rest of her life if she's an embarrassment.'

'Oh.'

Chrissie sat forward, 'Where is the rest room?'

Peggy clicked a finger and a servant appeared. 'Take her . . .'

The servant woman stepped back and let Chrissie into the house.

'I don't get what she lost,' said Peggy when she had left.

'Faith in people, maybe,' I suggested. 'Belief in herself. I think she was pretty in love with the woman who conned her. I don't know if she'd been in love before.'

Peggy approved of that, 'Girl on girl? Hm. Well, wouldn't have guessed that from meeting her.'

'The woman she fell for is pretty special.'

'Ah,' said Peggy, nodding at me, seeing that I'd been taken in too. 'Love ad hominem? Hm. I must say, I wasn't sorry to hear the Viscom name was left out of it. We can build a story around him now. The killer did me a favour really.'

'She wasn't trying to do you a favour, she was trying to do herself a favour. She was going to come forward with her own collection of paintings by him at some point in the future after you'd built him up, and claim the estate for herself.'

'Ma'am?' One of the servants stood by the balcony door with her head bent. It was the first time I'd heard any of them speak. It didn't seem to register with either of the women.

Pegsy said, 'She'll get nothing now.'

'Madam?'

'Viscom was a good artist but so are a lot of them. He doesn't really deserve to be singled out, none of them do. We decide –'

'Ma'am?'

'WHAT THE HELL IS IT?'

'The lady made a phone call, ma'am. It seems her father just died. She wants to take your car.'

40.

She had to see me at the house, said Errol Cooper on the telephone. Miss Montgomery was unwilling to simply wire me my fee without a face-to-face meeting. I didn't want to go up there again but the long-standing social convention of paying rent meant that I found myself driving past the Dancers on a slow afternoon and taking a right turn onto Montgomery.

The heatwave had broken. Somewhere out there, high above the wide, unthinking Pacific, a raincloud had slowly gathered until the weight of it pushed it landward and it fell over the filthy city, dampening down the stench and the dust, washing it clean. For a while.

I felt lighter and happier than I had in months. Moochie Ruud upheld his end of the bargain. Baby Maude was going to fry for what she did to Pasco Pete and Black Jack Beau had been released. Pavel Viscom had been identified from his photos and his attempt to fool Peggy Zimmerman soured her on him so much she magnanimously gave all of his paintings back to his long-lost daughter to see what she could do with them, which wasn't much. Evelyn was no Johanna Van Gogh.

Where the houses ran out on Montgomery Drive, the facing hills were wet and dark, silent now, the cicadas were all dead or in hiding.

I pulled into the driveway. The castellated gatehouse looked petty now, a hollow boast by a small man, easily disproved. I sat in the car with the rain pattering on the bonnet and watched as the door opened and a short man in Jimmy's uniform and monkey hat scampered over, around the front, to my door. I cracked open my window and gave him my name.

'Straight away, Mr Marlowe! You're expected at the main house. I'll let you through right away, sir!'

He went to the gates, all but doing a leprechaun kick on his way. It took him twenty seconds to get the gates unlocked, open and clear of the drive. Jimmy D. would have been astonished. He gave me a sharp little bow as I drove through and I heard the huge metal gates scrape against the brick, closing as soon as I was through. I turned into the jacaranda tunnel.

The flowers were all gone, leaving just the pods of seeds hanging and dropping like dead bats into the road. It reminded me that all parts of the jacaranda tree are poisonous, from the pretty tiny flowers to the heavy dark bark.

I followed the road up and saw the sights again but everything looked overstated, like a plea for clemency screamed into a baby's face. Nothing up here worked for me anymore.

I parked by the fountain and found myself chilled by the breeze from the water. I looked out over the rain-washed city. It was inviting from up here, all the smells and the small men and the crazy drunks and the Skid Row fights, it all looked good from this far away. It wasn't the lack of detail. It was the broader view.

I got out of the Olds and stood for a moment. Different. The garage doors were shut and locked. The gravel in the driveway had been raked evenly. No stray stones had washed up on the front step. None of the windows at the front of the house were open. All of the curtains were open and straight. The head of the family was no longer confined to a wheelchair. They could inspect the grounds, find fault at any time.

I rang the bell and one beat later it opened.

'Mr Marlowe, please come in, sir. You're most welcome.'

'Thanks, Cooper.'

I stepped in and gave him my hat, took my seat next to the Midas vase and tucked my elbows in like a good visitor.

Cooper stood holding my hat and looking at me.

'Congratulations. I heard.'

'Thank you. Anne and I aren't in any hurry but you'll be the first to know when we set the date, Mr Marlowe.'

I was pleased for them. My nose was a little out of joint but I couldn't think of a better guy for her. I wasn't it.

He went off to see if they were ready for me.

I sat and lit a cigarette for something to do but found I didn't have an ashtray. I made a little pocket out of a piece of paper I found in my jacket and was using that when I heard a voice.

'Hey.'

I looked around. I couldn't see anyone. I looked up.

'Well, if it isn't Piggy Poltroon.'

Piggy smiled down at me through the banisters. His teeth were awful cute, far apart and sticking out and white as a bleached collar.

'I'm not Piggy Poltroon.'

'No? Who are you then?'

He laughed. It felt odd. He laughed as if he was laughing at my attempt to talk to him. 'I'm going to grow up and I'm going to find you and I'm going to cut you up. Ha!'

Then he was gone, sucked back into the dark open door.

'Miss Montgomery will see you now.' Errol Cooper was back and waiting for me at the door. I didn't know what to do with my cigarette, or the little pouch of ash I'd made. Errol held his hand out and took them from me.

'I'm terribly sorry for the lack of ashtrays out here, sir. I'll remedy that at once.'

'No big deal.'

'It's most unwelcoming, Mr Marlowe, most incommodious.'

Errol was so into the part. I couldn't imagine his accent sliding anywhere south of Kennebunkport now. He didn't look me in the eyes anymore either. Even when he seemed to be making eye contact, his gaze settled a quarter of an inch below my eyes. It was unsettling but perhaps only to me. He seemed happy with it. Anne was happy with it. The only person it bothered was me and I had no business being bothered. Anne said it was because of me that he got to keep his job and land a substantial raise after all.

In the dark corridor he turned to face me, straightened his jacket, cleared his throat and knocked lightly on the door. I didn't hear the reply but he did. He opened it, stepped through, announced me and signalled that I could come in.

I could have walked away. I could have but I didn't. I stepped into the library with its lumpy floors and crumbling ceiling and I looked down to the desk and the two women behind it.

'Approach,' said Christine.

I should have walked away. But I didn't. I walked over.

'Sit down,' said Anneliese.

'I don't work for you anymore,' I said and lit another cigarette.

'Lieutenant Ruud arrested Evelyn for shooting her father,' said Anneliese.

'I heard. Mrs Dudek's interviews are all over the gossip papers and she's selling off the Viscom paintings to pay Evelyn's back rent.'

'She'll get a bit more than her back rent,' said Anneliese. 'Even Peggy Zimmerman can't undo the bump his prices got from the murder. It's a helluva story for an artist.'

'I'm not here to discuss that.'

They looked at each other. Anneliese smiled up at me, 'But you want your money.'

She was standing next to Christine Montgomery's chair. It was a new chair, not her father's throne. He had died in that chair, I'd heard, died of asphyxiation an hour after Anneliese let Chrissie leave the mansion. He'd fallen asleep in the chair and his big head dropped forward and his breathing was obstructed and he died. No one cared that he'd died.

'I want the money I'm owed,' I said. 'No more, no less.'

Anneliese was not happy that I was refusing to be played. She smiled a sickly smirk and attempted a put down. 'Do you need your money, Mr Marlowe?'

'Well,' I said, 'Sheil at Jane Jones' got my suit and I can't wear the same one all the time. I need another one for when this is in the cleaner's.'

Neither of them liked the mention of Sheil. I guess her Tennessee charms were lost on them. Christine looked up at Anneliese and nodded. Anneliese reached down to her neck with both hands and lifted a chain over her head. It had a small key on it. She used it to undo the lock on the desk drawer and opened it. She took out a brick of cash. She counted it, peeled off some notes and dropped them on the desk in front of Christine. I'd have to bend over the desk to get it.

Christine looked down and her mouth twitched a sneer at the money.

'Are you giving it to me or showing me it?'

'Take it,' said Anneliese.

'Give it to me.'

'Just take it, Mr Marlowe.'

I smoked my cigarette and looked at them. I undid a button on my jacket and slipped a hand into a pocket.

'You're not going to give it to me?'

'Take it.'

I dropped my cigarette on the priceless floor and ground it in with my shoe. 'I tell you what, Miss Baudelaire, you keep that money and spend it on your girl. See if either one of you can forget the soul-sucking compromise you've made . . .'

I may even have winked.

Who knows.

I walked out though, and got as far as the front door before Christine caught up with me. 'Roger Allan! Mr Allan!' She held out the money, 'Please. I owe you.'

There was a plea in her eye, a call to remember that hot afternoon a lifetime ago when we met, both liars but more honest than now.

She held it out. 'Please take it.'

'I can only find the truth, Joan Baudelaire.'

'That's why you'll never have anything, Mr Allan.'

'I know.'

'I won't hurt her and she won't hurt me. I'm not my father.'

I sucked my teeth in a hiss. 'Miss Baudelaire, what sticks in my throat, the thing that really chokes me? The cowardice of it.'

She looked at her feet, her swan-like neck bent steep.

'Because you deserve better and she deserves better. You deserve to take a chance and fail and take another chance. It's a shame.'

She looked up at me and she knew I was right. 'Please take the money, Mr Allan?'

I took it as Anneliese appeared at her shoulder. She stayed in her shadow. 'Goodbye, Mr Marlowe.'

I turned and opened the door to leave but turned back, 'You know who really bothers me in all of this, Anneliese?'

'Who?'

'Manny Perez,' I said. 'Manny really bothers me. You know why? Because he was just doing his job. He was just a no-account man driving a cab and he had some information Evelyn didn't want passed on. There's nothing I can do about it. No witnesses, no one saw anything, even his wife may be glad he's gone. No one really cares.'

Anneliese shrugged her perfect shoulders, 'He was just a cab driver.'

'The way I figure it, you should lose something. Even up the balance sheet. You need to lose something too.'

She laughed and stopped herself, her tongue stopping up the back of her teeth. 'I didn't kill him. Why should I lose something?'

I put my fingertips on the Midas vase and shoved it off its plinth. We all watched it tumble through the air and Anneliese leapt to catch it, throwing herself across the hall with her hands cupped.

She missed by ten feet.

It shattered on the stone floor, breaking into six pieces, the dull dusty thunk of it reverberating around the cold space. The pieces were quite distinct. They could put that back together so I raised my foot and stamped on it. I crushed it to dust. I made it so that no one anywhere would be able to fix it.

Then I looked at them and, in perfectly accented Spanish, repeated Manny's line from the basement bar, about the insult he would gladly suffer to his immortal soul if it got him out of the present company.

Then I left.

I never went back to the Montgomery place and they never came looking for me. I look up sometimes, when I'm driving down Santa Monica and the day is clear. For me, Anneliese and Chrissie will always be in that hall and I will always be repeating the words of the lowest, meanest drunk I ever met.

Manny Perez.

About the Author

Denise Mina is the author of seventeen novels, including the Reese Witherspoon x Hello Sunshine Book Club pick *Conviction* and its sequel, *Confidence*, *The Less Dead*, *The Long Drop*—winner of the 2017 McIlvanney Prize for Scottish crime book of the year—and the Garnethill trilogy, the first installment of which won the John Creasey Memorial Award for best first crime novel, as well as the Paddy Meehan series and the Alex Morrow series, among others. She has won the Theakston Old Peculier Crime Novel of the Year Award twice and was inducted into the Crime Writers' Association Hall of Fame in 2014. She lives in Glasgow.